W9-BEM-253

Out of
Xibalba

Liz Coley

Liz Coley

Xibalba /shi-bal-ba/ n. The Mayan Underworld

LizColey.com
LCTeen.com

ISBN-10: 1463556322
ISBN-13: 978-1463556327

ACKNOWLEDGMENTS

Thanks to my husband Brian for taking the family to Belize, a journey that started this adventure.

Thanks to everyone who believed in this story: my family; my first reader Rachel; my teen readers Maggie, Lena, Nathan, Ian, Connor, and Kate; my grownup readers Jorge, Lissa, Dee Dee, Heidi, Jason, Abby, and Marge; my production guru Deborah; my graphic artist Bob Worrall; and my final eyes and mother-in-law Barbara.

Thanks to Jason Yaeger, archeologist, for the first-hand information on Xunantunich excavations.

Cover Credit:
Special thanks to Jaime Lopez Wolters for permission to use his Mayan Girl/Guatemala photograph with my image of Barton Creek Cave.

A WORD ON THE
MAYAN COUNTING SYSTEM

Unlike our base-ten system, the ancient Mayans reckoned using a base-twenty system with compound symbols of dots and lines for the integers up to nineteen. A dot represents one, a line represents five, and a symbol resembling a closed fist represents zero. Example: the numeral consisting of four dots and two lines is fourteen.

Chapters taking place in the present era are numbered with our modern system. Chapters taking place in the past are numbered with Mayan numerals.

PART I - OUT OF XIBALBA

CHAPTER ONE
December 21, 2012

"Paddles up, please, girls," the guide Enrique said in his softly accented voice, "and I'll tell you about the end of the world."

Michelle felt his warm breath brush the back of her neck. By the glow of the cave-light strapped to her forehead, she watched her sister Maya lift her paddle from the dark water and rest it on the left edge of the canoe. Michelle placed hers on the right side, just to be different.

She twisted her arm to check out the back of her elbow. The fresh scrape had finally stopped bleeding. Entering the cave, she'd banged it hard on the rock walls when Maya over-steered the bow of the canoe.

Enrique had laughed when she began to swear and said, "No, no. Don't worry. This is good. You offered a blood sacrifice and you will return safely from our journey to Xibalba, the underworld entrance."

They'd heard a lot of jokes about blood sacrifice since they arrived in Belize, homeland of the ancient Mayans.

Enrique steered them out of the narrow, overhanging passage into a wide-open space, an underground lake deep in the cave system. The splashing echoes at a distance reassured Michelle that their parents were following. She tilted her head up, and her lamp flicked across the arching roof of the cavern. Colorful bands streaked the limestone formations rippling high above her. A bat darted through the beams and vanished into a deep crevice. Fragments of unwritten poetry ran through her head as she soaked in the ambience.

Enrique trailed his paddle, and the canoe spun slowly, turning the girls to face their parents' canoe, which had just glided out of the passage behind them.

"Let me show you some artifacts that by luck escaped looters. You see there?" He pointed to a pale brown ledge on the wall closest to the boats. "In that sort of dark pocket?"

Michelle squinted and made out the shape of three round pots nestled in a recess. "Oh, I see them. Wow. Incredible. This is so much cooler than seeing them in the museum."

"Where, Chel?" Maya demanded. "I don't see anything."

Michelle leaned forward and turned her sister's head the other way. "On this side."

"Oh, right. What's in them, Enrique?" Maya asked.

The flirty way she over-rolled the R made Chel cringe. They'd known Enrique for all of what, three hours? And already Maya was trying to snare him as another admirer.

Enrique stared right at Chel as he answered. Maybe he'd figured out she was the one genuinely interested. "These pots would have held dried peppers, spices, cacao seeds or perhaps even *aqa*, the Mayan corn liquor. When the ancient peoples came into the caves for rituals and sacrifices, they left these offerings to please the gods of the underworld...Xibalba." The word seemed to whisper itself as he spoke it, shi-bal-ba. "Now look over on that raised ledge, a natural flat place they would have used for ritual human sacrifices."

Again, Chel spotted it first. "Oh my God, Maya, look." She patted her sister on the right shoulder.

"Yes, there," Enrique said. "She has been there a long time. So long, her minerals have flowed into the rock itself."

Embedded in the ledge under a large stalactite, lay a prostrate skeleton. The bones blurred into stone, covered with an age-old layer of calcium that had dripped from the stalactite above it over the centuries. The skull emerged from the pile, grinning down at them as if she didn't really mind her condition. As if she knew a secret.

Chel's heart skipped a beat. The skull's empty sockets locked their blank gaze on her, and she found it impossible to look away. Her shoulders tingled with the sudden notion that a presence hovered near her, watching and guarding the cave. Chel shivered in the dank air, then shook off the spooky feeling. Caves were odd places.

"Powerful," Enrique said, as if reading her thoughts. "In the Mayan tradition, caves are the entrance to the underworld and places of great power. Gods and humans may meet here on the border between worlds." He paddled gently backward so the canoe moved out into the center of the lake. The mineral scent of the water rose as the surface was disturbed.

Dad took a few strokes to catch up and stopped his canoe alongside theirs. Chel noticed Mom wasn't rowing—she was gripping the sides of the canoe with clenched knuckles. Mom and tight enclosed places did not mix well, especially *dark* enclosed places—something about a locked closet and a game of hide and seek when she was a kid. But Chel and Maya had begged and pestered until Dad agreed to a private canoe tour through the caves.

This culture was an important part of the girls' heritage. Mayan blood ran through their veins, even if it had been thinned, diluted over the years. Grandpapa had left Belize—it was British Honduras then—before Dad was even born. Dad looked very much like the Mayans they had seen along the roads, not to mention the Mayans they had admired on engravings and pottery in the museum. However, he was culturally about as Midwestern U.S. as you could get, a corn farmer for the university. Chel knew he was learning just as much as she was about their fascinating ancestors on this winter vacation trip.

"Please turn off your lamps for a few minutes," Enrique said.

As Chel reached for the switch on her forehead, she heard Mom gasp.

Enrique must have heard it, too. "Don't worry, Mrs. Balam," he said. "Mine will be on while I tell you our story. A story of the beginning and the end of the world."

He sat on the stern seat, behind Chel, and as all the lights clicked off, she twisted toward him to listen. They were far from the cave entrance, deep in the heart of the mountain, and the only glimmer of light came from the three-inch lamp nestled in his ebony curls. His eyes were huge and dark, almost black even in daylight, now deepened by his wide open pupils. By contrast, his straight, white smile gleamed against the tanned skin of his handsome face. From his profile, his long aristocratic nose, she imagined there was noble Spanish blood in him, blood of the conquistadores.

Chel listened breathlessly as he told a story he must have told a thousand tourists before, but it felt as if he spoke especially to her. The only sounds in the cave were the liquid tones of his voice and the occasional plinking of water drops as they seeped through the ground above and into the cave, finally dropping fifty feet to add their tiny volume to the river which ran through. The soft smell of damp stone surrounded her.

"The world has begun four times already," Enrique said. "And ended three times."

Chel had read the story when she was doing research, but Enrique's version felt more authentic—less like a quaint myth and more like a metaphor for reality.

"In the first creation, there were only animals, who could not satisfy the gods' craving for worship. They were banished to the wilds. In the second creation, the gods made men of mud, the rich soil of the earth. But they absorbed too much water and couldn't stand or speak properly."

Maya snorted a laugh. "Floppy dudes."

Chel glared.

Enrique took no notice. "The gods began again. In the third creation, men were built of strong pito wood and women crafted from supple reeds. The people spoke and married and birthed children, but they were like dolls without souls or minds. Their faces held no expression. No sorrow. No joy."

His voice was hypnotic. The boat rocked ever so slightly, and Chel felt dizzy and disconnected from her body, surrounded by shadows.

"The sky grew dark, and a burning black rain fell; then everything turned against the men. Their animals refused them food and service; their tools refused them useful work; even their houses refused them shelter. Those who survived ran to the jungle and live now as monkeys. You have heard them howling in the night."

Backward evolution? Chel thought. Men became howler monkeys? Now *that* was an interesting myth. Maybe she could develop the idea into a story in sophomore comp class when she got home.

"In this, the fourth creation," Enrique continued, "men were created from a dough of white and yellow maize. Now we are strong and wise, some say even too wise."

He shrugged and reached for his paddle. The blade cut into the black water. "They say we displease the gods."

"Do you believe all that?" Chel asked.

"Well, no," Enrique answered. "I'm Catholic, actually."

"So is that it?" Maya asked.

5

"No, there is much more. I'll save that for the next cavern. Let's paddle across this one and through the next passage."

Enrique turned the boat and headed toward a place where Chel could have sworn the wall formed a solid barricade. "And Mr. Balam," he called back, "watch your head in this section. The water is high today, so the overhangs are quite low. Try to steer straight through the middle if you can. Oh, turn your lights back on."

There was an audible sigh of relief from Mom.

"So what about the end of the world?" Dad asked. "Our other guide, Hernán, said the Mayans scheduled the end of time, along with everything else, when he was showing us calendar markings on some stone monuments."

"Of course," Enrique replied in a loud voice that echoed in the cavern. He pulled harder, and the canoe surged forward. "The Mayans organized everything according to their sophisticated calendar. They predicted the phases of the moon and the cycles of Venus for centuries ahead of their time. So the end of the age is when the days run out."

He paused to look over his shoulder and check the progress of the other canoe. "Actually, it's like my car's odometer running out of numbers when I passed a hundred thousand miles. It reset to five zeroes. The bak'tun, one hundred and forty-four thousand days, is the largest unit in their Long Count calendar system. There will be thirteen complete bak'tuns in this Great Cycle, which began on the day of the fourth creation. Then that's it."

"That's it?" Maya stopped rowing. "What do you mean?"

"The last day of the fourth age is at the end of the thirteenth bak'tun. And that's set for the winter solstice of 2012. December 21. So we'll see what happens, yes?"

"Wait. Today?" Maya persisted.

"Yeah," Chel said. "Don't you remember when I was reading about it? How I told you what a cool time it would be to visit

Belize? That was like the whole point of coming for Christmas vacation."

Chel caught a hint of Dad singing to himself something that sounded suspiciously like "Belize Navidad."

"Maybe for you," Maya retorted. "But I'm here for the heat and sunshine."

Enrique laughed. "Yes, well, since the world is scheduled to end today, maybe you should be outside in the sun, enjoying it."

From behind, Mom's nervous voice asked, "Do you believe that, Enrique? Is the world really supposed to end today?"

He laughed again, that easy-going laugh Chel had heard so much today. His white smile said one thing while the dark intensity of his eyes said another. "That's what they say. But if it is, there's not much we can do about it, is there? Watch that stalactite formation on your right."

The wall that had appeared solid before opened up, and the narrow stream curved ahead. Chel paddled on, careful not to touch any of the flowstone formations, and glanced up at the tan and white stalactites hanging above. Some of them were huge, probably ancient. She hoped they were well attached to the ceiling. Everything was quiet again, except for the sound of five paddles dipping in and out of the water, completely out of cadence with each other. Five beams skittered over the cave walls in every direction as they all looked around.

The encroaching walls fell away, and they drifted into an enormous, spectacular cavern. Along one edge was a large flat area, like a landing, a stone beach. Crystalline white formations rose up from the solid ground, reaching toward their partners dangling down. Headlamp light reflected, sparkling through the gloom.

Enrique called back, "Okay, everyone. I'd like to take a minute to experience the heart of the cave. Mrs. Balam, are you up to this?"

"Of course I am." If there's one thing Mom didn't want to be, it was a spoilsport, or a chicken. "It's lovely."

"Okay. Let's all turn off our lights and listen. Listen to the cave speak."

Chel heard Dad whisper, "It's okay, honey. Give me your hand." Then all the lights snapped off and the darkness was overwhelming.

Chel's eyes were wide open, but absolutely nothing reached them. She passed a hand three inches in front of her eyes and saw nothing but black. The air was still, heavy, moist. Her ears throbbed with silence, broken only by the tiny sounds of moving water. She could almost believe this *was* the underworld.

Chel reached over the side of the canoe and trailed her hand through the water, which was surprisingly warm for being underground. A drop of moisture smacked her face, and she caught her breath. Her startled flinch rocked the boat.

"What happened?" Enrique asked.

"Sorry," Chel whispered. It was so quiet, she felt compelled to whisper. "I just got hit with a drop from the ceiling, that's all."

"That's lucky," Enrique said. "Cave drops, tears of Ix Chel, they're said to be a blessing."

Chel smiled in the dark and touched the damp spot on her cheek. She was blessed.

"As long as it wasn't bat pee," Maya said with a laugh.

Chel groaned. Her sister could happily suck the mystery out of anything.

Then Dad's watch beeped the hour. High noon. "Sorry," he said.

Finally, all was quiet again, and the silence felt darker. Chel's eyes strained for a hint of light. Mom was probably hating this, but it was really cool.

In the distance, Chel heard a low rumble, like a train passing far away. A ripple of water passed under the boat, and it rolled gently. Another train rumble, another ripple, this time larger, stronger.

"What's going on?" Mom's voice trembled. "What is it?" Her light snapped on, momentarily blinding Chel.

She blinked away the green spot in her vision. As her eyes adjusted, she realized the placid underground lake was choppy with overlapping wavelets. The boat pitched in several directions at once, and Enrique began rowing strongly with the underlying current.

"Come, follow me," he called to the rear boat. "Row, girls," he commanded. "With all your power."

"What is it?" Mom asked again.

"Earthquake," Enrique replied.

"Oh God, oh God, oh God," Mom moaned.

Chel clicked on her light and concentrated hard on paddling. They crossed the cavern quickly toward the next narrow passage. The rumbling sound continued, growing in volume. A large wave rolled upstream toward them, breaking over the bow.

"Shit, my camera!" Maya swore as the wave drenched her feet. Another wave followed the first, and Maya flailed toward it with her paddle. "Oh, shit," she screamed again.

Chel saw the paddle torn from her sister's hands. It vanished behind them. She doubled her grip and dug into the water, rowing hard against the current flowing the wrong way now, pushing them back into the cavern.

A roaring wind blew from the mouth of the passage, making it doubly impossible to exit. The sound rose in a crescendo that drowned out Mom's cries and Maya's swearing. The entire cavern heaved itself up and down again, and Chel's guts clenched. She turned to Enrique, to yell through the tumult, to plead for instructions. Behind their boat, she saw her father paddling furiously, the canoe turning in circles as Mom chanted helplessly and refused to row.

A ray of light glanced across the water, and Chel peered up at the source. A widening crack split the roof. A slash of brilliant blue sky shined through the fissure. Then an enormous stalactite straddling the crack wrenched loose and plunged toward the lake. Time slowed to a crawl as she watched the stalactite spin sedately through the air and soundlessly drive itself through the middle of her parents' canoe. Black water rushed into the gap. Bright orange life jackets bobbed away, empty. Chel scanned the surface desperately for any sign of her parents.

Water heaved upward from the recoil. The backwashing wave nearly capsized their canoe, which rocked and spun out of control. Enrique's paddle bit into the churning lake with no effect.

Chunks from the ceiling rained down around them with bruising ferocity. Maya turned and pointed at the water. What was she thinking? She was going to try to swim for it? Chel opened her mouth to scream, but her lungs refused to breathe. She shook her head, hard, but her sister ignored her as usual. Maya stood up to dive, and the boat inevitably turned over.

The edge of the canoe struck Chel painfully in the ribs and pushed her under the water without an ounce of air. The moment her cave-light submerged, it shorted and went out. Someone's leg kicked her hard in the stomach, and she sucked in a lung-full of water. She spasmed, her body trying to expel the liquid.

Brilliant sparkles filled her vision, sparks like underwater fireflies. Her chest burned with the effort of not breathing. Disoriented, injured, struggling for oxygen, she couldn't tell which way was up.

So this is what the end of the world feels like, she thought as she inhaled water. It's dark and it hurts.

This I have written.

I am Men Ch'o, he of the eagle's eyes, and I was the first to see the goddess Ix Chel when she came to us from Xibalba. We came to the river at the mouth of the cave where our boats waited. It was the day when the Jaguar-Sun climbs only to the top of the south temple and hurries down again into the night world, the day of shortest light. We came at first light, when the breath of the cave rises like a steaming pot and mists the river.

Our slaves carried small pots of seed that we promised to the gods. Today we asked them to return the days of warmth and long light and rain so our maize would grow tall. The maize of the past three tuns had been small and dry. The children of those years were thin, many staying on their mother's breasts far too long. Still, they had to be fed. We prayed now for much light and rain, a good tun, a good omen.

We filled the boats. The slaves steadied them as the *ah tz'ib* were seated. I, too, am *ah tz'ib*, one who writes, in training to serve as a scribe and priest, but I am also *ch'aak*, the second son of my Father-king, the K'ul Ahaw. It would not be proper for my brother heir, the *ba ch'aak*, to travel at dawn to the mouth of Xibalba to perform sacrifices, and that is why I was the first to see the goddess.

The morning was scarcely light, but the entrance to Xibalba was still darker, and the slaves lit the tips of the cotton torches drenched in maize oil. Black smoke rose from them, sliding through the long vines that hung from the trees along the river. We passed into the cave, and the smoke disappeared into the roof of the underworld, the rock floor of the world above.

Our captive warrior sat trembling in the first boat. Only his hands were bound. His pride kept him from fleeing. It was a strange sort of courage to display. I prayed it was pleasing to the gods. Our harvest depended on it.

The other *ah tz'ib* hummed a low chant, one I had struggled to learn. If only my ears were as sharp as my eyes. Their tones echoed off the walls of the stone chamber as if three-twenties of voices joined them. I sensed the presence of the underworld gods, and my skin was chilled.

Our boats entered the room of white crystals, and I looked to the landing place where we perform our works for the gods. A new gleam on the shore caught my eagle eyes. I pointed to it and called, "Look, what lies there?"

That is the proof I was the first to see the goddess.

We drew close enough to land, and I stepped from the boat before the others. The goddess appeared as a dark-haired woman sleeping on the rocks. Her coton, the dress she wore, was the whitest garment I have ever seen, and it clung damply to her young body. I placed a hand near her mouth. The slightest of breaths moved the air. While the others watched, I knelt and rested my head on her unmoving chest. I heard the steady beat of a heart. It sounded like that of any woman, so at that moment, I did not yet know her true self.

I supposed we would bring her to my Father Ahaw. He would decide what to do with this stranger. I slipped my arms under her to lift her into one of the boats. We would have room for an extra after we sacrificed our captive warrior. As I lifted her, she made a sound of pain. I held her still in my arms.

Her eyes opened then, and I nearly lost my hold. I ordered the nearest slave, "Come closer. Bring the torch closer."

Instead he backed away in fear, seeing what I had seen by pale, uncertain light. Her eyes were the color of the sky, the color of rain, the color of flowing water. It was the strangest pair of eyes I had seen in all my twenty tuns of life.

She stared at me, her eyes piercing straight ahead like mine, not turned inward, and those odd eyes opened wide with fear.

"You are safe," I said, not knowing why I chose those words. "But who are you? Why do you rest here?"

She began speaking sounds, words I could not understand, perhaps god-words. But one thing she repeated: "Ahm Ix Chel. Ahm Ix Chel."

Finally, her words pierced my understanding. Goddess Ix Chel, lady of rain, lady of rainbows. Goddess of fertility and childbirth and the moon.

How we were blessed! We had not even yet performed our rituals, but the pureness of our hearts and the courage of our captive must have pleased the gods before we even began. They sent not an omen, but a goddess.

I turned to the priest-scribes. "Look," I said. "This is Ix Chel, come to help us."

They fell on their faces before her. I, of course, still held her, and could not prostrate myself.

I called to the captive warrior, "This is a moment of great glory for you, specially chosen to honor the Lady Chel. Come show your warrior's heart and blood."

The captive knelt before me and held up his bound hands. Behind him, the elder priest drew his black knife and blessed it. The warrior fixed his eyes on the goddess as the priest pulled the blade swiftly across the wide rivers in his neck, first the left, then the right. His blood spilled onto the rocks as he held the goddess in his gaze. A single sound escaped him—"My lady"—as his last breath passed. He pitched forward onto the rocks, breaking his head, but his warrior's soul was already flown.

In my arms, the goddess fainted.

I remember dark. I remember soundless screams. I remember the world falling in on me, drowning me. I remember being flung onto a hard, sharp surface and puking my guts out, endless streams of water spewing out of me. Then everything was quiet and dark again and I sank away from consciousness. I wanted to stay there forever. The memories were too painful.

Physical pain woke me, a stabbing ache in my side as if my ribs were on fire. I figured I must have broken one. The agony doubled when I tried to breathe. I opened my eyes to the glow of torchlight. Not flashlights? A group of men lay on the ground, foreheads pressed to the stone. I was pinned in the excruciating grip of the only man standing, cradled against his chest. He was stripped to the waist, wearing some sort of cotton man-skirt, and his dark skin radiated warmth.

"Is everyone else okay?" I asked.

He stared at me blank-faced, clearly confused.

"My Mom and Dad, Maya and Enrique, are they okay? Did you find them, too? I'm Michelle."

"Michelle," he repeated, his eyes wide. He said something else to me in a soothing voice, but the words were garbled.

Maybe I'd hit my head on the rocks harder than I thought, possibly a concussion. I tried again. "I'm Michelle. I'm Michelle Balam. My sister and parents and our guide were in the cave when the earthquake hit. Did you already rescue them? Take them out of the cave?"

He didn't answer me. He spoke more strange words to the men on the ground.

They all stood and took a step back, except for one, nearly naked. For a moment, I thought he was a swimmer, maybe a lifeguard, wearing only a white Speedo, until I realized it wasn't a Speedo at all. The fabric was tied and tucked into a loincloth. Then he fell to his knees in front of me, raising his hands, which now I saw were tied together with a fiber cord. What the heck? What was going on here?

A flickering glint in the shadows caught my eye. A knife!

I was frozen, restrained by the man who held me.

Before I could call out a warning, a man stepped forward and slashed the throat of the bound one. And not a single person raised a hand to help him. Blood spurted everywhere as he knelt upright for an impossibly long time, locking his failing gaze on my eyes. My stomach heaved and my head spun painfully. He fell forward, his head hitting the white crystalline rock with a horrible wet smacking sound. Blood seeped into a black and red pool around him. The man holding me smiled his approval. I closed my eyes and my mind skipped off to somewhere bearable.

CHAPTER TWO
December 14, 2012

Two weeks of freedom and adventure lay just outside the door of the physical sciences lab, and Chel heard the irresistible call of winter break. Not just any winter break—Christmas in Belize!

Chel forced herself to take a breath and check over her multiple choice answers for the second time. She was *so* done with this exam. Why not call it a semester?

The lab test had actually been kind of fun. Mr. Spencer handed each student a box of wire, a strong magnet, assorted nuts and bolts and washers, strips of metal, and a handful of coins. His only instruction? "Make something interesting."

So she decided to combine two of their early experiments. First, she turned the pile of coins into a homemade battery with the help of some salty vinegar, paper, and foil. They'd done this one back in September. Then she coiled the wire around her pencil and attached it to the battery to create a weak magnet. In thirty-five minutes she built something like the world's most primitive electromagnetic switch. And it was working perfectly. Chel flicked it on and off, one more time for luck.

She glanced across the room. Hunched over her lab bench, Maya was creating a modern sculpture that had absolutely nothing to do with science—her version of something interesting. Maybe she was hoping for partial credit, points for sheer originality. In Spencer's class? Good luck with that.

Anyway, Chel couldn't wait a moment longer. She caught Maya's eye, mouthed "seeya" to her, and snatched up her jacket and backpack. As she burst through the door into the bright December sunshine, a snowball flew out of nowhere and smacked her in the face, knocking her breathless.

"What the…" she yelled, wiping the icy remains from her cheek. "Dang, that hurt!"

"Oh my God, I'm sorry. I'm sorry." It was Rand from her Algebra Two class. "Dammit, I was aiming for Jake right when you came out. I'm so sorry. God, I'm stupid." His face a picture of worry, he dusted the snow off her blue polar fleece coat with his bare hands. They were bright red from making snowballs for his deadly, frozen arsenal. A small pile of ammunition rested under the tree he was using for cover.

Jake emerged from behind another tree, laughing his head off at his friend's embarrassment.

Rand continued dusting off her hair.

"No really. I'm okay," Chel protested.

He put an icy hand under her chin and turned her head to the side. "Man, I hope that doesn't leave a bruise. It's all red now. God, I'm sorry."

"If anyone asks," Chel joked, "I'll just say you slugged me."

Rand's voice turned desperate. "Oh, please, no."

"Kidding. I'm kidding." In her effort to stop his frantic dusting, she grabbed his frozen hands in hers. Suddenly, he fell completely still, and there they stood.

Chel tried to read the expression on his face—it was cute, boyish. Under his mussed up auburn hair were eyes as blue as her own. The dusting of freckles across his cheeks framed his small nose, which was already glowing pink with cold.

"Hey," he said, his breath coming out in a puff of steam. "Are you hungry? Can I buy you an apologetic piece of pizza?"

"Chel!" Maya's voice broke from the building.

At that point, Chel realized she was still holding Rand's hands and loosened her grip, but Maya had already seen. Her eyebrows rose all the way up to her hairline. No doubt. She'd seen.

Chel dropped Rand's hands and reached for the gloves in her pockets. "Hey, Maya. We're going for pizza. Want to come?" Say no, she pleaded with her eyes.

The twin telepathy thing worked. Maya gave Chel a quick wink and a thumbs up. "Some other time," she said. "Mom's taking me driving this afternoon. I'll tell her you're going out for a while. 'Kay?" She whirled around without waiting for an answer and waved with the back of her hand.

Chel knew she'd be grilled later, but she smiled inside, and her heart beat just a little unsteadily. "My sister," she explained, for no apparent reason.

"Yeah, I know," Rand said. "You guys are really twins?"

"Well, yes and no. We're sort of broken twins. We have different birthdays. I was born before midnight and she was born after. Isn't that weird? We're fraternal, or rather, sororal. Is that the word? I don't think we look that much alike, actually," she confessed. She bit her lip to stop the nervous babbling.

Rand leaned closer and whispered in her ear, "I think you're much prettier." His cheek touched hers where the snowball had smashed.

A hot blush erased any leftover feeling of chill in her face. Chel had never remotely considered herself prettier. Except for her eyes, she had a more typical Central American look—broad, flat cheeks, a strong nose, round chin, and straight, thick, black hair—Indian hair, she called it. Ironically, Maya, who in no way resembled her name, had the delicate features of their Swedish Mom, exotically painted with Dad's rich mocha coloring, her silky hair like dark honey. Chel had always considered her sister the beauty of the family. Maybe a nurse with a vicious sense of humor had switched their name tags in the nursery.

"Are we going to finish this battle or not?" Jake asked impatiently.

"Not," Rand answered. "I owe Michelle a slice. Later, dude."

He picked up his backpack on his right arm and slid his left around her waist as if it were the most natural thing in the world.

It took all her willpower to control her voice. "It's Chel, actually," she said. "Michelle sounds too blonde."

"Shell," he echoed. "I like it. It fits you. A hard outer covering that hides who knows what delicacies inside."

"That's Chel with a CH," she said quickly. Good God. Delicacies?

This was all very new, very unexpected, very unfamiliar. In fact, the way her stomach was jumping and her mouth had gone dry, she seriously doubted whether she'd be physically able to swallow the promised pizza.

A blast of hot, garlicky air greeted them as they pushed into the cheap Italian restaurant in the strip mall near school. The tables were full, so Rand guided Chel to a pair of stools at the counter. "Four pepperoni slices and the XXL Coke," he requested. He fished for his wallet. "Much more cost effective to get XXL than two regulars," he whispered out of the corner of his mouth.

She reached for her purse, but he stopped her with a warm hand on her wrist. "My treat. I'm a working man, after all."

Her wrist tried not to shake. "Really? Where do you work?" She couldn't help noticing his wallet was fat with bills.

The server broke in. "Slices are up," he yelled, shoving two plates in front of them.

"Hardware store," Rand said. He shook a load of red pepper flakes onto his pizza. "Want some?"

Chel shook her head. "Wow, that's like a real job. I just do some babysitting. I can't drive yet. I mean, I can, but I'm still doing practice hours for my license. It's hard for my parents to fit them in with twins. Twice as many." She grabbed a steaming slice and stuffed it in her mouth to stop her runaway chatter. "Ha..ha..hot," she gasped.

Rand gestured to the world's largest pop. "Help yourself," he said. "I got it to share."

Only one straw. This was awkward.

He looked at her looking at the straw. A slow smile spread across his face. Without warning, he darted forward and planted a quick kiss smack on her mouth. She blinked.

"There," he said. "Now you don't need to worry about sharing germs."

"Good thinking," she said, blushing like crazy. Her feet tingled.

What was she going to tell Maya? That her first kiss was over before she knew what was happening? That she didn't even have time to memorize it?

Her lips tickled with the sting of the hot peppers from Rand's. Under the counter, her leg trembled just a bit as Rand's knee pressed up against hers. Her mind went completely blank.

But Rand began talking about his weekend job, and gradually Chel relaxed and shared a few stories about the wild Smith kids, her favorites. He told her about his family. She talked about the trials of assistant editing the school literary magazine—how she loved the challenge of organizing and being in charge, but what a lot of work it was, especially since the senior editor was too busy with college applications to do much. The pizza disappeared, along with the time. Customers came and went. December's early darkness surrounded the windows of the cozy pizza joint.

The server leaned in between them. "You kids gonna order anything else? We're getting ready for the dinner crowd."

Chel jumped off the bar stool. "Good God. What time is it?"

Rand pulled out his phone. "Almost six. Oh, wow."

Chel scarcely heard him. "Mom's going to freak. I'd better call Dad for a ride home."

Rand smoothed the panic off her face with a soft touch. "I can take you. My bike's still over at school."

Bike? That didn't sound like practical transportation in December, but Chel didn't protest. She could always call Dad from the parking lot.

Rand took her by the hand and intertwined his fingers with hers. She desperately needed to use the restroom, but there was no way she was letting go now. Too awkward, and he might take it the wrong way.

They walked outside into the cold night air. The moon was only the merest crescent, but the street lights made the falling snow sparkle with a yellowish-orange glow.

Rand's bike turned out to a be a dark red hybrid motorcycle with a seat just large enough for two. He fitted his helmet onto Chel's head and pulled a pair of leather gloves out of the cargo box. "Put on your gloves, too," he advised. "It's freezing once we get moving."

The ride home under the night sky was pure magic. Chel pressed close against Rand's back and wrapped her arms around him, just a fraction tighter than necessary. Inside the helmet, her chin rested awkwardly on his shoulder, her mouth close to his ear so she could give him directions. And even though she took the longest possible way home, it was over too soon.

Rand stopped the motorbike in the middle of her driveway, helped her down, and eased off the helmet. "So when can we do this again? Tomorrow night?" He rested his hands on her waist, pulling her close to him.

Chel's heart nearly exploded. She leaned against him, dizzy with crazy new sensations. He wanted to go out again. Tomorrow.

And she was already committed. Drat the Smiths. Drat this trip, she thought. "I'm babysitting tomorrow," she admitted with regret. "Then I'll actually be out of town till the day after Christmas."

"Seeing family?" he asked.

"Not really. More like seeing ancestors. We're going to Belize for a week and a half. My Grandpapa's full-blooded Mayan, but no one in my family has ever visited his homeland since he left it in the fifties."

"Belize," Rand said, his eyes lighting up. "That's really awesome. I'd love to travel around some day. See all the other ways people live. Ohio is just so ordinary, so boring."

Chel laughed. "I totally agree, but my Dad says sometimes boring is good. He likes that old Chinese saying: may you live in *interesting* times. The joke is it's supposed to be a curse."

"Cute. Very cute. I'll still take interesting, though," he said. He cupped her face in his gloved hands. The leather was warm, soft and fragrant. "And speaking of very cute and interesting, I want to take you out again. How about New Year's Eve, after you're home?"

The snow tumbled and swirled down on them. Rand's eyes held hers in a look that was possessive and soft at the same time. Chel melted inside. Man, he was a charmer. Confident, but sweet. She memorized this moment for her mental scrapbook of life.

"Yeah," she said. "New Year's Eve sounds perfect."

"I have a feeling it's going to be a very good year." Rand's steady, smiling gaze hypnotized her. Her lips fell apart as his head bent down toward her. She closed her eyes.

A loud honk from behind yanked her back to reality. They jumped apart.

Dad pulled into the driveway, his headlights illuminating them like a startled pair of deer. His window rolled down and his head poked out. "Chel, honey. Your Mom sent me all over town looking for you."

"Maya knew where I was," she protested. "Why didn't you just call me?"

"I did. Repeatedly," he said. "Did you turn your phone back on after school?"

Oh. Right. "Sorry, Dad. Shoot, I'm sorry. Is Mom really freaked?"

"I'll calm your mother down. Don't be long." He gave Rand a friendly look and nodded before pulling away toward the garage.

"Oops." Rand grinned. "Guess that's my cue to go."

He walked Chel up to the front door and stood in front of her, blocking the peephole.

"Thanks for everything," she said. "It was…I enjoyed…it was great. Everything." In case there was any doubt.

"Hey. I'm really looking forward to midnight New Year's Eve," he said.

"Me too," she confessed, letting her imagination run with it.

He leaned forward and kissed her softly right below the ear. He whispered, "I threw that snowball on purpose." Then he disappeared into the night.

Mom was standing, arms crossed, in the front hall, tapping her foot.

Chel ducked her head. "Sorry, Mom. I thought you knew where I was."

"Well?" Mom asked pointedly.

Chel looked at her blankly. What was the correct answer?

Mom filled her in. "I expected you to pack this afternoon."

"I'm on top of it, Mom," Chel assured her. "I've got a packing list. It'll only take five minutes."

That must have been the right answer. Mom's tight lips relaxed. She loved lists. Part of her *be prepared for anything and you won't be surprised* philosophy. It was the flipside of her other guiding principle: *expect the worst and you won't be disappointed.* Somehow Mom managed to have her glass half-full and half-empty at the same time.

"How did exams go?" she asked. "How was science?"

"Fine, Mom."

"And Spanish?"

"Bueno, Mom."

"Okay, great. Dinner's almost ready. Scoot upstairs and pack."

"Take it easy, Mom," Maya broke in, just when peace had been restored. "I'll help her." She dragged Chel by the arm toward the stairs.

"Are *you* packed?" Chel whispered.

"Are you kidding?"

As they climbed the stairs, lined with Maya's framed photographs of Baja, she quizzed Chel. "So who is he? What happened? When did it happen? Where did you guys go all afternoon? Why don't I know about him?"

Chel laughed, a giddy delighted sound. "I guess you really paid attention in journalism last year. You've got all the questions down. First, *who?* Don't you know Rand? He's in my math class."

They turned into Chel's room, and she reached under the bed for her travel backpack.

Maya snatched up the notepad from the nightstand. "Go on."

Chel tore off the top sheet—her packing list. "It was just pizza," she said casually, trying to play down her excitement. Then she couldn't help smiling. "But I have a date for New Year's Eve."

"A date?!" Maya yelled. "Get out. That's so cool. *Finally.* But New Year's? Why so long?"

"Hey, it's the best I could do." She pulled open the top drawer of her dresser. "He's working all day tomorrow, and I'm babysitting in the evening."

"Dang, girl. I'll cover that babysitting job for you. Call him and tell him you're free."

"But you detest the Smith kids! You said you never wanted to see them again."

Maya rolled her eyes. "Just the toddler from hell who eats marbles."

Chel giggled. "Yeah, Jody. She's adorable. Her brothers call her The Choker. Course it's their fault for never picking up."

"She scares me," Maya confided. "But I can handle it. Nine-nine-one, right? Come on. Call him."

"I don't have his number. I can wait. Really," Chel insisted.

Maya shrugged. "Okay. Whatever." She perched on the edge of the bed, watching Chel count out ten pairs of panties for the ten days plus one spare for emergencies. "Keep talking..."

Chel slid the pile of underclothes into the travel pack. "What am I up to? Oh. *When?* He threw a snowball at me right after exams. *Where?* We hung out at Donelli's. The time just flew."

She folded khaki and navy capris into her bag and ticked them off the list. Now, five sleeveless cotton blouses that matched either pair of pants would do it. She remembered an oversized T-shirt for sleeping and tankini for swimming in the resort pool. All she needed was one nice outfit for the Christmas Eve mass—a bright wraparound skirt and embroidered white blouse that looked striking with her dark coloring. She had the same perma-tan as Maya; she just didn't show it off. With her curvier body, she didn't want to look like a cheap advertisement.

"Did he kiss you goodnight?" Maya asked.

Chel blushed. "Sort of."

The last items slipped into the outer pocket—her leather-bound journal and the special engraved pen Grandpapa had given her for her fifteenth birthday. In six months, she'd already filled half of it with her poems. She zipped everything closed.

"What the hell is sort of?" Maya snatched the packing list and crumpled it into a ball. "Come on. My turn."

Chel followed her, stepping over the piles of discarded jeans and sweaters strewn across Maya's floor. She picked up a blue fuzzy sweater and began folding.

Maya took it from her and tossed it into the overflowing hamper. She swept a pair of panties off the unmade bed and scooped the contents of her summer drawer from her dresser onto the sheets.

Chel watched as Maya carefully chose the clothes that made the most of her small, slender build and naturally tanned skin. Almost all of it, Chel thought.

"Oh yeah. White beaches, here I come." Maya dangled the world's skimpiest bikini top from her pinkie finger.

Chel looked through the bedroom window at the snowstorm. Starlight sparkled on the white dusting just starting to accumulate on the lawn. Of course Maya hated the snow, hated cold, hated bundling up in thick, padded coats and wonderful bunchy, wool sweaters. But Chel loved a white Christmas. For the first time in years, they might finally have one, and she would miss it—her own fault, of course. She was the one, after all, who begged Mom and Dad to pick Belize for Christmas break. She was the one who'd been dreaming of it, literally, since she did that report on the Mayans for Ancient Civ.

"We're not on the beach," Chel said off-handedly.

"What are you talking about?" Maya demanded. "I checked out a website. Belize is like coastal Caribbean. Great scuba and snorkeling." She stuffed all the shorts, skorts, tank tops, and tube tops into her travelpack and pressed them down.

"True, but our resort is inland, on the Guatemala side."

"So we can drive to the beach. Whatever."

Should she say anything? Maybe not. Chel didn't feel like dealing with a pouting session. Maya would be really ticked that the resort was over two hours away from the coast. But that's where the really great archeological sites were—the ones she and Dad picked out together when they made their reservations. She'd even asked Dad at the time, "Should we warn Maya now?"

Dad's advice was, "I don't think so. What the eye doesn't see, the heart doesn't grieve."

"She'll see and grieve when we get there," Chel warned.

Dad shrugged it off. "Don't borrow trouble before it's due."

"You have one for everything, don't you?"

"Probably," Dad said. "Wisdom of the ages."

"Wisdom of the *aged*, you mean," Chel teased.

So Chel decided to drop it. She smiled as Maya's backpack grew chubbier. "Hey, it's only ten days. It's not like we're moving!"

Maya rolled her eyes, dark as her favorite black olives. "I like to have a choice. I don't know what I'll feel like wearing in the morning. Besides, this stuff packs down to nothing." She strained at the zipper until it closed the track of the bulgy bag.

"I'd rather take nothing," Chel responded. "Go native. Buy some real Belizean clothes when I get there."

"Be my guest. I'm not taking any chances." Maya tossed the backpack into a corner.

"You know what Dad would say. That thing about Destiny isn't chance. It's a matter of choice."

"Exactly what I said. I like to have a choice. And I choose to be well-dressed." Maya always claimed the last word on the subject.

The goddess still slept as deep as the dead when we came out of the cave. I did not trust the young slaves or the old men to carry her. She was light in my arms, only as much as a small cornerstone, perhaps ten or twelve knuckles on a side, no burden. We walked until the end of morning, until we could see the top of the temple gleaming white in the sun high above the trees. On the sunrise side, the huge carved face of Chaak, god of rain and thunder, god of planting and harvest, watched for our return. Grandfather had ordered construction of this frieze on the newest level of the temple when the rains first began to fail us even before my birth. Now Chaak smiled on us. Surely he had sent this living omen in my arms, moved by our devotion.

My heart beat fast within my chest. My Father would be pleased with what I brought home to him and to my elder brother K'awiil.

They sat inside the audience room, taking complaints and settling disputes on this, the smallest day of the year. The growing days of the year should be filled with good will between brothers and friends, not arguments. Ill feelings should be left behind with the darkness. K'awiil sat beside our Father the divine king, the K'ul Ahaw, listening to his wisdom and learning kingship. My place was not with them. I was the one who learned the stars and the calendar and the way we write our greatest deeds.

I saw that K'awiil had put on gold ear spools, large as a hand, larger even than our Father's. He wore a jaguar pati over his shoulder, also in imitation of the king, but his jaguar's maw was set open and snarling.

The few craftsmen and farmers waiting to be heard drew apart as I entered with the goddess and the priests.

"Send them away," I requested.

My Father frowned yet he gestured for all but his guards to leave. I laid the still sleeping goddess on the soft fur mat at his feet. His dog, Sac-tz'ul, so called for his unusual pale skin, rose from his sleeping spot and moved toward the goddess with curiosity.

"Keep him off," I said, forgetting politeness.

My Father-king waved the dog back with a snap of his fingers. "What is this drowned wench you drop before my throne?"

"She is the goddess Ix Chel," I replied. "She came to us from Xibalba in this, a young woman's form. The good omen we prayed for, Father."

"She's dead," he said with a shake of his head. The feathers of his splendid headdress fluttered. "Of what use is that?"

"No, she breathes, Father," I assured him. "She rests after her long journey through the thirteen underworlds." That was the only way I knew how to explain. "Receiving the noble blood of our sacrifices will soon revive her."

Father eyed her with a look of calculation. "How do I know what you say is true?"

I confess his distrust was a blow to my spirit. He had given me to the priests to train and now he doubted I could recognize one of the mighty?

"In four ways, Father Ahaw," I answered. "She came to us deep in the heart of the crystal cavern. She spoke the language of the gods. She spoke her name to us." I saved the most important for last. "And you will see when she wakes that her eyes contain all the sky—her true home—and the rain, which she will surely bring to us if we honor her properly."

Father raised himself from the soft jaguar pelts lining his stone bench. The jade bracelets covering his forearms clattered as he stepped forward to clap me on the shoulders. "Well done, boy," he said.

My eyes dropped from his blazing presence.

"Take the Lady Chel to my wife's room," he commanded the guards.

I hurried to lift her first. "I will," I said. "Which wife?"

"Ix Imul. The young pregnant one." A gleam lit his face. "Perhaps my next son will be birthed by the goddess herself." His laugh held a prideful sound.

My elder brother K'awiil also placed a heavy hand on my shoulder. "Tell Ix Imul to call me when the lady wakes. I wish to see her sky-eyes. And perhaps the first face she beholds on this earth should be mine, little brother, not your *chitam sotz'*."

Pig nose. His favorite name for me.

"She has already seen me, for a moment," I said in quiet.

"Perhaps that is why she swoons." K'awiil laughed till his handsome, bold face turned red. My Father Ahaw joined him.

In the night, howls came from the women's rooms. In the morning, I had two new brothers.

I can't say how long I was passed out. My watch had stopped at noon on December 21, and I had no sense of time. I had gone from darkness to darkness—from the cave to a windowless room, where I was eventually woken by a scream. It could have been my own.

At some point my blackout changed to regular sleep. I recognized it by the horrible recurring nightmare that held me in its grip again. In the dream, small dark-skinned, round-faced people crowded around me, calling my name, reaching toward me and pleading with me in a foreign language. I was just beginning to feel the confusing sounds that pounded on my ears separate into syllables. Almost into words that made sense. Here and there I caught the meaning of a phrase, and I struggled to hold onto the feeling. No use.

In the dream, a man stepped forward, bound just like the man in the cave. He bowed once to me, and I gestured to the man standing behind him. The captive stood motionless, fixing trusting eyes on me while a huge knife which swung like a scimitar sliced his head from his shoulders. His open eyes still watched me as his head rolled to my feet. And the most nightmarish part was that it all seemed normal.

Then the sound of screaming woke me.

I sat up, heart racing. Ragged, heavy breathing filled my ears, and I knew for sure it wasn't mine. I was scared breathless. "Who's there?" I called out in the dark.

From across the room, a long, drawn out, wailing moan rose like a lonely coyote's and faded away, human and animal at the same time. Beyond the walls, the scuffle of hurrying feet came closer. Two women burst into the room, holding flaming bowls. The fire lit their faces from below, coloring their smooth skin and dark eyes amber. They lit oil lamps in the corners of the room, and by the dim yellow light, I saw the poor girl who had made that unearthly sound. She looked about my age, maybe seventeen at the most, and her stomach was hugely swollen. She was braced in a sitting position against the wall, knees up. Her hands gripped the long hair of the animal fur under her as if her life depended on it. A loose cotton dress covered her to the ankles, but there was no doubt in my mind what was going on. This teenager was about to have a baby.

Sometimes I wake inside a dream but find I'm in another dream, like layers. It felt just like that. The flickering lights, the strange woman, the pregnant girl—all too strange to be true. But I knew I was awake, and this surreal scene was no dream.

Thank God the women had arrived, nurses or midwives who had heard the first screams of labor. At least they had competent staff in this hospital, even if it was the weirdest hospital I'd ever seen. The walls were plastered stone and white-washed, but there weren't any beds or gurneys or IV's or call lights or electrical fixtures or privacy curtains or sinks or anything like modern technology. The girl and I were several feet apart on animal skins on top of a woven rug that covered a stone floor. Not a sterile environment for patient care. The only light came from the bowls of burning oil, which gave off a resinous smell.

Where was I?

I took it all in while the girl caught her breath between moans. The nurses in their rough, woven shifts ignored me as they huddled round the girl, softly muttering encouraging instructions that sounded like nonsense to me. They stroked her belly, pushed her into different positions. The poor girl twisted and groaned, strained and panted. I was glad to hide back in the shadows with my little concussion, bothering no one. I desperately wanted to ask the nurses about Maya and my parents, but all their attention, with good reason, of course, was on the girl in labor.

I turned away and lay curled on my fur, dazed and disconnected. My stomach heaved dangerously, but I swallowed hard and managed to hold it down. I didn't see a bag or bowl nearby.

The nurses' unfamiliar words washed over me, making my head ache. What language were they speaking? English was the official language of Belize. Had I been taken into Guatemala or all the way to Mexico? But no, it wasn't even Spanish. I would have recognized that. So where the heck was I? How far out of civilization was this primitive hospital?

Urgent questions drowned me. I couldn't even get started on who, what, when, where, and why.

In spite of the heavy breathing and moaning, I drifted in and out of sleep as the hours went by. I'd never had a concussion before. I didn't know what was normal. And no one checked on me.

A loud, heated argument between the nurses roused me. They were pointing at me, one of them gesturing with anger, while the other one had a hand on her arm, trying to calm her. The angry woman stormed out, her last words hurled back at me: "...ichelle," uttered with contempt.

So they knew who I was? I shook my aching head in confusion. The exhausted teenager looked over at me now with heavy, pleading eyes and reached out a trembling hand. She was pale and drenched in sweat. This delivery was not going well at all.

The kinder nurse came to me and asked me something over and over again in gibberish. I stared at her helplessly, not understanding a word. Finally, with a frustrated sigh, she heaved me up by the arm and hauled me toward the other "bed."

The girl groaned again with the pain of a contraction, and when it released its grip she called pitifully, "...ichelle, ichelle."

The nurse pushed me even closer. What did they expect me to do?

I crouched beside the girl, frantic with concern, trying to offer her whatever encouragement and consolation I could. Stupid words that made no sense. "It's okay. Hang in there. You can do it." Stupid words. It never happened like this on medical TV shows. Someone always knew what to do or had a phone to call 911. Maybe the baby was breech, stuck upside down, and would never make it out. Oh, why wasn't the doctor here yet? "Doctor!" I yelled out. "Doctor! There's a problem."

The angry nurse came back with a small bowl, which she pressed to the girl's lips. "Ca cal tun," the nurse said. The girl sniffed and wrinkled her nose. She tried to turn her head away, but the nurse barked at her.

One word jumped out at me: *ch'obobej*—drink fast.

How did I know that?

The mean nurse forced her to gulp down every last drop of the pungent liquid. It reminded me of an Italian restaurant for no particular reason. Then I recognized the scent of fresh basil.

The nurse who had stayed with us pulled back the girl's gown, exposing her in a really embarrassing position and pushed me into the spot between the girl's knees. With her eyes and gestures she commanded me to take her place. A torrent of words came from her mouth, every few seconds, my name and another word repeated, *to'*—it meant *help*. Somehow I knew it meant *help*. I was supposed to help?

"Me? You want me to deliver this baby? You're nuts. You're all insane." My nightmares had never been this vivid, this bizarre.

She turned her back to me, to both of us, crossed her arms, and faced the wall.

Limp with exhaustion, the girl grabbed my hands as I knelt before her. I felt entirely useless, entirely helpless. Over my head. Out of my depth.

"I don't know how to help you," I whispered to her. "I'm so sorry."

She whimpered weakly. Oh God. Was she going to die in childbirth in front of my eyes?

Another contraction attacked her, and she squeezed my hands so hard between hers, I thought my fingers would break. Tears of pain, tears of frustration filled my eyes. "Damn it, why me? What am I supposed to do?" I yelled at the ceiling.

I placed my hand on her burning stomach, hard as a rock. The poor thing was too worn out with pain to do her part. I begged her, "Push, girl. Try to push. Please." Tears ran from my eyes, splashing across her taut belly as I pressed with her.

Suddenly, her eyes brightened. "Oh," she cried. "Ah...oh."

Her body heaved under my touch and a small dark head appeared between her knees. The nurse's hands darted between us, and she caught the baby as it slid free. Holding the child in one arm, she pulled a knife from her belt, ready to cut the cord, but her smile of triumph turned into a wail of dismay and disappointment. She dropped the unmoving infant onto the nasty, wet fur and flung the knife away. Blue. The baby was a dark ashen color, the umbilical cord wrapped around his neck.

"Oh my God, no!" I yelled. "Not after all that! Call a code. Code Blue," I ordered the stupid nurse.

I snatched the baby from the ground, unwound the cord, cut it free, and did what the Red Cross had drilled into me in all those babysitting classes. CPR on a plastic dummy wasn't even remotely close to real life. I blew sips of air into the tiny lungs and compressed the tiny chest, my fingers slipping across his slick, wet skin.

Breathe, breathe, press, press, press, press.

I couldn't remember my counts exactly, but I breathed and pressed like nothing else in the world existed.

The two women stared at me. Damn it. Why hadn't the nurse done this? Why weren't they running for a crash cart?

Finally, something twisted in my hands. The baby moved, opened his own mouth wide, and yowled. It was the happiest sound I'd ever heard.

The new mother reached out her hands to me with a cry of joy, and the nurse threw herself face down on the floor at my feet. I suppose I deserved it—I'd probably just saved her job. I was about to gladly hand off the little one to his mother when her face took on an odd expression. She arched back and yelped and another head appeared between her legs.

I kicked the prostrate nurse and yelled, "Get up and do your job, you old crone." At least, that's what I meant to say, but the words came out wrong. Even so, she leapt up and caught the twin who, thank God, was pink and noisy.

The mother smiled ear to ear, and the trauma of the past hours was instantly forgotten. She pulled off her sweat-soaked nightgown and held a baby to each dark, swollen breast as if she knew exactly what to do.

I had never seen anything so weird or so perfect in all my life.

CHAPTER THREE
December 16, 2012

The nightmares started the moment Chel fell asleep on the airplane.

Even though the Smiths had come home early the night before as promised, Chel didn't conk out until after midnight, and the alarm went off at four sharp. So as soon as the plane stopped climbing and hit that cruising altitude drone, Chel's heavy eyes closed. Against the backdrop of deep, constant hum, Maya's bright chatter floated as she flirted with the cute guy in the seat next to hers.

Their mingled voices faded away, and instead Chel heard different voices, many voices. A rhythmic drumming sounded, an echo of the slight pulse of the jet engines. A droning chant filled Chel's senses, strange syllables forming unfamiliar words. She relaxed into the random sound.

Then the visuals in her dream theatre clicked on. She stood on a broad plaza with a crowd of dark-skinned men dressed in the most amazing feathers and copper jewelry. The beating sun glared off the white-painted stone terrace underfoot, making Chel squint. Behind her loomed an enormous rectangular pyramid. Steep stairs led up to a high terrace on which waited a group of men even more finely dressed. From the plaza she turned and climbed the seemingly endless stairs, her legs never tiring.

The drummers were now far below her, but the percussive thrum of beaten skins and clacks of sticks on turtle shells rose up the sides of the pyramid, rebounding off the hard surfaces. The splendidly dressed men pushed forward another man, a bound captive, naked except for a loin wrapping. He held his head proudly, but his eyes danced as if he were drugged.

Chel nodded to the men presenting him. One of them drew a tremendous knife. The sun glanced off it brilliantly, blindingly. He swung.

Chel's eyes flew open. A startled yelp burst from her as she knocked Mom's tray table. Coffee sloshed everywhere.

"Oh, for goodness sakes," Mom said. "Now I'll be wearing coffee all day." She dabbed at her lap with a five-inch square napkin.

Dad offered his napkin as well, which hardly helped. "No use crying over spilt coffee," he joked.

Mom shot him an exasperated glare.

"Oh, Mom. I'm sorry. Really sorry," Chel said. "I drifted off and had an awful nightmare."

The dream had cut off mid-scene, but Chel still had the sick feeling in her stomach that something awful was about to happen. That sense of gloom hung over her, even though she was fully awake now. Well, the travel clinic had warned them that the anti-malaria pills could cause vivid dreams, even nightmares. Maybe she was extra susceptible.

"For goodness sakes," Mom said again. "A nightmare? I knew I shouldn't have let you stay out so late last night."

Which was quite unfair, Chel thought, since it wasn't like she was hanging out with friends—she'd been working. And besides, she got home at a perfectly decent hour, and any sleep she lost could be blamed on her excitement about the trip.

"Do you have anything you could change into?" Chel asked.

"Don't be ridiculous. Of course I do," Mom replied. "But I can't imagine changing in those tiny bathrooms, and heaven knows how long it will be before we land, get through customs, and get to the resort." She sighed.

"Remember, honey. What can't be cured must be endured," Dad interjected.

"Sorry, Mom," Chel said again.

"Oh well," Mom said. "I'll manage."

Chel wasn't sure whether she was supposed to end up feeling bad or cheered up by this announcement. She stared out the window at the tops of the clouds and refused to let the engine noise change back into drumming in her head.

December 17. This morning, I woke up in Belize! Chel wrote in her leather journal. *Today's adventure is an ancient Mayan city near the resort. It's called Xunantunich, shoo-nan-toon-eesh, which according to the guidebook means Stone Maiden. I love all these words that start with X.*

Chel and her Dad had spent hours on the internet poring over the tourist options before they chose a resort in the Cayo District, right on the western border of Belize. Dad had arranged a private guide for all the side trips. It wasn't hard. Tourism was a booming industry, and Belize was the one country in Central America where English was the official language. You could even pay for things in dollars.

Hernán, their guide, was a short, solid young man with more than a little Mayan in his ancestry. His resemblance to Chel was undeniable, and, of course, Maya insisted on posing them together under a palm tree and snapping a picture.

"You can say he's your cousin a hundred times removed," she said. "It's probably true." She laughed naturally, not the usual flirty trill.

Chel blushed uncomfortably as Hernán put an arm around her waist in a cousinly way, but she humored Maya, who could be completely charming when she wasn't putting it on.

Hernán smiled at the tiny image on the back of the camera. "Yes. Very nice cousins. Okay folks. Now we can go."

He steered the van down the Western Highway, a two-lane paved road, past native Belizean homes.

Chel watched out the windows as the view bounced past. Kids on bicycles steered along the sides of the road. Men sat smoking on front porches of one- or two-room stuccoed houses. Half-dressed tots ran around the dirt lots surrounding their homes. Lazy black and brown dogs lay in the shade, their floppy ears twitching mosquitoes away from time to time.

The road ran along the Mopan River, and Chel noticed five men in blue jeans and no shirts hanging out in the water, staying cool. Nearby, women washed clothes by hand, in the same river water. Two kids splashed in the shallows.

Chel glanced back and noted electrical lines running to most of the homes. TV antennas topped a few roofs—some evidence of modern times. Rickety, narrow wooden structures that were obviously outhouses were tucked behind the houses. So. No indoor plumbing. She turned to watch the bathers in the river and wondered what they did for clean, fresh drinking water.

The tour van pulled to a stop in front of a sign that read "Xunantunich Ferry." At the landing, local women sold beaded jewelry and red-fired pottery from several stalls.

"Oooh. Can I look at the bracelets?" Maya asked.

"Maybe later," Mom said, which meant she didn't particularly want to and they'd never get around to it. "The ferry's here."

The ferry was only a motorized raft, which carried them across the calm waters of the Mopan in a couple minutes. Chel stepped off first, startling a large black iguana, which ran off into the underbrush.

"Wow, did you see that?" she asked Maya. "That's the biggest darn iguana I've ever seen."

"Oh, sorry," Maya said, examining her nail polish. "I was distracted."

Chel sighed quietly. What was the point of going to cool, exotic places if you were more interested in looking good for the good-looking tour guides?

Hernán laughed. "Big fellow. He'd make a feast for a family."

Chel shuddered. "They eat iguanas?"

"If they can catch them. Free protein is always welcome. Otherwise it's tortillas and beans for supper again, you know?"

"Bet it tastes like chicken," Maya quipped.

"Yes, you know," Hernán said, "it does."

But Chel thought about Hernán's comment and the poverty she had seen—not dire, abject homeless poverty, but certainly not the way she'd like to live or raise a family.

"Is it served in any restaurants?" Dad asked. Like Chel, he was interested in the authentic experience.

The traditional Belizean soup they'd had last night, full of unfamiliar spices, tasted absolutely wonderful. Mom and Maya had ordered chicken noodle to be on the safe side. Iguana noodle? Now that would have been interesting.

Hernán led the way along an unpaved road toward the promised ruin. "So, this place, Xunantunich, means 'stone maiden.' That's not the original name, which nobody knows yet."

Amazing, Chel thought. An entire city in ruins, the thousands of people who lived here forgotten forever, even the name of the city lost in time. It was cool and sad, all rolled into one. There should be a special word for that.

Maybe she'd compose a haiku. Yes, that was it, a haiku.

Forgotten city,
Abandoned by your people,
Who once walked your steps?

"Nineteenth-century archaeologists discovered this site," Hernán continued, breaking into her mental wandering. "Many times over the years, the ghostly figure of a young woman dressed all in white has been witnessed on the stairs of El Castillo, the tallest temple in Belize. She runs up the stairs and vanishes." He grinned.

Chel's imagination soared. "Have *you* ever seen her?"

"Not yet," he said. "But who knows, I come here on many days, and one of them may be lucky."

"I bet it's just a rumor for the tourists," Maya said. "It makes the place seem more romantic."

"It *is* romantic," Chel insisted. "Just look around!"

A toucan, more beautiful than any she had seen at the zoo, flew past from treetop to treetop, right in front of them.

Hernán pointed out its mate in a nearby tree, and they stopped to wait for the second toucan to follow the first. While they watched, he told them, "So this site I'm going to show you was abandoned at the end of the Mayan Classic Period in the late 800's. The last actual dated stone found on the site has been translated to the year 849 A.D."

The 800's! That was six hundred years before Columbus even thought about traveling West to go East. While Europe was in the Dark Ages, this civilization was flourishing in the Americas. The ruins at the top of this hill above the Mopan would be the oldest things Chel had ever seen outside a museum.

"Okay," Hernán said. "Let's keep going so we get done before the big storm blows in."

43

Chel looked up through the trees to the cloudless sky. There was a little breeze, but no sign she could see of a big storm.

"When grass is dry at morning light, look for rain before the night," Dad offered.

"What are you babbling about, Dad?" Maya scolded. She punched him in the arm. "That's totally lame. It doesn't make sense."

"Hey, we agronomists have a second sense about these things." Dad defended himself.

Chel punched him from the other side. "Dad, you're a professor, not a real farmer."

"Then what do you call all those corn stalks in our back forty?" he asked.

"A fire hazard," Mom said to Hernán. "About the storm, though, is there one predicted? We don't have a TV in our room to get the forecast."

"No, not on the TV weather," Hernán replied. "But you can smell it coming. The leaves are starting to curl, so it looks like thunder, too."

Dad nodded in agreement.

"Well, by all means, let's hurry, then," Mom said.

They climbed the hill, Maya complaining how uncomfortable her new high-heeled sandals were. She'd bought them just for the trip, and she'd have blisters for sure. Chel was glad she just brought some comfortable old shoes, even if they were a bit worn around the edges.

They turned the final corner on the rough road leading up to the site and stepped onto a mowed lawn stretching across what was once an open plaza. Chel felt the shock of familiarity as her eyes came to rest on the largest intact structure.

"What's that?" she asked. Her chest heaved with the effort of breathing, though not from the climb.

Hernán followed her gaze. "Yes, that is El Castillo, as we call it. Over six hundred feet tall. Can you imagine? Built with only stone and wood tools and the sweat of men's labor. This is our tallest ancient monument in Belize."

"El Castillo?" Chel thought she knew it by another name, a name she couldn't call to mind. But this was the temple of her nightmare, the temple she had climbed with the chanting crowd behind her. Why was it so familiar? What was it doing in her head?

She'd never been—oh, of course. She must have seen it in a guidebook or on a webpage. Maybe that planted the idea, an image that her malaria pills had dramatized. Blame the chloroquinone. That made sense.

Her feet led her to the middle of the plaza, and she spun in a circle, taking in the whole scene. She forgot to breathe. This place spoke to her on some weird level. Before Hernán pointed out the buildings, she already knew—*that* was the main palace complex to the north. There was the palace where the king's left-hand advisor lived with his three wives. Over here was where vendors set up their market stalls. This tall stair was where her son tripped and broke his wrist.

Hold the phone. *Her son?*

"Chel! Chel!" Maya's voice broke in. "Get over here before we lose you."

Chel was jolted back to reality. Good God. Those pills must cause daymares, too.

"C'mon. We're headed over to the ball court, Hernán says." Maya grabbed her arm and dragged her to catch up.

Hernán waited for them to arrive before starting his narration. "The ball game was a very important ritual sport for the Mayans and other Central American cultures like the Azteca. A combination of sport and war. You know, they had the rubber tree, *chicle*, and they made a heavy hard rubber ball and tried to get it from one end to the other, we think, like American football with no protection except a hard leather helmet."

The ball court. Two sloped areas were separated by a court of grass. It wasn't always that way, Chel knew. She closed her eyes and saw the grounds teeming with shouting and jeering spectators. The area between the sloping walls was hard stone, not grass, paved and marked with the zones of play.

She opened her eyes. Grass.

She closed them and saw near naked men in scant loin wraps, black tapir leather shin and arm guards, leather helmets. They dripped with sweat under the hot sun as they battled for control of the ball, which they passed with amazing skill using their calves, hips, and shoulders, never touching it with their hands. The crowd yelled, cheered, and cursed in a strange language.

"Are you okay? Chel, are you okay?" Maya tugged her arm.

Chel opened her eyes, dizzy at the sudden return to normal. "Holy crap, those pills are making me crazy!"

"What do you mean?" Maya asked.

Chel put her hands to her head. "I'm having the weirdest daymares."

"Like what?"

"Like I'm imagining what this was like when people actually lived here."

Maya patted her shoulder with a sisterly smirk. "You know, you might like to think of yourself as the practical one, but you've got a vivid imagination, girl. C'mon. While you were off in whateverland, Hernán said we're going to the top of the castle. I hope this is authentic enough for you."

"Is Mom freaking?"

"What do you think? Freaking on the inside, smiling on the outside."

46

Chel turned her back on the ball court, the echo of voices clamoring in her imagination.

"Keel, Keel," they called, like a blood thirsty mob. Or maybe it was more like, "Kweel, Kweel, Ka-weel, Ka-weel."

Chel covered her ears. Crazy. Just crazy.

On their path to the long stairway up El Castillo, Hernán pulled a handful of leaves from a small, round tree. He handed one to each of them. "Go on. Bite it," he ordered, demonstrating.

Maya took a tentative nibble and announced, "Spicy."

Chel put the whole leaf in her mouth. "Whoa, has that got a kick! Watch it, Mom."

"Oh, honey. It's just allspice," Mom said.

"Yes, that's right," Hernán said. "Very good for fresh breath and upset stomachs."

"Also good for pumpkin pie," Mom added.

Chel chewed her leaf, enjoying fresh breath and maybe even a calmer stomach, as they climbed up a steep stairway to the main level of El Castillo. From the high vantage, Chel could look out over the tree tops. Nothing showed of the hundreds of homes that once stood here. According to Hernán, all the small stone foundation mounds were overgrown now, the leaf mould decomposed into a rich humus that in turn allowed a new understory to take root and grow. You'd never know how far the original settlement stretched from the air.

They entered the ruin partway up through a triangular opening and continued the climb through an internal staircase. Chel's legs danced up the stairs as she hurried to the top, following Hernán. Mom trailed behind, carefully placing her feet. Heights bothered her more than she would admit.

Dad kept asking "Are you sure about this, dear?"

"Don't fuss," Mom hissed down at him. "I don't want to hold everyone back."

Dad climbed behind, ready to catch her if she stumbled. Nice to know someone had your back, especially when you were terrified. Maya and her blisters brought up the rear.

Chel popped out on top of the building, on top of the world. While the others panted up the stairway, Chel and Hernán stood side by side looking down at the plaza and across to the palace. It was crushingly familiar, yet different.

"I've been here," Chel murmured.

Hernán picked up her comment. "Oh? I thought your father said this was your first trip to Belize."

"It is," Chel said. "That's what's weird. There's no way I've been here before, but I have."

Hernán smiled. "Perhaps your soul travels a circular path."

Chel was about to ask what he meant when her Mom burst through the opening to the upper level. "Oh my God," she said. "No guard rails. Honey, there's no guard rails."

Chel turned away from the embarrassing scene of Dad trying to calm down her mother, who had insisted on coming up in the first place.

Either conquer your fear, or don't, Mom, she thought. This is lame.

She stood two feet from the edge, back far enough for safety and close enough to raise Mom's blood pressure. She spread her arms, closed her eyes, and let the wind caress her. The breeze lifted her heavy hair and tossed it across her face.

In her imagination, thousands of people crowded the plaza below. Their voices rose as one to the top of El Castillo, calling "Michelle. Michelle. Ichelle. Ichelle. Ix Chel! Ix Chel!" and she knew what she needed to do.

She lifted her hands to the clouds and called out, "Shock!"

A crack of thunder rang out across the sky. Chel's eyes flew open. Rain started to fall.

"Get down quick, everyone," Mom ordered. "We can't stay up here in the open if there's lightning. Come on, Chel, Maya. There's a storm coming on!"

At first light, a slave came from my Father, instructing me to bring the goddess to his presence. He had been told that she woke to bring my two brothers into the world; more, that she had breathed life into the first-born, who was born still. My Father Ahaw strutted about, the slave said, proud father of living twin boys even as his own hair was completely gray. I wondered if that piece of good fortune was due more to the youthful strength of his third wife, not even one *k'atun* of years.

Good omen piled on good omen, whatever the cause. We had reason to be hopeful.

I hurried to the women's rooms. The sight that met me brought new and unknown feelings to my chest. My breath caught, half in, half out.

By the unsteady lamp light, I saw the two dark-haired girls leaning against each other as sisters. My Father's wife Ix Imul suckled one of the boys. He was hardly larger than her breast. The goddess, looking down, cradled the other sleeping son, her fingertip in his mouth. His tiny pursed lips pulled on her finger as he slept and sighed. With her head bowed, she looked like any other maiden of the city. But when she lifted her head and eyes to me, I was pierced again as if lightning bolts struck from the clear blue day in her eyes.

I swallowed surprise and found words. "Lady Chel, if you please, K'ul Ahaw, the divine king my Father, wishes to thank you." In the quiet room, my voice echoed harsh and loud. She put a finger to her lips, and I fell silent.

"Take him," she whispered, and held the child toward me, who had never handled anything so small and weak.

Her first words, I had to obey. Well enough. I was not destined to be a warrior king, it seemed. Performing this gentle woman's task would not un-man me more. And there were no witnesses to tell.

The child weighed no more than a warm pup. My hand easily cupped his head and shoulders. He stirred, waking, and I tucked him against my chest before he could fall to the floor.

The goddess rose and stretched like a jaguarondi arising from a sunny nap. She watched me with approval, and I felt weak when I should have felt strong. Her gaze held strange power.

"Let me put him down," she said, and took my tiny brother to wrap him in cloth and rest him against the warm side of his mother. Ix Imul turned a worried face, but Ix Chel promised to return. I did not understand this by her strange god-words, but I felt the sense of them.

"What is this place?" she asked me as I led her through passages and stairways. She spoke this to me as a mix of words, some god-speech and then a simple question, just as we speak.

I would not appear too foolish, but I could only reply in my own tongue. "We go to the reception room." My Father Ahaw would be there, surrounded by splendor to show his most powerful presence. He was not one to humble himself, even, it seems, to a goddess.

"My Father Ahaw attends us." I explained. "This is our palace."

Ix Chel paused by a window and looked out at the sight of our fields below, lit by the rising sun. "What city? What is it called?" she asked.

"Green-hill. Yaxmuul. Do you not know?"

The goddess breathed heavily and said, "I fear I am lost to my family. You found me? In the cavern?"

This time, I understood all of her words. "Yes," I said.

"Were there others, others like me?" she asked.

"I saw no other gods with you," I replied.

She fell silent. Her head hung low in sorrow. It was unbearable to see.

"I can return and search again," I suggested.

Her words were too rapid for me to understand, but her face showed gladness and excitement. One part of her expression was hope, and so I feared failing in my search. I feared seeing the light of that hope returned to misery.

We came to the reception room where my Father waited with K'awiil.

"Here is the Lady Chel," I said, and to her I said, "Here is my Father K'ul Ahaw and my elder brother, his heir, our prince, K'awiil."

I was careful to observe all proper formality even though she had just seen me hold an infant and I had just seen her shed tears.

"For the safe delivery of my twin sons, I must thank you," Father said. "Welcome goddess. You honor us with your attention. You will make your earthly home with us."

Lady Chel regarded him in her guise of frightened young woman. I stepped closer to her.

I watched my Father's eyes fill with hunger, as did K'awiil's.

We were in an interior room without windows, and morning came unnoticed as I helped Imul handle the two newborns. Between gestures and half-understood words, we spoke and kept each other company. Her quiet, cheerful presence kept me from breaking. Later, I told myself, I would get oriented. I was sure I hadn't drifted unconscious far from where the canoes capsized or I would have drowned. My rescuers had somehow separated me from my family. But by daylight, I'd find them. I had to believe that.

The longer we whispered, the more sense I got of Imul's language. I recognized the pattern first—the language I'd been hearing in my dreams for months. The rhythm, the stops, the alternating vowels and consonants—the pattern must have impressed itself on my imagination. And the words? If I let my mind drift, the sounds translated into actual words. Part of my mind struggled with the unfamiliar sounds while part understood the sense without translation. The same with speaking. There was no logic to it, of course, but if I answered without thinking, my mouth formed words in her language, as if I'd always known them. My tongue knew how to wrap around the unfamiliar syllables, but if I thought too hard, it all fell apart and English came out. My head buzzed strangely as we spoke, making me slightly nauseated. Still, we managed to communicate.

That's how I learned that her name was Imul, that young as she was, she was married to an important man here. I had to ask myself why he hadn't attended the birth. Something cultural, I guess. Sure, I knew that girls married younger in Mexico and Belize, but I was shocked when Imul confessed that at age fourteen she had been offered by her father, some other local leader, to become engaged to her husband, a man she had never met. That was ruled child abuse in Utah and Texas, but here in Belize, Imul considered it normal. She gave every sign of being content, happy even.

I couldn't wait to tell Maya and Mom about my nighttime adventure when we were reunited. I imagined what Dad would say, something about clouds and silver linings. If I hadn't been half-drowned and dragged off to this place, this baby in my arms would never have made it. My heart filled with gratitude that I'd been here for Imul, known what to do. The baby sucked my finger, and I stared at his perfect little face while Imul slept between feedings. His brother had fallen asleep in the crook of her arm. They were so tiny, they might have been preemies, like me and Maya. Twins always come a little early, but Maya and I had spent our first month in side-by-side incubators while our lungs matured. These little dudes were breathing fine.

When Imul stirred and put the sleeping baby down on his stomach, I rolled him to his back. They'd taught us about SIDS in Red Cross babysitting. I wasn't taking any chances after all the effort I had spent jump-starting his big brother.

A sound at the doorway startled me, and I looked up to see a vaguely familiar face. The man at the door watched us closely. He was stocky, about my height maybe, five and a half feet, and clearly Mayan, though his nose was small and slightly upturned. Imul smiled at him and made no move to cover herself, so I thought, this must be the proud father. He didn't appear terribly kingly, the word Imul had used to describe her husband, but, hey, love was blind, or at least a little blurry.

He spoke loudly—I wasn't used to his voice and couldn't understand a word—and the baby in my arms startled. I shushed him and handed him the child I held. I had to smile at the awkward way he clasped it at arms length. He had no clue how to handle this little miracle. Did he have any idea how close he'd come to losing one of them? Had anyone told him? Maybe so, because he pulled the baby against his wide chest and hugged him carefully.

"Hey, congratulations," I said with a smile. From his quizzical expression, I could tell it came out in English. Try again. "Here, I'll put him down," I offered. This time the words flowed out of my mouth with that double sense.

He understood me and gestured for me to come with him.

"I'll be back soon," I promised Imul. "Try to get a little more sleep."

I tried to release and relax my mind so that I could talk to this man. I was pretty sure he was the one who found me. I asked about the rest of my family. Where were they now? Were they injured or okay? For all I knew, they might be in the very next room. But from the look on his face, I got the impression that I had been found alone.

Alone. I wasn't ready to hear that.

Okay, then. That was okay, because maybe my family had made it all the way out of the cave through another opening. Maybe Mom and Dad floated out on the broken wreckage of their canoe. And Maya was a strong swimmer. And Enrique knew all the passages. So maybe they'd been able to go all the way through. Maybe anything except the worst possibility.

Tears filled my eyes, and I blinked them away. To cry would be to let myself believe the worst. So I wouldn't cry.

He touched my arm gently. "I can return and search again," he said.

I understood him clearly, every word, and my hope bubbled up. Yes, he could search again. I gave him a fluent description of the crystal cave, of our canoes, of Mom and Dad and Maya, even our guide. I said Enrique's family was probably frantic looking for him. Unless he'd made it out and they were all frantically looking for me.

I followed Imul's husband through a maze of rooms and stairs. We passed several triangular windows, which brightened our way. The big red sun was just rising over fields filled with dry stalks of corn, past harvest time, I suppose. My throat closed at the familiar sight. Our own small organic farm was taking a break for winter, but two months ago, it looked just like this in the mornings as I left for school, the soft glow of the rising sun turning the dry stalks a pinkish-orange.

Fresh air blew through the rooms, and it struck me as strange that, even in this warm climate, a hospital would have open air windows with no barricades to prevent falls. Not even screens to keep out the hungry mosquitoes. Mom would totally disapprove.

We turned a corner and came to the largest room I had yet seen. First I noticed the windows, with a commanding view of the acres of fields below and the tropical forest beyond them. Next, my eyes flew to the beautiful murals on the white-washed walls. They were as fine, or rather finer, than anything we had seen in the museums or the guide books—perfectly executed paintings of native warriors in combat, of kings and captives and the famous ball game. The colors of the dyes were brilliant yellows and oranges, deep reds and black. An unusual theme for a lobby, and rather violent, actually, but this was Mesoamerica. They were very proud of their cultural heritage.

Finally, my glance fell on the two men who dominated the room, and I couldn't believe they were the last to catch my eye. The older man, dressed in a brilliantly colored cloak of feathers, wore a matched headdress that must have topped him by another foot and a half. Although the man himself was hardly over five feet, the towering headdress gave the impression that he was huge and powerful. A jaguar skin wrapped his waist, and the sharply fanged head hung at his side, magnificent and horrible all at once. Authority and command poured from his face.

The most bizarre dog I'd ever seen lay at his feet, totally hairless except for the bristles on his large, upright ears. From his size and the look of his muscles, he appeared more hunting dog than lap dog.

At his side stood a tall, noble-looking man in his mid-twenties, his lean body all muscle. A collar of iridescent shells lay across his otherwise bare chest. He stood a few inches taller than me, even accounting for the raised platform, and looked down a sculpted nose that was straight off a piece of pre-Columbian art. Slightly crossed eyes gave him a puzzled look, and I noticed that his father wore it as well. Perhaps a family trait? Or, maybe he was, in fact, puzzled at my sudden appearance.

For a moment, I was utterly lost. The story my imagination had constructed of a primitive hospital in a corner of Belize somewhere near the Mopan River was disintegrating before my eyes. This scene had an unmistakable genuine feel, like a movie set that never ended, and extras who were the real deal.

The elder man spoke first, and every word fell crystal clear on my ears. "For the safe delivery of my twin sons, I must thank you," he said.

His sons? Did he misspeak? Mean to say grandsons? I thought back to Imul's description of her husband's kingly bearing. Light broke through my stupid blindness. This elderly man, not the young man who had escorted me, had fathered those two babies with Imul. Oh help. What kind of back-country cult had I landed in?

"Welcome, goddess," he continued.

Now I knew my delusion was complete.

"You honor us with your attention. I am pleased you have chosen to make your earthly home with us."

He examined me up and down with a look he really should have reserved for Imul. I shivered in my light cotton dress.

The man at my side took a step closer to me, and the heat of his broad body radiated across the inches between us. He must have a metabolism like a furnace.

The king, the K'ul Ahaw, I suppose I must call him, called to the man beside him without removing his probing gaze from me. "K'awiil. Offer the goddess some fruit. You eat food in this form?" he asked me.

This form? How was I supposed to answer that? The way he was looking at me, I hesitated to argue that I was a lost teenaged girl, separated from her family, not some goddess. It didn't seem the wisest move. I took the safest route and merely nodded.

The one he called K'awiil stepped forward with a bowl of fresh fruits. My hand reached for the only one immediately familiar and easy to eat—a humble banana. He caught my eye as I wrapped my hand around the fruit, and a slight smile tilted his lips. His canine teeth showed, flashing me a glimpse of green jade grillz. His eyebrows lifted as I blushed beneath my tan and my breath caught.

He leaned toward me, breaking into my comfort zone, and paralyzed me with his confident gaze. "I think you would prefer a bigger one," he offered. A burning sensation flooded my belly as I imagined he might not be referring to the fruit.

"I would...I will take one also to Imul," I managed in their language.

"Of course," the K'ul Ahaw said abruptly from the dais, and I felt his dismissal.

So much for the power of being mistaken for a goddess.

K'awiil thrust the fruit bowl at my guide. "Men Ch'o, brother, take this to our little mother."

Little mother? Oh. Imul, of course.

Men Ch'o. He finally had a name. How stupid of me not to have asked. But maybe he had told me when all the words were jumbled. Now they came more clearly, as if God had downloaded updated software into my brain.

When we were out of hearing, Men Ch'o said, "I apologize for the rude behavior of my brother."

"Oh, I didn't find him rude," I said to reassure him. Unsettling, unnerving, for sure.

"Ah. That is good." Men Ch'o sounded doubtful.

I still clutched that stupid banana, and as we walked I peeled it. My stomach growled at the first food it had seen in I don't know how long. Men Ch'o paced silently beside me.

I grabbed an opportunity that might not come again soon. "Can you take me to a window? Or outside? I need...I need to get my bearings."

I don't know what I hoped to see, but these stone floors, stone walls, stone ceilings were making me claustrophobic. I needed to look out over the jungle and see how close we were to something recognizable—San Ignacio or the border crossing into Guatemala, the Mopan River, the Western Highway, anything.

He glanced at my cotton dress in a very different way than his father and brother had done. "You will be chilled," he said.

"No, I'll be fine," I said. "I'm tough."

His smile flickered, a look that completely changed his usually serious face. "I believe you are," he said.

He took a new turn and paused before the doorway. "The people have been awake since sun up." He touched my arm, trying to convey a meaning I totally didn't get.

"They have been told that you are here," he said.

Well, that was good, wasn't it? Maybe someone would have news of my family.

I stepped from the darkness of the building into bright morning sunshine. I squinted and shaded my eyes. The terrace on which we stood overlooked a broad plaza filled with people. Vendor stalls around the edges were conducting business. Children playing a game of tag knocked their way through the crowd. My family hadn't been to this town, I was sure, but I had a sudden sense of déjà vu.

One woman carrying a loaded basket glanced up and saw us. Her eyes widened. At her cry, other heads turned, and the crowd pressed toward us. I stared across the plaza, past the crowd, over their heads. El Castillo rose up before me. My mind seized up, refused to comprehend. There loomed El Castillo as no one had ever seen it—stuccoed, painted, intact, magnificent in the full light of morning. The pyramid temple dominated the plaza beneath it, stretched high toward the clouds.

"Xunantunich?" I whispered.

Men Ch'o looked at me, puzzled. "Stone maiden? I do not understand."

He didn't understand? I almost laughed. *He didn't understand?!* All around me I saw Xunantunich alive, perfect, bustling with activity.

A chant rose from the crowd, echoing the soundtrack of my nightmares. And now I could finally understand the words. "Chel, Lady Chel. Welcome, Lady Chel. Be with us, Lady Chel. Bless us, Lady Chel."

They went on and on, and I waited anxiously for the next part of the nightmare, because I knew this had to be an elaborate dream and, even knowing that, I couldn't make myself wake up.

Maybe I was awake, but I had fallen back into the same hallucinations that kept stealing my mind when we visited Xunantunich. I pinched myself, hard. But nothing changed.

Maybe I was in a coma. Maybe I hit my head so hard in the canoe accident and came so close to drowning that I was in a coma. Okay, that made some kind of sense. This was the story my brain was telling me while I lay in critical condition with lines and breathing tubes coming out of me.

It had to be one of those things. It *had* to.

Because if I were actually awake and all of this real, then I was truly lost beyond finding. Lost in the deep past.

And that was unthinkable.

PART II - SUCCESSION

CHAPTER FOUR
December 18, 2012

Chel woke with the sound of birds. She lay in bed listening to them sing the sun up. Maya was still dead asleep, her covers thrown off sometime in the middle of the night. She wouldn't bother to pick them up till she needed them tonight. At home, Maya could make all the mess she wanted and close her door on it. Their old brick Victorian farmhouse had plenty of high-ceilinged bedrooms, enough to spread out. They'd had their own rooms ever since their Mom separated them at a week old. Maya, the fussy sleeper, irregular, and on her own schedule interfered with Chel's nice, predictable cycle. How had they ever gotten along for almost nine months in less than one cubic foot of space? After only two days in the same room, Maya's free-spirited slob lifestyle was beginning to wear on her.

Chel slid out of bed and stepped on Maya's wet bikini, which lay dumped on the floor between their beds. It was still soaking from their late night swim, and they were supposed to bring a suit with them on the horseback ride. Sighing, she carried it into the bathroom and hung it over the shower rod. It would never dry in time, anyway.

She grabbed her notebook and quietly unbolted the door. She slipped out into the dewy, pink morning just to wander around. The gardeners were already awake and working. One snipped dead flowers on the ornamental native shrubs. The other raked fallen leaves and blossoms out of the flower beds. He picked them up by hand and tossed them into a wheelbarrow.

Chel realized what was missing from this picture—the obnoxious sound of a leaf blower. That realization made her stop and listen. Four or five distinct bird calls rose and fell. But there was no roar from the road, as there was from the highway that ran across the back of their farm. Nor was there the long hoot of a coal train from West Virginia rumbling through. At this time of morning, Belize sounded as it had for hundreds, even thousands of years. Very peaceful. Chel smiled to the world at large and jotted down a quick poem.

Late arising birds
Call to their diligent mates,
"Did you save me worms?"

When she got back to their cabin, Mom was on the porch, hanging out hand-rinsed clothes over the railing and humming. "Mornin' honey. I didn't realize you were up already. Is Maya awake?"

"I don't think so," Chel said. "She stayed up kind of late going through her pictures. She was still doing stuff to them when I put out my light."

"Well, you look ready to ride," Mom said cheerfully. She was wearing jeans and a lot of pungent bug spray, and she smiled her approval at Chel's clothes, her mid-calf capris and a long-sleeved cotton top. Mom had grown up with horses. She'd even talked about getting one since they had the acreage and the girls were old enough to help. It was a good idea. Plus it would give Mom someone else to look after in a couple of years when they left for college.

"Hey, Mom, later this afternoon, can we go into town and do some clothes shopping?"

"What do you need, honey? Did you forget something?"

"No, Mom," Chel replied. "I'd just really like to get some sort of authentic souvenir, like one of those pretty embroidered dresses we saw people wearing. Maybe some sandals? I have room in my pack."

"Well, I don't see why not."

Chel cheered. That was Mom's way of saying yes.

Even though she considered sticking to fruit for breakfast, Chel allowed herself to indulge in two good-sized pancakes—she could count on burning them off. She knew from experience that riding was quite strenuous, and they'd all feel hungry long before lunchtime. Plus the guidebook said to plan for a swim in the river, and that was good for more calories.

When they were done eating, Mom asked, "How long will it take you to change into something appropriate, Maya? We're supposed to be down in the horse pasture in about fifteen minutes."

"What do you mean—change?"

"You can't wear those short shorts on horseback, honey. You know that."

Maya pouted. "These are all I have. I didn't bring anything long. Remember, you said it would be hot."

"You want to borrow my other pants?" Chel asked.

"No way. You've already worn them. They're probably sweaty and gross. I'll just deal."

"That's lame. You're going to get chafed like crazy."

"No I'm not," Maya argued. "I've got a good seat. I'll be fine."

"An ounce of prevention," Dad suggested.

"I'll be perfectly fine," Maya insisted.

After about an hour of riding across meadows and along a high mountain trail, she drooped miserably.

Chel rode alongside her at a wide spot. "Are you okay?"

Maya just pointed to the red raw skin on the insides of her thighs.

Chel winced. "Holy crap. That looks hideous. Are you going to make it?"

"No one's offering to turn back, are they?" Maya whispered fiercely. "I'll just deal. Forget about it."

"You should've borrowed my pants," Chel said.

"No shit," Maya said. "Too late now."

"Maybe the swimming will make it feel better."

"I didn't bring my suit," Maya growled. "It was still wet even though I hung it up to dry."

"You—?" Chel stopped herself just in time. No amount of I-told-you-so's could turn back the clock.

When they reached the inviting edge of the river, Chel avoided Maya's glare as she shed her own clothes to wade in while Maya watched from shore. The cool water relaxed her leg muscles, which were tensed up after a couple hours of clenching the horse.

Tiny fish slipped by, tickling her feet. The river was overhung with lush green trees. The water was clean and clear—no industrial waste, no fertilizer run-off from lawns. She closed her eyes and allowed herself to imagine for a moment actually living in this paradise. What luxuries from home would she really miss?

"Can we go already?" Maya's voice broke her trance.

What was worse, Chel wondered. The pain? Or knowing it was all her silly, stubborn fault? Oh well. She bit her tongue. But by the fifth time Maya muttered loudly enough for everyone to hear, "I knew we shouldn't have come on this stupid horse ride," Chel couldn't hold back.

"It's not the horse ride that's stupid. It's you, you idiot. We all tried to help you this morning."

That just about killed any possibility of salvaging Maya's mood, which predictably got worse and worse. When Chel tentatively asked her if she wanted to come into town to look at the shops, she snarled back, "I am not taking another unnecessary step today."

So Chel was alone with Mom as they wandered through the colorful streets of San Ignacio. They caught lots of smiles from the local men, but Chel wasn't sure whether they were directed at her or at her tall, blond mother.

At last Chel found a perfect traditional dress, a coarse white cotton weave that fell below her knees. Hand stitched red and blue embroidery circled the neckline. When she caught sight of herself in the store mirror, she was a portrait of a local Mayan girl, except for the blue eyes, of course.

For a moment, she considered asking Mom to buy a second dress for Maya, but then she held back. Maya didn't deserve it after the bratty way she acted today. Besides, this was her own special memento of the trip. Maya had her pictures. Chel wanted the real thing. She'd wear her new outfit when they went to the caves. She could hardly wait.

This record I hesitate to write.

The goddess behaved strangely over the next four k'inal. She kept to the chamber she shared with Ix Imul. Ix Imul's women slaves brought their food and took away their chamber pots. Lady Imul rested most of the time, the women reported. When Lady Imul waked, the goddess spoke with her and helped her tend to the babies. They sent the women away, so I do not know of what they spoke. When Lady Imul slept, the slaves told me, the goddess sat quietly weeping. And while the goddess wept, the clouds gathered and the rain fell on the fields, softening the cracked, dry ground.

On the fourth day after her waking, I met a slave who was returning the goddess's untouched food to the preparation kitchen. Before she saw me, she popped one of the sweet cakes into her rounded cheek.

"What is this?" I asked. "Is this plate not to her taste? Then prepare another."

The woman dropped her eyes to the ground, swallowed, and answered. "Your pardon. Nothing is to her taste. Lady K'uk' sends many tempting dishes, but the goddess will not eat." She turned her eyes up to me. "Perhaps she has no need of mortal food?"

Perhaps she drank only mortal blood, which we had failed to provide. I grew concerned. Or perhaps she planned to leave us as suddenly as she had come and did not need to eat. The thought filled me with despair. We urgently needed her favor. I went to the women's room to try to speak with her, to ask what we might do to please her. I would gladly bleed for her, if she desired it.

Two attendant slaves stood outside the door whispering together. Lady Imul and the infants were sleeping within.

"Please ask Lady Chel to step out," I asked.

I was shocked at the change that had overcome the goddess. Our careless slaves had shamed us. How could they have stood by and watched this transformation? Had they no hearts?

Lady Chel's eyes were swollen with tears and dull as a gray puddle after rain. Her rumpled clothes stank of sweat. Her cheeks were narrowed and pale from lack of food, lack of sunshine. Her shoulders folded forward. She crumpled in on herself.

"Fetch fresh clothing from my sister's room," I ordered one slave. My sister had cast aside her maiden clothes when she left us to marry a nobleman of Saal, our nearby sister city where my Father's elder cousin, Ub'aah K'awiil, rules.

To the second servant, I said, "Bring fresh sliced papaya and mango and honeyed maize cakes. And kakaw."

The goddess stood unspeaking while all this took place. She did not meet my eyes, but listened with no interest. The first maid returned with an armload of cloth.

"Dress her," I ordered, and turned away.

When the second slave arrived with fruit and cakes, I took the bowls from her.

"Lady Chel, come with me," I requested. "You must walk outside a while."

Life sprang to her eyes, but it was fear I saw there. "The people...," she whispered.

"We will go the private way. No one will see us."

I found a solitary and peace-filled place for the goddess to sit. She stared out across the treetops and took notice of the macaws and toucans flying among their branches. She tilted her head at the sound of howlers in the trees below. The wind lifted her matted hair, and I thought to order a brush for her. How could the servants have disgraced us so?

I pushed the food at her. "You must eat this," I said.

"Thank you," she whispered. "I'm not very hungry."

How could one order a goddess? But I did so anyway. "You must eat, or your body will die. Perhaps you have forgotten the needs of the human form you wear."

"What difference?" she asked. "We'll all die. The world will end whether we eat or not."

This melancholy puzzled me. "But today we are alive," I said. "And tomorrow." I broke a piece of maize cake and gave her half. "Please."

She took a bite from the cake, and the crumbs stuck to the honey on her lips. She licked them clean, and I wished I had thought to order *aqa* or fermented juice as well. Many people found it cheering.

"My parents died," she said. "My sister died. Enrique died. In the earthquake, the cave-in. In fact, Men Ch'o," she said looking straight at me, "I think everyone died. Why not me?"

"I cannot answer a question I do not understand," I said.

"Me neither," she said, and fell back into silence. But as she sat, she picked at the fruit until it was all eaten, and that was good.

I pushed the bowl of sacred kakaw to her.

She sniffed it. "Koko?" she asked, mispronouncing the word.

"Yes, kakaw," I answered. "But if you would rather take blood..." I held out my forearm and gestured to the blue rivers.

She made a terrible face, scorning my offer. "No, no. Kakaw is fine." She sipped the hot, bitter, spicy drink of royals and her eyes brightened with life.

I would have been content to stay all day, but I had not yet made my daily visit to the cavern to look for whatever the goddess sought. It was a long run, and I knew she herself did not yet have the strength for it. I soon took her back to Ix Imul, who was awake and feeding the infants.

"Lady Imul," I said. "I ask you to make sure she eats and walks about. Also see that the slaves brush out her hair and bring her water to bathe. She is not strong enough to go down to the river." I left, hoping to bring back something that would give her peace, if not joy.

For four days, I pinched and slapped myself black and blue in a stupid attempt to wake from my hallucination or coma. Finally, I stopped. Not only was there nowhere left to hurt, but it was obvious I was deluding myself.

Enrique's words came back to me then. "You will return safely from our journey." Great news, I told myself, slamming my fist into the wall. I'm safely out of Xibalba. Fabulous. I escaped the end of the world, but my bloody elbow didn't buy safe passage for the rest of my loved ones.

Hernán's odd words taunted me. "Perhaps your soul walks a circular path." A circle. Somehow not only my soul, but my body had circled back, back in time to when Xunantunich was a living, colorful city, not hauntingly familiar ruins. A shiver ran down my sides. What had he known, or sensed, or guessed?

I tried to breathe calmly and take stock of my situation, journalism style. How else could I stay sane? First, *who?* Me, Michelle, apparently mistaken for the goddess Ix Chel, which might be my only protection in this world. Second, *what?* Tossed like a piece of driftwood back in time. Third, *when?* God only knows. Or should I be more contemporary and say, the gods only know? Fourth, *where?* Yes, at least I knew that much—Yaxmuul, the true name of the ruins, in Belize, a country that wouldn't exist for...for centuries. Fifth, *why?*

Yeah, why? Why me and not my more aptly named sister Maya? Maybe the gods had made a cosmic error, snatched the wrong sister in their incomprehensible scheme. But *I* was the one who had picked Belize, not Maya. *I* was the one with nightmares. *I* was the one who insisted on going into the caves on the last day. It was all *me*. Me—running toward my own destruction, planning it, driving it.

So here I was.

Trapped.

Now what?

I had no idea what to do next. I'd seen and survived the end of the world. Was I supposed to run around warning people, like some poor, mad Cassandra?

Anyway, what was the point? What, after all, was the point of doing anything?

I lay facing the wall in my dimly lit chamber. The babies' cries of hunger and gas and wetness were a mockery of the death and destruction that awaited us all.

Feed them, I thought; it doesn't matter. Change them; it doesn't matter. Watch them grow to manhood, fight wars, marry, father children. Watch the crops harvested, eaten, and replanted again and again and again. For how long? A thousand years? And then the universal timer would expire. Regardless.

And these people. How many more glory years did they have left? They would abandon their cities and retreat to villages, weak and ripe to be conquered by the Europeans. They would be absorbed or marginalized. They would end up living poor but honest lives with little electricity, some modern medicine, maybe running water, and television to show them how marvelously their conquerors had fared.

What was the point? Because even then, if you believed the Mayan cosmology, this mysterious long-predicted cataclysm would wipe the slate clean for another try. Mud men. Wood men. Corn men.

The gods still weren't satisfied, I guess. As a species, we weren't working out too well. We'd been judged lacking... something...again. Shit. Pardon me. I mean, Xit.

What would the whimsical Creator try next?

I watched Imul, the babies, the servants going along, unaware we were already discards. Dust.

I decided not to eat. It wasn't hard, actually, since the sight of food turned my stomach. So did the stink of my body, still wearing the same underwear and clothes after four days and nights. And so did the stink of the closed chamber. The birthing sheets had been removed, but the air still held a tinge of blood and chamber pots.

I decided never to leave this room. There was no way I would show myself to the people again. Just like my nightmares, the chanting crowd had been at my feet adoring me. I had fled inside before the next part of the nightmare could come true, the beheading that somehow I would order. Would I know what I was doing when it happened? Would I enjoy it? Would I become one of them?

Refusing to eat was the most reasonable course. I lacked the guts and will to hurl myself off the top of El Castillo. Though that would be quicker.

I lay facing the wall, muttering lists of the things I would never see again: television, movies, my iPhone, an alarm clock. No more final exams, book reports, math problems, lab write-ups. So much for my education. Oh gods. I'd be a high school drop out for the rest of my short life.

An end to roller skates, skis, a bike; elastic, nylon, aluminum foil, Saran wrap, polar fleece; a real toothbrush, Crest, deodorant, conditioner; ice cream, popsicles, grande lattes, Twinkies, peanut butter, apple pie, Snickers, biscotti.

So many things. Lost forever.

I said a bitter goodbye to everything familiar and useful and, until this moment, completely taken for granted.

I shrank a little bit with everything I let go. I faded away a little more with every plate I pushed away. A calm, limp feeling smothered me. My plan was working.

I would die soon. I hoped.

I squeezed my eyes shut and tried to picture Mom's and Dad's faces as hard as I could. All I could remember was Mom's final terrified look of confusion, Dad's final look of helpless astonishment.

I'd already lost the innocent memories of comfort and familiarity and love.

It was Christmas morning, I think, if I had calculated the passage of time by meals correctly. Farewell to stockings, trees, and gifts. No scrambled eggs and cheddar and bacon, no fluffy biscuits and honey butter, no midnight mass and candle-lit singing of "Silent Night." Maya always sang alto while I sang the melody line. Could I ever say goodbye and let go of Maya? I could scarcely breathe past the choking sobs.

A man's voice sounded outside the chamber, and one of the servant women touched me.

I curled tighter, ignoring her.

"Come, Lady, you are summoned," she said, roughly jostling my shoulder.

Who summons a goddess like that? I thought briefly. Show some respect.

But I rose with a huge effort and went to the doorway, wiping my eyes on my bare arms. Men Ch'o waited there, his straight gaze boring curiously into me. He ordered the women about while I stood like a doll with no will of my own. One of the women took away my filthy dress and put a cool, homespun shift over my head. She held my only pair of bikini briefs at arm's length and studied them dubiously.

"Wash everything," Men Ch'o ordered. He gestured around the room to all the sleeping linens and mats. "Lady Chel, come with me. You must walk outside a while."

Oh my God, please, no. I couldn't bear the chanting crowds. "The people..." I whispered.

But he promised to take me through a secret, private way, and we came out on the backside of the complex, away from the plaza. We sat on a breezy terrace with an endless view of the tree tops. He handed me a yellow piece of cake, dripping with brown goop. His serious eyes forced me to take a careful bite. My mouth exploded with sweetness. It wasn't biscuits and honey butter, but it was close.

"Why am I alive?" I asked, but he couldn't answer. I ate anyway.

Hours later in Imul's chamber, a servant brought the evening meal of spicy stewed meat and maize tortillas. Men Ch'o followed right behind. His black eyes gleamed with excitement, and he breathed heavily. Sweat glistened on his broad chest.

"Goddess," he said. "I hope you will be pleased. I have found...something."

"What? What is it?" I asked, noting he said something, not someone. And pleased, which meant, thank the gods, not a body.

He handed me a bright orange bag, rolled up and clipped shut. "I have never seen such a cloth, such a color," he said. "Is it from the god-world?"

A dry bag. It was a dry bag from one of the canoes! I snatched it from him in my eagerness to see what flotsam had washed up in this ancient world. With all his attention, Men Ch'o watched me work the snaps.

I unrolled the bag and looked inside. Oh, Grandpapa. "Oh thank you."

I pulled my leather journal from the bag and kissed it as if I were kissing Grandpapa himself, on his soft leathery cheek. I reached in again and pulled out a granola bar and an apple, the extra food I'd thrown in for our snack. "Oh my God, I don't believe it," I said as I pulled the last item from the bottom corner of the bag—a Coke, the only known can of Coke in the world.

"Thank you, Men Ch'o, thank you," I said, my cheeks stretching painfully with smiles. I would have hugged him right then, sweat and all, but his earnest, serious look held me back. "Thank you," I said again in a matching tone. "This is the best Christmas present I've ever received."

It wasn't just stuff. It was two things, really. Connection and hope. A connection to my real life, to all I loved and remembered. That gleaming red Coke can with its bold silver stripe was my anchor in unfamiliar waters, something so simple and normal in a life turned upside down. The granola bar wrapped in a material that wouldn't be invented for more than a thousand years connected me to all the industry and technology I'd never noticed, that operated in the background all my life. And the journal was a connection to my words. I opened the first few pages and stared eagerly at what I had written in a language no one here could read or understand.

Hope? The apple was firm and fresh, as though it had just come through, not fermented in a bag for days. The apple was hope itself—the possibility that something else could pierce whatever rift between worlds and times I had come through.

My stomach growled. Men Ch'o laughed out loud, a shockingly joyful sound.

"Come," he said, handing me a bowl of stew. "It is time for you to eat again."

I admit, it was delicious and warming. Venison, I think. It filled the empty space for a while.

Long after Men Ch'o left, I sat with my Christmas gifts, humming quietly to myself, "Silent Night, Holy Night. All is calm, all is bright."

Imul and the babies slept soundly.

CHAPTER FIVE
December 19, 2012

The next morning, Chel was up and more than ready for another adventure. The minivan came for them at the crack of eight o'clock. Chel had eaten her fill of mango, banana, and jicama fruit salad for breakfast. Maya, who always ate as much as she liked of anything and never gained an ounce, wolfed down three large pancakes with oceans of syrup. They smelled wonderful, but Chel resisted, knowing she would regret going home five pounds heavier.

An hour later, bumping down an unpaved road after the border crossing into Guatemala, Chel was thrilled with her decision to eat light. Next to her, Maya was looking green around the gills in the back seat of the minivan. Mom reached back and handed her chewable motion sickness pills, which was a good thing, because Chel did not want a pile of half-digested pancakes on her lap before the end of the trip.

"Oh my God," Maya complained. "Why do we have to go so far for another damned ruin? Wasn't that X place enough?" She huffed. No one said anything. "My butt still hurts," she added. "And my thighs are ruined for the rest of the trip."

Chel tried to ignore Maya's pointed groaning, but finally she couldn't help herself. "Tikal isn't *just another damned ruin*. It's one of the most powerful ancient cities. If you'd looked at the pictures—"

"The rubble, you mean." Maya's voice was full of scorn.

Chel knew half of it was Maya's motion sickness, but did she need to ruin everyone else's day? She bit her lip and tried to feel sympathetic. The scenery bounced by.

As soon as they crossed the border out of Belize into Guatemala, Chel realized that what she had judged as near-poverty in Belize was unbelievable comfort and wealth compared to the way these people lived. The houses here were ramshackle structures of boards that didn't quite fit, one-room houses with no sign of electricity at all. People sat on their front stoops, a few brown and black chickens clucking around their feet, hoping for a fistful of corn. She wondered, what would it take to get them going? How could you take someone whose priority was keeping their family fed and interest them in books or the internet?

The van rattled on and on until they reached their destination, Tikal, one of the most famous and beautiful ancient cities of Mesoamerica. Following a busload of Japanese tourists up a steep hill, Hernán paused to explain. "The rich and important people, they got to live up high in the breezes, away from the mosquitoes and close to the center of things. You can't see now with all this jungle, but once all this land was cleared and developed."

As they walked through lush, overgrown jungle, Chel caught sight of a tall pile of what might have been quarried stone, still rectangular in spite of erosion. Moss, humus, and new trees almost completely obscured it, but it had an unmistakable pyramid shape. "Was that once a building?" she asked.

Hernán followed her pointing finger. "Yes. The base of a building. A pole and thatch one-room house would be raised on the flat top. Of course, those materials are worn away with time, but the base stones remain to tell us that a family once lived here. There are more than eight thousand building mounds already discovered, so they say maybe two hundred thousand people lived here."

"Two hundred thousand?!" Maya squeaked. "What happened to them? Did they all die?"

Hernán shrugged. "You know, we think some died of diseases of hunger. The most recent skeletons show malnutrition—not enough food or not the variety they needed. These many people ate from only four large fields. And they stored water in these cisterns they dug out of the ground, but when there was a long drought, of course, it would run out with so large a population. So many of the people would have spread out to small household farms on new land that was not depleted."

"Hmmm," Dad grunted. "I could've taught them a thing or two about sustainable organic farming. That's my specialty at the university, Hernán—agronomic crop management. Teaching and research."

"So I guess they could have used your advice, Mr. Balam. Yes, they could."

"It's so sad," Chel said. "How could two hundred thousand people just fade away?"

"Oh, it was many more than that across Central America. You know, when the Spanish arrived, all these large cities were fallen and the people who still lived had moved closer to the coasts or to the north. When we get to the top of the hill, you will see an idea of what this place once was. They called it themselves Yax Mutul—the first topknot. You know topknots?" He gathered his shiny black hair into a high ponytail with his hands.

"So they thought they were pretty important," Mom said.

"Yes, and so they were. There was a great rivalry among the three cities which controlled so much land and people. But eventually, as you see, they all fell."

"Ah, how are the mighty fallen," Dad quoted.

Chel and Maya both glared at him.

"Pride goeth before a fall?" he suggested.

"Dad, no offense," Maya said. "But shut up."

Hernán climbed the steep slope without losing a bit of breath, but Chel was puffing when they crested the hill and saw the first of the great plazas. Surrounded on four sides by enormous temples, the plaza was a huge, grassy open space filled with tourists.

"Okay, Chel. I'll admit this is kind of cool," Maya said. She set her camera on wide-angle and marveled that she still couldn't get it all in. "You can use some of my shots for the magazine. Yeah?"

Chel rolled her eyes and accepted Maya's version of an apology. "See. Told you, stupid." Her smile softened the words.

She took a deep breath and immersed herself in the spirit of the place. Matched pyramids rose at the north and south ends of the plaza. Hernán explained that deep within the two-hundred foot tall monuments were the tombs of a king and queen who had loved each other. Now they spent eternity facing each other across a broad green lawn.

An ancient romance. Chel's imagination stirred, and the wind sounded a little too loud in her ears, blowing a minor melody. She braced herself for another hallucination attack, but the feeling passed as she clung to reality. Her mental vision of royals gathered on the temple ritual platforms with crowds below them were based solely on pictures she had really seen.

"Come together," Hernán said. "We can climb the south pyramid complex." He pointed to where a tall wooden stairway attached to the side of the pyramid. The steps were so thin, it was more like a ladder than a stair.

"I think I'll sit this one out," Mom said. "I'm going to find a nice shady tree and have a Coke."

No one argued.

Chel, Maya, and Dad climbed the narrow, steep staircase to the platform level. Here at least there were guard rails. Mom would have been happy about that.

Chel asked, "Dad, do you think Mom's having an okay time? Is this too much for her?"

"Oh, she's fine, kiddo," Dad said. "She wouldn't want you to worry about her. Just enjoy yourselves."

"Have you talked to her about the caves? When we're going? They're supposed to be one of the best things. Part of our plan. Right?"

"I said we'd have to see about that," Dad said.

"Yeah, I know," Chel said. "I know that's what you told us, but we have to see about it soon. We have to make a plan."

"We'll see," Dad said.

And that usually means no, Chel thought anxiously. She *had* to see the caves. It would be so stupid to come all this way and spend all this money and not do the most important, coolest thing. So when they climbed down and rejoined Mom, Chel asked Hernán, "Which of the caves would you most recommend if you could only do one?"

"Do you want to go tubing or use canoes?" he asked.

"Hey, Mom," Chel asked. "Which would you prefer, canoes or inner tubes? We can actually swim in the cave water with tubes."

Mom shuddered and put on a tight little smile. "I would most prefer dry land. You know there's a nice nature walk we can take."

Chel persisted. "So a canoe, where you don't actually have to get wet would be better, right?"

"Michelle, please. Can we talk this over another time?"

"Mom, there isn't that much time. It's running out faster than you think. It's already our third day, and with Christmas coming up, don't you think Hernán will take some days off? We need to decide at least."

"You know I'd really rather not," Mom said.

"I know that," Chel replied. "But you'll do it anyway, right? Or can me and Maya sign up on our own? You and Dad could go look at flowers or butterflies or green iguanas or something. Or go nature walking without us. Can we do that? Can we split up?"

Dad intervened. "No, Chel. I don't like the idea of you two girls on your own in a strange country."

"Dad, it's not *strange*. It's foreign and everyone speaks English. We'll be fine. Right, Maya?" She elbowed her sister. "Looking for a little support here," she hissed.

"Sure, Dad," Maya agreed. "We'd be fine. Hernán always takes good care of us." She entwined her arm through his.

"We are not splitting up," Mom said in that very definitive voice she could put on.

Hernán caught Mom's glare and slid out of Maya's grasp. It would have been funny if Chel wasn't so desperately worried that Mom would ruin everything.

"Can't you see, Mom? That's so unreasonable. Why can't we ever do what I want to do?"

Mom paused and glared back. "I thought I had been doing that. I thought we were doing all the things you picked out."

"Well, I've done a good job so far, haven't I?"

Mom was as silent as stone for a moment. Then she turned to Dad. "What do you think, dear?"

Dad shrugged. "Whatever you want to do, honey. I've read good things about the caves. But only if you feel up to it."

Maya and Chel both put on huge, toothy smiles. "Puhleeese," they begged as one.

Mom heaved a sigh. "Okay. Tomorrow the nature trail. Next day, we'll go to the caves."

"Thank you, thank you, thank you," Chel exclaimed. "I love you, I love you. This is so great. It'll be so cool. I *swear* you won't regret it, Mom."

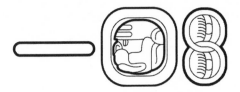

The pouch I found for the goddess must have held treasures. She came back to life that day.

On the next morning, I went to her again, early before I set out. She asked if I would take her with me to the cave, to the place where I had found her, to the place where I had found the sack. I agreed and sent a slave to prepare a carry-meal.

The goddess walked beside me, her strides matching my own as we were of just the same height. When she tired after a time, I offered her rest, but she refused.

She said words that sounded like, "I forgot. No jorses, no ouweels." God-words that were strange to me.

When we came to the creek, she gave a startled cry. "Yes," she said. "I recognize this place." She pointed to the boats tied to the trees along the river's edge and laughed. "Some things never change, even in a thousand years. This is where we tied up a few days ago."

I did not understand her precise words, but from her laugh, the first time that joyful sound had come from her mouth, I understood that she was pleased. I suggested that we eat our carry-meal before going on, and she praised my idea. I gave her a maize cake wrapped in mint leaves and a small pot of squash pudding seasoned with *naba-cuc*.

"My gods," she said. "This tastes like pumpkin pie." She devoured the simple fruit pudding as if it were a rarity for royalty, like the pineapple.

When we finished, I lit an oil torch from the supply that we kept near the cave. We rowed into the dark, and she looked all around, speaking quiet words that only she could hear or understand. We came at last to the crystal cave where I had first seen her. She pointed up to the roof, to the large hanging rock.

"Look at that," she said. "It will look the same for the next thousand years until it falls."

"Twenty and twenty and ten k'atuns!" I wondered. "How would you know...?" Then I stopped myself, realizing that the goddess would know the before and after. Perhaps this was why she had worried so about the end of the Great Cycle, something so far beyond my years that I could not feel its weight as she did.

She searched every crevice of the flattened out place above the water where I told her she had been sleeping. I had moved the corpse of our warrior captive to a high niche on one of my returns to the cave. The river had licked clean his blood from the ground. It was bright white again when Ix Chel examined it. She touched and pressed on the stone walls, all she could reach. Then we floated back and forth across the entire cavern. She peered down into the water, holding the torch high.

When we had swept the entire space with our boat and our feet and nothing was found, I feared she would fall into sadness again. But she said in a firm voice, "Not today, I guess," and motioned for us to leave. Once outside the cave and into the late afternoon light, she thanked me for the effort, and we began the long walk back. I wished I could have done more.

The day after Christmas, I woke to the sight of a granola bar and a Coke next to the scratchy folded blanket that served as a pillow. My neck ached.

I had eaten some kind of poultry stew on my second day here. There must be ducks or chickens or turkeys around. I'd definitely speak to someone about stuffing a nice, soft sack of down feathers. As goddess, I sure as heck deserved a pillow.

Just the fact that I could joke with myself showed me a doorway out of my depression.

And, now that I'd decided to rejoin the living, there was another step I could take, a positive step. I washed myself with a bowl of water. Daily bathing was a luxury, no doubt, and daily showering just a dream, but I had to keep up my standards. With a stiff bristle comb, I brushed out my thick, greasy hair. I put on a clean dress. After eating fried dough balls that tasted coconutty, I felt ready to meet the day. I just didn't know where to go to meet it.

Fortunately, Men Ch'o interrupted whatever was his usual work and came to see whether his orders for my comfort were being followed. He was so kind that I dared to ask him a special favor, to take me to the cavern where he had found me and the dry bag. We set off by mid-morning through hidden ways until we were clear of curious townspeople. We walked for hours, first heading east across the Mopan River, then crossing through jungle. He set an even, quick pace.

"You take this route often?" I asked. "The trail is very clear."

"I have worn it out the past days, since you came to the world. I have been searching for your god-companions. The ones you cry out for in your sleep." He turned sad eyes to me. "I am sorry I found only your pouch."

My heart swelled. "Men Ch'o, that was a true gift. I will always be grateful for that, even if we find nothing else."

His dark eyes brightened, and his pace turned even quicker. I had to push myself to keep up.

The sun had passed noon when we came to a familiar place, the river widening where we had rented our canoes by the cave entrance. My heart beat just a little bit fast, hoping against hope that I would discover...something.

We spent hours exploring the crystal cavern, but of course there was nothing new. No splintered pieces of canoe, no floating oars, no life vests. I don't know what I hoped to find, really. A shimmering portal? A hidden passage in the rock that led to the future? Why not go for a magic lamp and genie? But it wasn't a cave of wonders; it was just a cave.

I clicked my heels three times together, for luck, and said Dorothy's magic words—no place like home—but nothing changed. A warm tear ran down my cheek and I brushed it away. No point in that. I refused to let despair take hold of me again. It hurt too much.

"Thank you, Men Ch'o," I said to him at last. "We've tried everything. Let's go now."

The torch he held reflected in the damp glimmer of his eyes, dark as cave water. I think he might have stayed in there with me forever, had I asked.

We walked what I estimated to be ten miles, following the west-moving sun. Even my comfortable sandals had rubbed blisters on my heels and pinkie toes by this time. I asked to sit on the bank of the Mopan, near—I almost said home—near Xunantunich, and soak my tired feet. Men Ch'o sat beside me, his presence peaceful. He was very calm, very still, and soon an iguana walked right up to us, crawled over my legs, and slipped away. Swallows flew low over the water, eating the mosquitoes.

The day was done. The sun was setting behind the hill that Xunantunich dominated. I had spent most of this short day walking, and the rest inside a cave, but today my exhaustion was well-earned, by hard physical work instead of depression.

Beside me, Men Ch'o rubbed his stomach.

"Me too," I said. "I'm starving. Do you think food is ready for us yet?"

"The stewpot is always ready," he answered and helped me to my feet.

In the evening I had to explain my long absence to Imul, who was annoyed and fretful after a hard day alone with the babies.

"Why didn't you ask the servants to help you?" I asked.

"The boys are more quiet with you. They feel safe in your arms."

Well, it was sweet of her to say so. I had done a lot of babysitting, and I was fairly confident. On the other hand, I had mixed emotions about her feeling so dependent on me, especially when later in the night one of the serving women interrupted a feeding session to summon her. Imul passed me the drowsy baby without hesitation.

She apologized as she covered her breasts. "I must go for a while. I hope they do not wake and fuss at you."

"Where are you going in the middle of the night?"

"The King calls me."

"Can't he wait to see you until tomorrow?" I asked.

"Not when this mood is on him," she said, laughing and blushing.

I suddenly understood why she had been called, and I couldn't help showing my concern. "But you just had a baby. Two babies! Can't you tell him no?"

She looked at me like I was a mad woman. "But he is my husband," she said plainly. Then a thought occurred to her. "You should have a husband. Perhaps he will marry you, too. So we would be as sisters. I will suggest it."

I was torn between horror at the idea of marrying the old king and unexpected gratitude that the young queen Imul considered me as a sister. I settled for, "Please don't bother him with that now. Just try to come back soon."

"I expect I will," she said with a sly smile. "He is rather an old man."

After she left, I lay awake, thinking hard about her words. What was to become of me? Time to face a little reality.

I'd seen for myself that the cave didn't conceal a pathway back. If I were truly stuck in this time and place, I couldn't live forever as Imul's idle roommate and occasional babysitter. I needed a role, a job, a way of providing for myself. Except I don't think women did that. Did goddesses?

One thing was clear to me. I had to keep up my role as goddess for now. Otherwise, I was nothing but a captured peasant with no useful life skills. If they realized I was a fraud and threw me out of the palace, onto my own resources, I'd end up as the property of the first man who claimed me. Imul was right. In this culture, I would need to find a husband.

But that's so...so calculated, my modern mind objected.

Sorry, Chel, it's just the mathematics of survival, I answered myself. *You must find a good husband, protector and provider.*

But I couldn't marry the old king. No way.

Then I remembered the way my pulse had raced and my breath had caught when the prince K'awiil was near, how he had teased me with his eyes. Was he possibly interested? Could that tense little moment have been a starting point? Maybe I could capture his attention. He was young, strong, handsome, with excellent prospects. Better him than the old king, who I suspected would jump at the chance to grab another young wife—to grab me.

Besides, what better protector for me than the heir apparent? And what better consort for the future king than a goddess? It made sense.

But could I learn to love him?

I hadn't seen him since the first day, but the memory of his powerful body, his noble face, his confidence jumped immediately into my head. He was all of a man, that's for sure.

I thought wistfully of Rand's sweet smile and boyish freckles. What a contrast! At my age I was supposed to be dating, holding hands, flirting, gradually getting to know my first crush. Skip all that. Reset. I had no time for adolescence.

Unfair? Yes.

Reality? Yes.

In this culture, I was a full-grown woman, not a girl. That could be helpful. Or dangerous.

So maybe I had a chance with K'awiil. I might be playing with fire, but what better way to keep warm. Maybe I could become queen of a midsized Mesoamerican city-state.

Oh, get over yourself, Michelle, I told myself. *You're supposed to be a sophomore in a large public high school. K'awiil is way out of your league.*

CHAPTER SIX
December 20, 2012

Another thunderstorm rolled through well into the night. Chel would have happily slept with the deep rumbles lulling her and the patter of rainfall blocking the sound of Maya's heavy breathing. But Maya was a little afraid of storms, and she jumped out of bed at the first crack of lightning. She bounced onto the edge of Chel's bed and shook her.

"Shit, I hate this," she said too loudly.

Chel didn't answer.

"Do you miss your new boyfriend?" Maya asked.

Chel rolled over. "What?"

"I just asked if you miss your new boyfriend. You know, anything you want to know about guys, I can tell you." Maya, who'd already had three short-lived boyfriends and one very serious one, was apparently the expert on the subject.

"What do you mean, anything?" Chel murmured. She wasn't exactly in the mood for this kind of pillow talk.

"ANYthing," Maya said in a meaningful voice. "Budge over." She lay down on her back next to Chel and stole half the pillow.

"Do I really want to hear this?" Chel blushed in the dark.

"I know you're a late bloomer, girl, but you're not hopeless, you know." Maya elbowed her in the side.

"I'm only fifteen," Chel answered somewhat weakly.

"Hello, sister. I'm fifteen, too. In the olden days we would have been married by now."

"In some *countries* we'd be married by now," Chel added. "But the point is, we're not."

"Like that matters," Maya said.

She wanted Chel to ask her questions. Clearly she wanted to be pressed for details. It was like when you can't tear your eyes away from something squished in the road. Or when you hear on TV that someone was murdered and part of you really wants to know how.

A flash of lightning lit the room, and Maya sucked in her breath.

Chel counted. "One, two, three—" A peal of thunder rattled the window. "Wow. Only half a mile off."

Next to her Maya was completely still.

"Breathe," Chel ordered. She heard a stifled breath. So, more to distract Maya than to satisfy her uncomfortable curiosity, she asked, "Who was it?"

"The first time? Franklin, a guy who did the photography program with me in Ensenada. God he was cute."

For their special summer treat, while Mom and Dad had some parent time alone, Maya had chosen an exotic, expensive summer camp on the west coast of Mexico. She came home with tons of gorgeous photos, fluency in Spanish, and, apparently, a secret boyfriend.

Chel had chosen to attend a teen writing retreat at Walden Pond. Except it turned out it was in Concord, not actually in Walden, which wasn't as authentic.

Maya continued reminiscing. "He had the best abs. Totally buff. In the buff." She broke off, giggling.

"When did you...when..." Chel couldn't stop herself. It's not like she was jealous, because she certainly wouldn't, couldn't imagine.

"It was like the third night we were there, I think. Or maybe the second. Well, the first time, anyway."

She was so matter of fact about it, Chel was shocked. "So are you guys going together? I mean, do you text all the time or what?"

"Nah. We haven't really been in touch."

She said it like she didn't care. Really didn't care.

How weird. How totally weird. And maybe kind of cheap and easy. But Chel didn't want to think *that* about her own sister. She asked herself for the millionth time, how could they possibly have come out of the same womb?

"Can I please sleep now?" she asked. "It sounds like it's moving off."

"Oh, sure," Maya said. "I was just being social, you know. We don't have to get up early or anything."

"Mmm hmm." Chel burrowed under her covers, into the warm spot Maya had created. The smell of Maya's musky-sweet perfume lingered on her pillow, and maybe that had something to do with the crazy dreams she had as she dozed for the rest of the night, dreams about Rand and—how weird was this?—a black-haired, cross-eyed man.

By daybreak the storm had passed on, and everything wore a freshly washed look.

Maya cheerfully told everyone she planned to spend the rest of the morning with her camera, taking pictures of nature beaded with droplets, from the glossy yellow coconuts to the bright red parrot's beak flowers to the sparkling spider webs.

Mom was happy to hang by the pool with a detective novel, and Dad sat beside her, engrossed in one of his serious books, one about how empires always end in collapse.

Chel lay on a deck chair, eyes closed. In the far distance, the howler monkeys were waking up, calling to each other with their distinctive throaty barks. From close range, Dad made funny little "hmmm" sounds, every time he came across a thought-provoking fact.

"Listen to this, Chel," he said from time to time.

She made "hmming" noises back at him without really listening. Thank God Mom didn't read excerpts from her book.

When the light breeze wasn't enough to cool her, Chel slipped into the pool. She swam ten lazy laps, then clambered out. "I'm going to shower."

"Okay, honey. Why don't you meet us for lunch in an hour? We've got our short tour this afternoon."

"I know," Chel said. A guided jungle walk. At least this one didn't threaten Mom with one of her phobias—no high places, no dark places. Well, maybe there would be big spiders or poisonous caterpillars. Poor Mom.

Lunch featured a heaping plate of spiced rice, beans, and chicken, which made Chel wish she had done thirty laps instead of ten. Maya brought her camera to the table and showed Chel her photos on the three-inch screen. Hard to appreciate at that size. Chel kept her own full-scale photos in her head.

Hernán picked the family up in the restaurant just as they finished. "You looking forward to our walk?" he asked.

"I am, no doubt," Mom said. "I need it after that wonderful lunch. How come I haven't seen anyone overweight?"

Hernán laughed. "We don't have a lot of labor-saving devices, you know? Washing in the rivers, walking and biking to get around. No fast foods, just real food. We got a good balance, here."

Chel nodded. The people she'd met who lived here seemed more in touch with the earth. Life was more basic—simpler, and in a way, more real.

Hernán was as knowledgeable about the jungle as he had been about history. Did people just grow up knowing these things or was there a tour guide university?

"Hernán," she asked, "who taught you about all these plants?"

"My grandfather. He is a traditional healer, a h'men."

"Is that like a shaman?" Dad asked.

"Yes, same idea," Hernán said. "He knows the plants to use and the words and chants to say to help with physical and spiritual ills."

"How did he learn?" Chel asked.

"It is passed down, from parent to child for hundreds of years."

"And he taught you? Are you going to be a...a traditional healer, too?"

"No," he laughed. "There's no money in it. No retirement plan. He helps people for no fee, and maybe they bring him some of their guava jelly or chicken stew or something when they get better. I have to work and save money for university. One day, I'll be doing research in medical biochemistry, and I can work for Ix Chel."

"For me?" Chel asked.

"For her?" Maya echoed. "Seriously?"

"No, no. With the Ix Chel Tropical Research Foundation. They study the ethnobotany of traditional Maya medicines. With my grandfather's healing knowledge, they have already asked me to help them. I plan to study biochemical pharmacology so we can figure out the active chemicals in these plants that give them their effect. There's big money from the drug companies for this kind of information."

"I can well believe that," Dad said.

"What's ishell?" Maya asked.

"Yes, she is spelled I-X-C-H-E-L in regular letters. She is the goddess of the moon and healing arts and weaving and childbirth. So this medicine project is named for her. She is also Lady Rainbow, so she helps the rain god Chaak with rainfall. Sometimes she is shown as an old woman, like a waning moon or an empty vessel, and other times as a young girl. Many of the Mayan gods have more than one aspect like this."

Hernán took them along the trail, pointing out the most fascinating stuff. There was a tree with sap so deadly it would burn a hole right through your skin, and the only way to survive was to take a nine-hour bath in tea made from another tree nearby. There were berries that were good for diarrhea, and other ones that gave you the runs. There was a tree with leaves that made men more manly, but the bark prevented pregnancy.

"Smart balance, yes?" Hernán commented. He pointed out plants that helped soothe cranky babies, that cured snakebite, that stopped bleeding, that made childbirth faster, that unplugged stuffy noses or cured asthma, that helped with fevers, and cramps and gas. "There's a wild pharmacy out here if you just know what to look for."

"Does this stuff really work?" Maya asked. "Or is it just like traditional stuff for fun?"

"Oh yes, it works," Hernán said. He showed them a scar on his arm. "This is from a venomous snake who caught me by surprise. In the hospital, my arm was completely black. I was near death. The doctors called a priest, a Catholic priest, you know, to do the last rites. But grandfather came with his great friend Joe, who is a brilliant snake doctor. Joe knew the right herbs to burn and chants and prayers. So, you see I recovered."

"Wow. I'll say," Maya said, stroking his muscular arm. "Cool."

Chel's feet tingled as she watched Maya's manicured fingertips trace Hernán's scar. She scrubbed away the snapshot that popped into her head of Maya's slender figure pressed close against Hernán's sturdy one.

The tour went on. Chel stuffed all the interesting facts into her head to scribble down later in her journal. The palmetto palm provided thatch for roofs. The Cohune tree nuts contained a coconut-flavored cooking oil. The fruit of the monkey-ball tree oozed white glue like Elmer's. It was more than cool. It was fascinating—the green canopy overhead, the vines creeping up the trunks, the shrubs in the undergrowth, and the wild flowers poking out between them. Everything was full of magic, medicine, and secrets.

I have recorded the first blow struck by son against father.

The goddess Ix Chel began to live among us as a woman, as a teacher, and most strangely, as a pupil.

My Father Ahaw had not sent messengers even to Saal to announce her presence here with us. I believe he waited to make sure of her favor toward us. It might tempt the larger, wealthier court there to steal away her favor. I wondered if he would send messengers to Yax Mutul, the knot that ties this region together. Probably not until he had made her fully his own.

I confess this idea pierced me as I began to know Ix Chel.

After her two weeks of resting, Ix Imul returned to her public position. She presented the babies to our Father at first-meal one morning. K'awiil gave them only a passing look. Then he noticed how the goddess's soft glances rested on them, and he made great show of admiring them. He toyed with one baby's jade brow-bead, tied between the eyes to train them to cross, to mark him with beauty and nobility. As K'awiil did this, he sent me a look of pity for my ugliness.

I needed no reminder that my eagle's eyes had stared straight ahead and refused to cross when I was an infant. I had the common look, to my Father's shame. Until the babies grew, K'awiil was sure to be the only one of Father's sons who bore his royal stamp.

My Father Ahaw smiled on the boys, tapped his chest proudly, and sent them away with servants before they could cry and disturb his meal. He leaned close to Ix Imul at his side and said loudly enough for others to hear the boast, "I would wish for another twenty such sons." Then his eyes moved to Ix Chel in a way I could not like. "Twenty may be too many for my one little wife."

Lady Imul waved her black lashes at her husband king.

Lady K'uk', mother of K'awiil, now barren with age, looked to the ceiling.

Lady Chel cast her eyes down in a modest, becoming way. Her lashes drew long shadows across her cheeks.

K'awiil grinned like a stalking jaguar, scenting the air. "Twenty may be too many for you, old Father. Perhaps you would better wish for twenty such grandsons."

Such a look sparked across the K'ul Ahaw's face, like lightning. I expected his voice to roar like thunder at such a comment. Then I saw the thoughts moving behind his eyes, and he turned the insult aside with a joke. He held up four fingers and a closed fist. "I believe I lead with a score of four to zero."

All at the breakfast table laughed loudly. A lesson in kingship, but one that K'awiil may not have enjoyed.

K'awiil used the laughing time to gather his wits. He raised his own clenched fist up and down. "The late rising star may keep pace with the first one up."

The courtiers burst with humor at the lewd joke and gestures. Yes, he had taken the lesson. I could never think my brother a fool.

After the meal, I noticed the goddess clutching the brownskin tablet I had found for her. I followed when she left, taking our private way to the outdoor terrace. She sat and scratched the tablet with an odd tool, slender like a brush, but without hairs. With her hairless brush, she painted symbols between the lines.

"What is that?" I asked. "God-writing?"

She jumped around in surprise. My feet were so quiet, she never knew I had followed her with curiosity.

"God-writing?" she said. "Yes. Yes, I suppose it is. Do you...do you know writing?" she asked me.

"Yes, I do." I replied. "I am one who writes histories and tracks the cycles of time."

"Show me," she said, handing me the hairless brush and the tablet.

I saw with great shock that the tablet was not a single page or folded book, but twenties of slim pages tied together, whitened without whitewash, and so thin I could not even see the edge. I held the brush awkwardly.

"Like this," she said.

She touched my hand and the point of the brush slid over the page, leaving a narrow track of paint, thin as a leaf-bearing ant's trail. It was marvelous to see.

"Please," she said. "Show me your writing."

I drew the glyph for my Father king, Ahaw, a warrior facing left with the face of the sun rising from his brow.

She took the brush from my hand and copied my writing.

"Yes," I said. "That is the king."

"Kul," she said, a god-word I did not understand. "Another one," she demanded.

I drew the date. "This is today," I said. "Eight kib' nineteen kumk'u."

Her fingers traced the number signs and her eyes glowed. "I remember," she said. "Bars for fives, circles for one. It works." She copied the words as though she had practiced for years.

A bold thought came to me. "If I show you my writing, will you..." I stopped, ashamed of my impudence.

"If you show me yours, will I show you mine?" she asked. Her eyes shone like polished bluestone and her voice laughed, so I was not afraid to nod.

"That is a wonderful idea," she said. "But before you can learn the god-writing, you must learn the god-words." She broke into a flood of words I could not understand, but that was the beginning of our new purpose in meeting after every first-meal.

We were both teacher and we were both student. I told no one of this.

My decision to live after all gave me several goals. If I were going to be an effective moon goddess, I needed to hide my ignorance and learn as much herbal lore and midwifery as I could. The few notes jotted in my journal about Hernán's medicinal plants barely scratched the surface. A least it was a start I could expand on—just had to meet the right people and transfer everything they knew into my brain.

Maybe I should start with something easier.

Imul and I eventually came out of our seclusion. She woke me very early one morning and led me by the hand to a dim, hot room. "It is my purification time," she explained, as we edged along one wall and sat in the stifling dark.

Soon the maids came in with pots of water and emptied them. A loud hiss rose from a small central hearth, and as the room filled with steam, the maids removed our clothes and waited beyond the door curtain.

"No one's going to come in, are they?" I asked.

"No, no. We will be undisturbed until I am cleansed."

I wondered how getting completely sweaty was supposed to be cleansing compared to my morning wash, but sitting in complete relaxation in the dark allowed me to think. I had been lost for two weeks now. Without my journal, a tether to reality, I could easily have lost track of time in this world where every day seemed the same. I always dated my entries according to the date it would have been. By now I'd missed New Year's Eve—the New Year that never came.

My left hand rose and brushed my lips. I sighed silently. The promise of Rand's sweet midnight kiss was broken for eternity.

So I wondered. Had the world gone on without me and my family? Did the headlines say we were tragically lost in a cave accident? Or had time and creation come to a complete halt at the moment the cave collapsed?

On the cosmic remote controller, which button had the gods hit? Pause? Stop and Eject? Or Rewind?

Imul and I were thoroughly scrubbed and lightly scented with her vanilla perfume when we came to breakfast that morning, bringing out the babies, who had proved strong enough to survive this long. Days ago she had removed the awkward boards from their foreheads, a strange device that molded their heads into a sloped-back shape. Now they looked just like the little clay images I had seen in the museum so long ago. They had no special names, other than the traditional name of their birth date, but we couldn't call them Akbal the First and Akbal the Second, so Imul now called the first child Born-twice, to commemorate my successful CPR.

The king strutted like a rooster and bragged about his virility, which caused a lot of good-natured laughter among his court.

I meant to catch K'awiil's eye, to see if he might take me for a long walk outside the palace. I needed to get to know him better, maybe hint that he interested me. What passed for a romantic courtship in these ancient times? I suspected it was nothing but a handshake and a drink between the fathers. Well, I had no one to act for me. Maybe the king would play both roles in my case.

Before I could gather my courage to make a move, K'awiil invited several other young men to wrestle and practice spear throwing. He churned with manly energy this morning. So much for a romantic walk.

After breakfast, I found a quiet spot to update my journal. I nearly fell off the terrace when Men Ch'o's voice sounded behind me. He was very curious about my pen and notebook, so I asked him to show me his writing. He held the pen awkwardly in his big hands, but he drew the date for me, and seeing the care he took with it, I remembered what Hernán had told us about the Mayan calendar. To the priests and scribes, every day wasn't the same. Each day was so important, so unique, it had a name that wasn't used again for fifty-two years. If I learned this system, I thought, maybe I could keep my bearings in this strange world.

Men Ch'o asked even before I could suggest the exact same idea. Cultural exchange. I would teach him English and he would teach me writing.

Having decided to live, I had so much to learn.

At noon, I found the food storage and preparation area in the palace, two rooms behind the room where we had eaten. I peered in and recognized the old woman who sat beside Imul at breakfast. She had been very helpful, holding the babies and cooing over them so Imul could eat. No one had introduced us, so I figured she must be quite an important servant to have eaten with the royal family. She was seated on a three-legged stool, peeling and slicing papaya at a rough wooden table.

As I watched from the doorway, she scooped the black seeds into a small pot and mashed the fruit in a larger bowl. She took three small round seeds from a jar and ground them with a mortar and pestle. The scent of fresh allspice filled the air. She mixed the spices into the papaya. Nearby, a small hearth fire heated a water pot on a triangular stand. The woman tossed in a handful of some kind of dried fruit. She sat back to wait for it to soften.

"Hello," I said softly.

The woman turned to me, startled. She dropped to the floor, her head touching the earth.

Would I ever get used to this? "Please. Please stand," I said. "Will you show me your kitchen?"

"Yes. At once, Lady Chel," the woman said.

She took me through the adjacent storeroom, showing me the preserved fruits and vegetables from another season, her spice jars, and sacks of ground corn meal. Dried peppers hung in racks from the ceiling. A dark corner held stored roots, cassava and tiny wild onions in woven slings above the ground. I pretended to nod my approval as I made a mental list of all the foods available to her.

Why had I taken for granted the variety of dishes that had appeared in our bed chamber over the past two weeks? Why had I sent half of them back untouched? She had worked so hard to produce a nice selection for the queen and the goddess. With more than a twinge of guilt, I thanked her quite sincerely. Surely it would have been easier to send in tortillas and beans every day, peasant food.

"Will the men return for a noon meal?" I asked. "They are practicing war arts."

She made a snorting noise. "Bah. No. They will come back at sundown, each with the hunger of three."

"May I take some food to them?" I asked, not sure if this was a terrible breech of protocol.

She grabbed a woven basket from a ceiling hook and filled it with a pile of tortillas and several banana bunches. "This will do," she said. "The goddess is very kind."

"I do my best," I said. "Where shall I find them?"

She told me how to find the ball court, where, she said, they practiced all sport. Once I was outside, I remembered. I walked slowly across the plaza, trying to blend in and look like any other woman with a basket. The noises around me faded away as I remembered the last time I walked this way, across a mowed lawn that covered this ancient paved plaza. The ball court had been excavated, and Maya and I had stood in the shade of a palm tree while Hernán explained the ritual games that had once taken place here. The game, played with a hard rubber ball the size of a skull, could cause severe injuries, even accidental death. And then the losers were sacrificed at the end of the game. The games were rigged, of course, so that the captured enemies lost and the home team always won.

I listened to the yells of men at play and their grunts of exertion. The noon sun beat down on them, their bodies glistening with sweat, as they rolled with slippery holds. K'awiil pinned his opponent and grinned down at him, a look of friendly triumph. He laughed as I had heard him laugh that morning.

"K'awiil," I called.

He turned at the sound of my voice and jumped to his feet. "Goddess," he said. "What brings you out here in the hot sun? Do you come to judge the strength of your warriors?"

My warriors? Had I been promoted to general?

"I brought some food from the kitchen maid," I said.

"Kitchen maid?" he echoed. His slightly crossed eyes pressed closer in puzzlement. "Kitchen maid? Ah. A crone missing this tooth?" He gestured to his canine.

I nodded.

"Yes. My mother," he said. "I hope you were polite." He reached into the basket and grabbed the stack of tortillas. He began tossing them like Frisbees to the other men.

"Good gods. Your mother?" I hoped I was polite as well. "Why is a queen cooking in the kitchen?"

He laughed at my embarrassment. "She enjoys mixing things. She creates new foods. It gives her a useful way to spend her time now that she is of no use to my Father."

"No use?" I asked stupidly.

"He has his pretty little wife who can bear him many sons. She is past that. I was the only son of hers who lived." He rolled a tortilla in his long, slender fingers and devoured half in one bite.

"Oh. What about Men Ch'o?" I asked. How stupid—I had been living in their home for two weeks and had no notion of the royal family tree.

"He is only a half-brother by the second wife, that small-nosed brother of mine. His mother died when he was born. Some say of fright," he joked.

Sibling rivalry. As old as time. And I'd give anything to see my sister again, in spite of it all. I blinked back a tear and pushed that sundered feeling back down to where it hides.

K'awiil rolled another tortilla. "Poor mother has no grandchildren to occupy her. Yet." He studied my face, tilted it to the sun. "You would make beautiful children."

I blushed furiously. My cheeks burned where his hands had touched.

Then he put his hands on my hips. "You would carry them well, I think."

My mind froze up. What was a girl supposed to say to that? I was half pleased that my wide hips passed inspection, half terrified that I was being judged like good breeding stock.

I twisted away with a forced laugh. "That will be far in the future, I think," I said lightly.

"Not so far, *I* think," K'awiil said.

My chest tightened at the look in his eye. No doubt there was something there.

You are playing with fire, I reminded myself. Oh yes, he wanted something from me, but was it the goddess he wanted or was it my heart?

"Heya," he called to his friends. "Lazy ones. Back to practice."

Clearly, I was dismissed. No one even thanked me for bringing the food. If this is how they treated incarnated goddesses, it must really suck to be a regular mortal woman.

It was best, I learned, to follow Imul's example and stay indoors during the hottest part of the day. The thick stone walls of the palace kept it a constant temperature.

When I asked her about K'awiil, she was all admiration, in a not very motherly way. Not that there was anything weird going on there. She was loyally attached to the king. I think she quite loved him. But she thought the world of K'awiil. She praised his looks, his strength, and his cunning in war. I was surprised. I hadn't thought him old enough to command, but I suppose rank came with his birthright.

"So, does your favor run that way?" she asked at last. "The son and not the father?"

How to answer diplomatically? "Dearest Imul," I said. "I believe you are all the woman the king could ever wish for. I will not aim so high."

She laughed, clearly pleased at my flattery. When a woman has just spent nine months full of twins, a little bit of appreciation goes a long way. I learned that from my Mom.

In that moment of memory, I realized with a stab how deeply I missed her and all her funny ways. My throat tightened, ached. Tears started to gather in my eyes, but I pushed away the lost child terror. I had to.

Mom would have found a way to make me feel good and bad about K'awiil at the same time.

Actually, I think I was managing that on my own.

When we all gathered for the supper meal, it was already dark through the windows. The western sky showed the last glimmers of red and purple across the clouds. Dozens, or rather, twenties of oil lamps were lit to cheer the room. After a very spicy turkey stew, the old queen's papaya pudding made an appearance. It was a creamy, cooling delight, but I still could have gone for a huge glass of ice water.

One more thing to add to the "never again" list—ice cubes. The drinks set with supper had a sour fruit taste that stung the back of my throat and warmed the stomach. Even though I really didn't care for it, I chugged it down to quench my peppery thirst.

Some flute players had been asked to entertain this evening, maybe to celebrate Imul's recovery. The haunting sounds of their trills and melodies filled the stone room. I closed my eyes and imagined myself in a concert hall, red velvet seats and gold-painted carving on the walls. I imagined a maestro in tuxedo tails and women in glittery black dresses. I breathed slowly, allowing myself to be hypnotized, feeling my head roll gently with the sway of the music.

When the music stopped, my head continued to spin. I opened my eyes, and the room bobbed gently. Xit. The sour fruit drink must have fermented. I hoped to God I wasn't drunk.

K'awiil, looking pretty relaxed himself, sat across from the Ahaw. His eyes swept the room, and when they landed on me, he gestured for me to come closer. I rose hesitantly.

"Goddess," he said, with a lift of one black eyebrow. "You have proved your healing gifts once already. Could you favor me with another demonstration?"

I sank back into my seat. "What are you asking?" I said as clearly as I could. He'd better not be asking for mouth to mouth resuscitation, I thought.

He raised his right arm. "This shoulder," he said, rotating it with a pained look. "I foolishly agreed to a three-men-on-one drill. I was the one," he added, unnecessarily. "Can you lay your healing hands on it?"

Ah. This I could do. When Maya needed six weeks of physical therapy on her shoulder after that gymnastics injury, I often helped rub it at night. It was hard enough for her to sleep when she thought about how close she'd come to qualifying for States, never mind the pain. I was an okay amateur massage therapist, at least according to my sister.

But without any herbs? Oh, for the natural equivalent of Ben-Gay. I blew out one of the oil lamps and tipped the heated oil into my palms. Taking a deep breath, I placed my hands on the sore shoulder. I was acutely aware of the king watching me from across the table.

Keep it professional, I told myself. You're a goddess of healing.

By this time all eyes were on me. I closed my own to escape the pressure, listened only to the flute sounds, and rubbed the knots out of K'awiil's shoulders and back, navigating the taut muscles by feel. I disappeared into the music, my hands performing a dance all their own. My palms tingled with fatigue by the time I was done.

"A miracle," K'awiil sighed. "I would wish your healing hands forever in my service."

I blinked with gratitude at the compliment and allowed him to take my small right hand between his, there in front of everyone. I placed my left on his good shoulder, warm and gleaming with oil. The Ahaw, sitting across from him, lifted his shoulders in a tiny shrug and inclined his head in a nod.

K'awiil stood then, reaching into a leather pouch at his waist. He pulled out a necklace and draped it across my palm. It was stunning—large round pearls alternating with blood-red iridescent beads, from some sort of shell, I supposed. K'awiil folded my hand around the necklace. "Will you have this?" he asked. So close to me, his dark eyes focused intensely on my face.

"Of course," I said. "I thank you."

His face suddenly glowed with delight, and something else that brought a blush to my cheeks. He stood behind me to fasten his gift around my neck, and his legs brushed against the backs of my thighs. My belly tickled with anticipation.

Imul's eyes twinkled with joy as they met mine. Men Ch'o was distracted, looking anywhere but where I stood. Lady K'uk' rested a mother's soft, proud gaze on her bold, warrior son.

I'd taken my first step forward. Part of my mind stood up and cheered at my bravery. You can do it, it said. You can make it here.

CHAPTER SEVEN
December 21, 2012

By the time Maya finally cracked open her eyes, Chel was already showered, dressed in her new Belizean clothes, and excited to get started.

"Going native?" Maya asked sleepily.

Chel heard a hint of sarcasm, whether Maya meant it or not, and she snapped back defensively. "Well, *I* like it."

"I didn't say I didn't like it," Maya protested. "It fits you."

Since the embroidered dress was straight and shapeless, Chel assumed her sister meant it suited her—at least she preferred to take it that way.

"So, are you going to get up in time for breakfast?"

Maya stretched and snuggled into her pillow like they had all the time in the world.

"We're meeting Hernán in less than an hour, you know," Chel nagged.

"Mmmhmm."

Chel exhaled loudly. Her glance fell on the four-day accumulation of clothes between their beds. All Maya's, of course. Without a word, she scooped everything up and dumped it on the end of Maya's bed. Maya kicked at the weight on her feet. The clothes slid back to the floor. Chel clenched her teeth and retreated to the bathroom to brush her teeth. Maya's make-up was scattered across the counter, and another exasperated sigh escaped.

From the outer room, she heard a gentle knock followed by Dad's muffled voice. "Ready girls? Mom and I are headed down to breakfast."

When Chel came out of the bathroom, Maya's sleep tank and shorts lay in a twisted heap next to her bed. The rest of her had vanished. Great.

"Thanks for waiting," Chel said to the empty room.

Everyone was already seated with a glass of mango juice when she stepped into the dining room.

"Sleep in, honey?" Mom asked. "I thought you'd be up first after the way you pestered all of us about this canoe trip."

Pestered? Chel held in the words that sprang to mind. As far as she was concerned, this was the highlight of the trip, and she refused to get into a bad mood and spoil it.

"We ordered pancakes for you," Maya said.

"Okay...thanks," Chel responded flatly. She wanted fruit and yogurt, but when the syrup-drenched pancakes appeared, she ate the entire stack.

After breakfast, they went straight to the resort office to meet up with Hernán.

"Are you the Balam family?" an unfamiliar man asked.

Maya elbowed Chel in the ribs. "Whoa. Serious cuteness approaching."

"Sure," Dad said, extending his hand. "Dave Balam."

"Enrique," the man said. "I'm Hernán's partner. His little boy is sick today, so I'm taking your tour."

"Nothing serious, I hope," Mom said.

"Oh no. Just a low fever and an ear ache. Anyway, who is excited for today's trip? You all have sandals or waterproof shoes?"

Maya stretched a glossy, tanned leg toward Enrique and pointed to her white-heeled sandals. Her painted toenails gleamed red between the straps. "Are these okay, Enrique?" she asked, rotating her slim ankle.

"Well, as long as you can walk a little way along a trail...."

"Oh, no problem," Maya replied. She touched her bare shoulder and tilted her head. "Do we need sunscreen, too?"

"Well, not in the cave," he answered with a straight face.

"Oh, I'm so silly." Maya giggled. She ran her fingers through her honey brown hair and pulled it up into a pony tail then shook it loose again.

Chel watched for Enrique's response to Maya's way too obvious flirting. To his credit, he was immune, or he hid his reactions well. She couldn't deny that Maya was right, although *cute* was totally the wrong word. More like *stunning*, in a tall, dark, mysterious, foreign way.

Even Mom was affected. Her eyes lost their usual worried expression, which instantly made her look ten years younger. "I told the girls I couldn't wait to go into the caves," she confided.

Maya and Chel glanced at each other. What?

Mom rested a hand on Enrique's arm. "They sound so mysterious." She let Enrique help her into the front passenger seat. "You've done this many times before, I take it?" she asked.

Chel laughed inside. Okay, that was more Mommish. She rested her head on her hand, elbow on the window sill, and let her mind drift as the countryside sped past. The regular bump of the tires over the seams in the road took on the overtones of a low, steady drum beat in the background. A tone like distant chanting rose in harmony with the pitch of the engine noise. Chel shook her head hard to erase the sound. No way was she going to let her brain go off to that other place today.

Enrique pulled the jeep into a parking area under the shade of some tall trees. Chel recognized them as Cohune trees from the clusters of large hanging nuts. Enrique dashed around the front of the jeep to help Mom out. The rest of them unbent and clambered out of the back seats. Enrique handed around bright orange bags.

"Put anything you need to keep dry in here. Like that." He pointed to Maya's camera.

"But I want to take pictures in the cave," she protested.

He shrugged. "Your camera might be splashed by our paddles."

"Oh. Okay then," she said. "Shit. I wanted a good picture to remember this by. I know! Chel...?" She handed the camera off to Chel. "It's ready to shoot. Get a good one of me and Enrique. Okay?"

Chel peered through the viewfinder and waited for Maya to strike a pose. Never shy, she pulled Enrique close, cheek to cheek, and grinned. He cooperated with a brilliant white smile. Click.

While Maya put her expensive camera away in the drybag, Enrique opened the cooler strapped onto the back of the Jeep. He handed out Cokes and granola bars. "Put these in your bags for a snack later," he said. "Anyone want fruit?"

Chel grabbed an apple and added it to her stash. She copied the way Enrique rolled and secured the drybag.

"Everyone set?" He gestured to the food Maya had returned to the cooler. "You're not eating?"

"I only drink Diet," she explained, tracing her slim waist with her hands.

God. Would she never give up?

Enrique turned away for a moment, but Chel could have sworn his shoulders were shaking with laughter. "Okay, folks. Grab a life jacket and let's go find our canoes," he said with just a hint of amusement still in his voice.

Chel smiled to herself. So he was onto Maya. Serves her right.

She slid one arm into her life vest and gazed up at the sky through the leafy canopy. For just a moment, she heard the distant sound of reed flutes and caught a faint scent like sweet burning pine. Her heart swelled with joy. Her feet tingled with excitement as the caves of her ancestors called to her. She suddenly had the sense that her entire life had led up to this moment. This place. This time.

"I'm coming," she whispered.

This I have written of the goddess's betrothal. My hand shakes and so shames me.

On the eve of the Wayeb, the five dark days that have no name, the goddess chose my half-brother K'awiil. My Father Ahaw gave way to his heir with some regret, I believe. Lady Imul hung close to the king for the next few k'inal. As she touched him, flattered him, flashed her eyes at him, and visited his night chamber, he soon forgot his regret. A wise woman, Lady Imul.

How else could the goddess have chosen? To bestow her immortal favors on mortal man, K'awiil was the only choice. He and Lady Chel would create a dynasty to last until the end of the age, 1183 haab years from this time, as I had calculated. It would be my fate to write of their deeds and wars and monuments for as long as I lived.

I confess that these thoughts came later. When I sat at the feast table watching the goddess pour holy healing into K'awiil's wounded shoulder, my thoughts were shameful and impure. Some of them involved slicing my elder brother into pieces with a knife. Others that I cannot write involved the Lady Chel.

To discipline my thoughts, I fasted and prayed and pierced myself daily. The other priests thought my penitent observance of the Wayeb time a fine and pious example. Daily we went to the caves to burn copan and leave offerings to appease the gods of Xibalba. The curtain between the worlds grows so thin during these days that gods and mortals may meet. For the five days I searched in vain for the god companions Ix Chel would have me find in the caves. And so, when the named days returned, I still had no further hope to offer her and nothing to increase my favor in her eyes.

My Father Ahaw instructed me to choose an auspicious day for their marriage. I could not force myself to the task until my Father Ahaw grew angry at the delay.

"Is this task too hard for you, boy?" he asked. "Must I ask our highest priest?"

While I struggled to answer, he persisted. "Is there another reason you cannot find the date? Are the omens so ill?"

At that, I had to tell him the proper date. "No, my Father. The omens could hardly be better, but it is so soon, I had to be sure. Zero Ahaw Eighteen Wo. The seating day of Ahaw is most auspicious for the start of the dynasty of god-kings."

Not only was the chosen date the very seating of the month of kings, it was only one turn of the uinal before the turn of the tenth bak'tun, the most holy day in our lifetime.

"Then let it be so," my Father declared. And so it was to be.

Lady Chel had little to prepare. My sister's fine dresses and huipils would be hers. The mantle maker had been told to weave a fine cloak trimmed in jaguar tails. Three jewelers were hammering copper and setting jade and quartz into bracelets and anklets. The duck-boy was given a special job collecting down feathers for something the goddess was planning as a marriage gift for K'awiil—a *pi'lo*. This word she told me as we continued our morning teachings. She learned our sound signs so fast, I could only admire her wisdom. She showed me the twenty-six sound signs of her god-writing, and I practiced drawing them in sand so as not to waste my tablets.

These days together passed too quickly. I wondered what would become of our lessons when K'awiil commanded her.

The palace atmosphere was changed the day after the famous massage. Even though my head was pounding and my stomach felt wretched, I was aware enough to feel a strange energy in the air. I asked Imul if she sensed it, too.

"It is your marriage to K'awiil. All are in great excitement to prepare the festival."

I gasped. "My marriage? Did I miss something? What happened last night? I don't remember him asking me to marry him."

Imul laughed and fingered the beautiful necklace at my throat. "It was you who asked him. With your eyes, with your body, with your hands. You cannot pretend now to be so shy. We all witnessed."

The light dawned. "It was just a backrub," I protested.

Imul pursed her lips. "Hmm. So you say. But I was there. It was not just a backrub. The heat in the room became unbearable. The water boiled."

"Oh hush," I said, blushing.

So maybe it wasn't just a backrub. Maybe my body knew something that I hadn't admitted to myself yet. Maybe the tremors I'd felt weren't just nerves. Maybe they were the stirrings of genuine attraction. Maybe the satisfaction I'd felt at K'awiil's sighs were the beginnings of love. Maybe I really was falling in love with him. And if we loved each other, then it would be okay.

Only that thought reassured me about this whole sudden engagement thing.

Still, I needed some time to figure it out—time for my feelings to grow more certain, more permanent. I hardly saw K'awiil, and never alone. I spent far more time with Men Ch'o.

How much time did I have?

"Is anyone going to tell me when this marriage is supposed to happen?" I wasn't omniscient—just a goddess. Ha.

"Men Ch'o will choose the date. You must ask him."

So I would, but Imul's words led me to believe it wouldn't be for a while, and something held me back for the next few days. Men Ch'o was so focused at our lessons, I found it impossible to bring up.

He was such a quick student it was a joy to watch his progress. I hoped he felt the same way about me because I was working incredibly hard to learn their complicated writing system. Sometimes the glyphs were pictures that sort of resembled what they were supposed to mean. Sometimes they were completely abstract. Sometimes they had other pieces tacked on to them that gave pronunciation hints, like the first letter of the word if you needed that as well. I decided to concentrate first on the symbols for actual sounds. Each one represented a vowel and a consonant—one syllable. If I learned all of them I could at least write things out phonetically if I couldn't remember the official glyph. Or glyphs. Some words had more than one.

One day, I noticed that Men Ch'o had written the symbols for a date over and over again.

"What is that?" I asked. "Zero King Eighteen Wo?" I could read the numbers and month names by now, almost fluently.

"A lucky day," he said. "Your marriage day."

Ah, so there it was. Out in the open, just like that.

"How long?" I asked. "How many days?"

He did a quick calculation, using his fingers and toes. "Uinal and one more day."

Twenty-one days! Only three weeks. Was I happy? Well, I must be. This is what I had hoped for, and it had fallen right into my lap.

Three weeks.

And then I'd be safe, secure. Protected.

Hopefully in love.

Although I hardly saw him otherwise, K'awiil's increased attentiveness to me at suppers made my belly tighten. His eyes held a world of emotions when they met mine, tender and triumphant and possessive and impatient all at once. I think I was impatient, too. But strangely we never spoke of it. He never touched me.

At night, Imul, sweet as she was, drove me crazy. She would leave me watching the twins and disappear into her husband's room. Almost every night. When she came back, I'd be dropping with exhaustion and she wanted to talk. About men. And what they wanted, expected, liked. In bed. I suppose she was trying to be kind, to educate the virgin goddess, but for the gods' sakes, I was from a twenty-first century public high school. There probably wasn't anything she could tell me that I hadn't picked up from Maya or some of her wild friends. In fact, there were probably a few things I could tell her that would knock her socks off, if she wore them.

Of course, my worldly knowledge was all theory. I was, actually, a virgin goddess. Rand's passionate smooch on my neck was all the experience I could claim. K'awiil hadn't even made a move to kiss me, and I didn't want to imagine anything beyond that. I really didn't.

At fifteen I could officially get married with parental consent in about six states. What would mine have said about all this? It was easy to picture an encouraging but nervous look on Mom's face. Dad's was only a blur. I concentrated hard on remembering his voice and his smile as he delivered his silly clichés. My failure to bring him into focus drove home the truth. I was totally alone. I didn't have any parents now, and it was likely that the only state I'd be married in was the state of Panic.

So my mind avoided going there, and I tried to get Imul to drop the subject. In exasperation one night I said to her, "Look, Imul. I know all of this from my sister."

"Your sister?" she repeated. "I didn't know you have a sister. You never speak of her. We must send a messenger to tell her of the marriage festival. She will be so excited. How far?"

"Too far," I said. "Much too far. She...she's dead. All of my family is dead."

It was the first time I forced those words out of my mouth, and the taste they left was bitter.

In that moment, though, I realized that I really would go through with this marriage. I *had* to. I knew with certainty that there was no going back...forward. For me, at least, the twenty-first century no longer existed.

I write of the second blow struck by son against father.

The days drew closer to the marriage of my brother and the goddess Lady Chel. It was expected that I would show joy at allying our house with immortals, and so I showed my Father Ahaw joy on my face. It was my good fortune that his old eyes could see no deeper.

Without Father's knowledge or consent, K'awiil sent runners along the sacbe for ten bakaanes in all directions to boast of his new alliance, his new conquest, his first wife. I feared the reactions of both our allies and our enemies. I do not know which I feared most.

An answer had not yet returned when the goddess Lady Chel spoke to me with a troubled heart.

"Is there something wrong with me?" she asked. "I am so plain by your standards? I know my forehead is straight and my eyes aren't crossed..."

Here she stopped, as if she wondered that I would be shamed by her words.

"Lady Chel," I said in reply, "you are a goddess. What do you care for this body you wear now? At times, they say, you wear the figure of the crone. At other times, the swollen body of the moon."

She breathed heavily. "Suppose I were not the goddess. Would K'awiil still wish to marry me? Or does my goddessness provide enough reason even if he dislikes my looks?"

I tried to find my words. "Ix Chel, how should he dislike your looks? Such clear, soft skin, eyes like the noon-sky when the clouds are gone, brows that arch like rainbows. And more valuable, you have clever hands and a quick mind. Even if your face were as strange as mine, he should honor you."

Lady Chel mistook the tremor in my voice for self-pity, perhaps. She asked, "Strange? What do you mean, your face is strange?"

"It is nothing. I do not mind," I said, which was not the truth as I stood before her. "They call me chitam sotz'—pig nose. Have you not heard?"

The goddess's anger rose like the whipping wind that arrives before thunder. Her face darkened. "Who called you that?" Then her words fell rapidly into the god tongue, so fast I could not follow, but her wrath was clear.

I did not name K'awiil, inventor of the insult. It was not my hope to cause trouble between them.

"You came to me with a question," I reminded her. "What did you really wish to ask?"

She calmed her own storm. "Is there a reason K'awiil has not...has not embraced me?" She turned her head aside as she spoke. "Or kissed me?"

Then it was I who could not meet her eyes, imagining that embrace. I could think of no reason why K'awiil had not done more than that, now that the marriage date was declared.

If I were he....but I could not allow my mind to wander there.

"Perhaps, fearing your power, he waits for your invitation?" I suggested.

"Is there a way you could let him know that it would be welcome, that it would make me anticipate the marriage, um, even more? But can you be….there's no word for it in your language." So she taught me the sense of the god-word *sutl*.

"You are my true friend," she said, and to my shock, wrapped her arms around my neck.

I stood as if paralyzed with venom, but of the sweetest kind. I might have died happily at that moment.

As she walked away, soft raindrops began to fall. An early rain. A good omen.

It was incredibly awkward asking Men Ch'o for premarital advice, but I had no idea of the customs between men and women in this culture. Imul was no help here either. When I asked her about the early days of her marriage to the king, a quick calculation suggested she was pregnant already at the time of their marriage festival. Why didn't the Belize guide books have any of these details?

Pregnancy. No matter how much I liked K'awiil and planned to be a good queen-wife, producing an heir wasn't in my immediate plans. I wasn't old enough yet, emotionally, physically, the works. Drug stores were a millennium off. I wracked my mind, but I couldn't remember what Hernán had told us about contraceptive trees. I couldn't imagine that Men' Ch'o would know about these women's things. Asking would be horribly embarrassing. Imul, the dutiful young wife, would never understand. I needed a mom's advice. I really did.

There was only one mature mom I knew in the palace. I walked to the kitchen area, wondering if I could possibly ask my future mother-in-law how to avoid getting pregnant with the grandchildren it was my duty to produce. Of course, I would have them eventually, I argued in my head. The timing was just very bad.

I found K'awiil's mother baking sweet potatoes over hot coals. What wonderful surprise did she and her servants have for us tonight?

She smiled widely at me, revealing more than one missing tooth. She'd stopped throwing herself on the floor whenever she saw me, but I still towered over her. I dropped to sit on the floor mat. She came to sit nearby and waited quietly for me to speak first.

"Ix K'uk'," I said, having made a point of learning her name. "Since I have no mother, you must be both my mother and K'awiil's mother. I need to ask you a question as only *my* mother."

She nodded gravely.

"I do not want to have children. What are the remedies?"

Her eyes filled with tears, but she said, "Goddess, a tea made from the ground seeds of the *on* or the *put*, the avocado or papaya..." Her voice trailed off. Then she asked with a pleading tone, "No children? Never?"

"Oh gods. No," I said. "Not never," wondering if double negatives came out the right way. "In a while maybe....Soon," I added, seeing the desperate hope in her eyes.

Her worried brow cleared. She rose and showed me a basket of cedar strips. I thought they were there to keep away moths from the grain supplies, but she told me she would make me a tea "three days before the bleeding time, to drink three times each day."

And that brought up another uncomfortable question that had to be asked in a way to cover my ignorance and preserve my goddess cover. I was due to hit any day now if my body was still on schedule.

"Mother K'uk'," I said. "I have not worn a young woman's body in so long, I cannot remember what to wear for the bleeding time." Tampons. Stick-on disposable sanipads with wings. I sighed. The never-again list just grew longer.

"Ask the servants for a basket of cloth strips and a basket to take them away. They will take care of all for you."

Now that was a job I would hate to have. Laundry. So many invisible workers took care of us. I would have to remember to thank them thoroughly. The dresses I changed daily and discarded reappeared rinsed fresh and wind dried. It never dawned on my conscious mind that they weren't just running out to the laundromat.

I was just about to ask Lady K'uk' about studying more plant lore, when shouts and a huge commotion erupted. Without hesitation we both headed toward the audience room from which the shouts were coming. Both of us hung back in the doorway when we saw the face of the king, scarlet with anger, screaming at K'awiil.

"What has he done?" I whispered to Lady K'uk'.

She put a finger to her lips.

Two messengers, wet with perspiration and dark with road dust, knelt abjectly before the raised platform. Four advisors huddled against a side wall. At this point, though, all attention was focused on the argument between the king and his eldest son.

"What do you know of statesmanship, you small pup?" the king shouted. "Nothing! You do not speak for me. Not while I am breathing. You incite our friends and enemies against us with your boasting! Bah. You are an idiot."

He shook a clenched fist in K'awiil's face. K'awiil glared down at his father and enclosed the bony fist in his broad hand. Without a change in his deadly calm expression, he forced the king's hand down, pulling it so low that his father was forced to bend. All eyes were on them, and a terrible silence filled the room. K'awiil waited for the king's stillness to speak for him before he spoke again. He lifted his right hand toward me, and the electric intensity in his eyes sparked a current of white hot energy in my heart.

Through the sudden rushing in my ears, I heard his proclamation: "This is *my* triumph. And I choose to announce it in the face of all. If our enemies hate us, then who cares.

We will take them and offer their heads and hearts to the bloodthirsty gods. If our allies envy us? Who cares. We will slay them and install our cousins in their place. I care nothing for your statecraft if it means sitting in a small room in a small kingdom answering the problems of farmers and bothering no one. For that, Men Ch'o could do. I am made for better things. I am made to conquer and to rule."

Lady K'uk' whispered beside me. "Oh no. Silly boy."

Boy? He was no boy. Not the seething, towering warrior that K'awiil had become before my eyes. Something inside me swelled in response, growing and surging in harmony with K'awiil's passion. My heart raced. He was frightening. He was magnificent. His eyes shot bolts of fiery determination.

I saw the future in his gleaming face. A new future.

With such bold ambition, I thought, with such strength, we could take Naranjo. Tikal. Caracol. We could take all the cities nested in the plains of the Maya Mountains. We could unite them and make them strong. We could sweep through Mexico and Central America before the Azteca grew powerful. We could build a dynasty that would send the Spanish packing when they arrived in seven hundred years. We could bring a golden age to the New World.

K'awiil beckoned with his outstretched hand, summoned me to his side. His nostrils flared like those of a proud stallion before he rears up and shakes off his rider. I lifted my chin proudly, and he read the flash in my eyes that said, *I am the goddess. Together we will do this.*

It was to be war. The message brought by the two runners was clear. They had delivered K'awiil's announcement that he was soon to marry Ix Chel, the goddess incarnate, and thereafter command both the moon and the rainfall. He had demanded immediate surrender of the kings. If they proved their loyalty to him, they might keep their places. Otherwise, he would behead them and replace them with men of his choosing.

On the roadways between the cities, the *sacbe*, our messengers had met coming home, each warned by a different king that they would unite against Yaxmuul and reduce our fine temples and palaces to rubble. My Father Ahaw was not pleased.

He called together the *holpop*, the nine men of the round mat, his most trusted counselors. I sat near them, yet not with them, in the *popul na*, the house of counsel, my brush and ink ready to take note of their decisions. Painted images of our ancestors' greatest deeds surrounded us.

As heir and captain, of course, K'awiil sat among them, cross-legged on the woven mat. K'awiil argued, "Now the enemy kings have revealed their intent to attack. We must attack first and conquer them one after another before their men can join forces. We hold this moment of time before their kings can agree who will command."

My Father Ahaw scowled at him and pointed. "This is your fault. There would be no intent to attack if you had not made such demands in my name."

K'awiil mocked him plainly. "You speak as if you wanted peace with bad neighbors."

My Father Ahaw said more gently, "K'awiil, it is hard enough to keep our strength and feed our children when the harvests are so poor, year after year. Now you would send our strongest out to be killed in war?"

"You think so little of your own men?" K'awiil demanded. "I tell you they are ready to fight and to die with honor if the gods will it."

"You may think me an old man," the king said, "but I would prefer they lived. What do you say, Men Ch'o?"

I was unused to having my words asked for at the mat, and I stumbled. "Living, yes, it is preferable to dying."

"You would say that," K'awiil said. "You who prefer scribbling to wrestling."

Father's left-hand counselor stood and stretched his arms wide. "Enough of this. What has been said, has been said. What has been threatened, has been threatened. There is no going backward and unsaying. If armies are coming together to meet us, we must stop them on their separate roads. There is no longer a choice."

My Father Ahaw stood also. "There is no longer a choice." He let silence speak loudest and left the room. Only his faithful hound Sac-tz'ul followed, his lowered head a mirror of my Father's.

K'awiil clapped his hands once. "The harvests will be no problem this year," he announced. "I will command my wife to see to that." His eyes followed our Father's footsteps. "Now, the old one is gone, let us begin to plan strategy."

Not being a strategist, I asked leave to go. K'awiil dismissed me with a wave, then called me back. "Chitam sotz', you will begin writing the words for this date. The stone honoring the start of this campaign will be dedicated at my marriage festival. Tell in stone how it all began."

I bowed my head to agree while I wondered if this stone would, in the end, tell how it all finished.

Lady Chel found me working with brush and ink on a white-washed fig bark tablet, planning the words for the stone monument which would be carved with all haste and raised before seven suns had risen and set. She pointed to the date glyphs in pairs, left to right, top to bottom as I had taught her. Her lips moved silently, forming the words for the numbers of the Long Count and the day names below.

"That date," she said. "Today?"

I agreed.

"What about the rest?" she asked. "Or is it a private writing, a xurnal?"

"Not a xurnal," I said. "An announcement that today K'awiil sat at the head of the mat in my Father Ahaw's place and planned war against our neighbor Ux B'alam." This part tells how the council, the holpop, stood with him. This part tells of the two hundred men he will take. This part tells of their proud victory and the sacrifice of their captive princes on the day of his marriage. This part tells how the gods were honored and rewarded us with plentiful rain."

"That has not happened yet," she said.

"No," I answered. "But it will. It must, as the stone masons begin work on this stela tonight."

I did not tell her that K'awiil had chosen his time poorly, that the War Star moved swiftly toward the sun, soon to disappear from the morning sky. To battle while the War Star wandered invisible through the realms to the night sky was the choice of a very brave or very foolish man. K'awiil had little time left under its protective watch.

"War!" she said. "Who will K'awiil send to command?"

"He will go," I answered.

"But what about the marriage? In seven days?"

"He plans to win very fast," I said.

Men Ch'o told me of the war preparations. I could hardly believe it. Yes, I had seen K'awiil's bold plan. More than anyone else, I'd been caught the excitement of it. But right now? Terrible timing!

My Dad went skydiving the week before his wedding. Mom had sworn to call the whole thing off if he came back in pieces. That was nothing, I thought. Nothing compared to leading a small army into battle with obsidian spears and knives. What was this fiancé of mine thinking?

The entire city shifted into a new mode. Watch dogs on the grounds kept up a constant alert as messengers came and went all afternoon. I walked into the plaza amidst great scurrying and activity. Women were carrying small pots of ground maize and donating them to grain barrels set out in the public square. The tanner was wrapping the barrels with deer leather straps to fit around the waists and foreheads of the poor porters who had to carry them. Other women brought large cooking pots and baskets of dried beans. Strings of dried, salted fish hung waiting to be packed. I wondered where the water would come from to turn these dried supplies into food. Surely they weren't going to carry their own water.

"Trucks," I muttered to myself. "Why don't you have trucks! Or at least carts. It would be so much easier." How a people this smart in so many ways could have overlooked wheels and axles was bizarre. They paved their roads, then dragged or carried all their goods. I put that project on my mental to-do list. When K'awiil and I were married, we'd give the people a gift that would make them spin. Literally.

Finally at supper, I saw K'awiil. Surrounded by his men and the king's advisors, he was too preoccupied with war plans to send me a glance. I was forced to admire him from afar. Copper bangles ornamented his arms and legs, and a spectacular jade collar adorned his broad, tanned chest. Plumes of iridescent quetzal feathers sprang from his glossy topknot. He looked every bit the future king. My breath caught at the knowledge that soon he would be mine, and I would be his. This strange new life of mine had pushed me forward faster than I could have imagined. The old life I remembered was now the dream.

Tonight a fine meal had been prepared, a celebration with roast peccary and smoked peppers wrapped in fragrant husks. A hearty bean stew was ladled into bowls over *ul*, the usual maize gruel, and I watched as Lady K'uk' moved a few peppers from the tamales into the stew—she did like things spicy. The men ate twice as much as usual. I remembered the old saying about an army marching on its stomach. They needed to start their trip with full stomachs to lighten the load for their porters.

They also drank much of the soured fruit drink. I sure didn't envy the hangovers they would have the next morning, having accidentally experienced my first one just a few days earlier. I mixed mine with water. As goddess, one with no head for alcohol, I now insisted that water be available at the table. It was gratifying to see the ceramic pitcher appear reliably at every meal after that. The pitcher was painted with glyphs that I actually recognized and read: *Ix Chel it is her water*.

After the supper banquet, servants with torches were summoned to lead a procession into the central plaza. A whole band of drummers and flute players sounded loud and flashy tunes. Dancers in high-feathered headdresses spun madly in the moonlight. Keeping a respectful distance from the court, the common people danced and drank in the cool of the night. Imul and I danced as well, abandoning ourselves to the drumbeat rhythm of the tunkul and our high spirits. I was more thirsty than ever, and eventually I drank from the intoxicating cups the servants brought us, unwatered, of course. The celebration went on and on as the stars crossed the night sky. A poem slipped out of my subconscious:

> *The whirling heavens*
> *Join now in celebration*
> *With mortals below.*

The men's voices grew louder, the more they drank. My ears filled with the overwhelming sound, which bounced off the faces of the pyramids and palace. El Castillo rose before me, turning the whole scene magical, mystical. I drank again, and the other-worldly feeling grew stronger.

Then the instruments stopped. The silence rang. K'awiil strode up the lower steps of El Castillo so that he was above the level of the crowd. A servant hurried to bring a torch, to light his face in the darkness. Reflections of the dancing flames appeared as sparks in his dilated pupils. K'awiil began to shout the story of his future victory, his face flushed with excitement. All eyes were on him, thousands of eyes, and I understood why these nobles would follow him into battle and why the common soldiers would fight for the privilege to be in his advance force. He proclaimed a vision of such triumph, glory, and power that we all were swept up in chanting.

"Victory...K'awiil...! Victory...K'awiil...na-k'....na-k'!"

As the crowd reached a frenzied peak, he pulled something from a pouch at his belt, something that glittered long, dark, and sharp by torchlight. He drew the slender spike through the flames. The crowd gasped as one in anticipation. A smile lit his face. Then he drove the spike with all his force through the skin of his right breast and the crowd erupted with a roar of approval. A second spike appeared. The crowd hushed. And with another show of unbelievable bravery and strength, he pierced the skin of his left breast. He raised his arms to the sky, calling on the gods to witness his blood sacrifice and grant a swift but noble victory. The dark red rivers streamed down his chest.

I, who had always gone faint at the sight of blood, instead longed to race to him and run my hands through the royal outpouring that flowed from his self-inflicted wounds. This is what a king did for his people. He fed the gods his blood, the eternal bargain.

Unable to control myself any longer, I ran to the steps below him and raised my arms toward him. "K'awiil," I shouted. "Victory! K'awiil!"

He signaled the drummers, who started beating a rhythm to fill the crowd with bloodlust for their enemies. He came down the steps toward me, a hot and dangerous look in his eye. "I leave in the early morning," he said, and swept me up into his arms as if I weighed nothing.

He carried me all the way back into the deserted palace to a room I had never seen. The scattered furs and cotton blankets reeked of man-sweat. My heart still raced from the thrill of the crowd. My head still rang with the soaring sounds of men and music and madness. K'awiil steadied me on my feet against the wall then carefully drew the spines from his flesh while I watched in breathless fascination.

Fresh blood welled up, but he took no notice. I grabbed the hem of my dress and pressed against the wounds with the fabric, hiking it up above my waist to reach his chest.

His hands reached behind me to stroke the curves I had accidentally uncovered. My body tensed with an alertness I'd never experienced.

"Now," he said. "I hear I have disappointed you with my restraint." His eyes studied mine for a response as he pulled me against him. "So much so that you complain to my brother."

His voice took on an uncomfortable edge. "That will be a problem no more. Goddess. Wife." His breath was hot and sour in my face. "The time for restraint in all things is past."

His muscled, hard body pressed me against the wall and a hand slid inside what remained of my dress. My own hands pressed uselessly against his chest, a moth trying to move a mountain. The coppery smell of blood between my fingers made me dizzy. His other hand held my chin tightly, forcing my face up to his. I read a purpose in his eyes that frightened me more than anything.

For me it was too much, too soon. I tried to back away, to plead with him to let me go. His mouth covered my scream, absorbed it, swallowed it whole. No one was near enough to hear. No one was near enough to care. In everyone's eyes I was already his wife.

Oh gods. What had I done?

K'awiil released me to undo the clasp of his half-tunic.

I stood like a trembling rabbit in the path of onrushing disaster. I was as still and silent. My bruised lips throbbed with the beat of my racing heart. My eyes dropped, and the sight of my dress, soaked in blood, was the final shock to my overloaded mind and stomach.

I bent over, retching, and passed out cold.

This is the history of the darkest days.

Messengers ran to and from the city, seeking news of the battle. For three days the news was good. Our warriors pressed through the farmland surrounding Actuncan to our north. At the sight of K'awiil in all his splendor leading a band of two hundred men painted in the red and black of war, the farmers kept to their homes and offered no resistance. In the centre of the small city, a show of fifty warriors engaged bravely but hopelessly with our well-trained band. It was only a short time before their ruler stepped forward to prevent the slaughter of those who still lived. He swore his loyalty to Yaxmuul, to K'awiil, and to my Father K'ul Ahaw.

As the messengers told it, the ruler Ux B'alam, with his six sons beside him, removed his neck jewels and quilted armor and bared his chest to K'awiil. He offered his royal life as sacrifice to please the gods and preserve the two twenties of his men.

It was K'awiil's right by conquest to take them all for slavery or sacrifice, but the ruler bargained. His city had urgent need of these men.

K'awiil agreed with the calculation. One royal life for two twenties of warriors. He drew his sharpest obsidian knife.

The youngest son, a boy of only four or five tuns, shouted with anger and ran in front of Ux B'alam. He raised his fists in defiance to K'awiil and shouted, "You will leave my father alone."

As they tell it, K'awiil showed his own style of mercy, cutting the throat of the youngest son as he stood there. So quick, the boy had no time even to cry out in surprise.

K'awiil said to the conquered one, "There. A royal life has been given and two twenties spared. Rule honestly, loyally, and long. Go to your queen now and plant another son to replace this fine little warrior. His boldness honors you."

As the messengers tell it, Ux B'alam gathered up the small body, swallowed his grief proudly, and bowed low to K'awiil. He provided a feast for all the Yaxmuul soldiers and salves for their wounds and forty sacks of kakaw beans in tribute. That was the third day.

The goddess pressed me every day for news. When she heard of the city that yielded in three days, she asked, "Will K'awiil return home? It is only four days until our marriage." Her voice trembled like poplar leaves in light wind.

"Do not think that he would forget," I said. "I know he is counting the days as well as you. But the messengers say that he plans to march one more day to challenge Ux Ch'akan. Word of his overpowering army and Ux B'alam's submission will make that small city an easy conquest."

"K'awiil the conqueror," she said in a strange voice. "It would not be wise to anger him."

I had to laugh at her solemn face. "No, Ix Chel, it would not be wise to anger him. I have felt his wrath a few times myself, and it is not a pleasant memory." My hands moved of their own will to the scars on my arms and shoulders.

It was on the fifth day that the messengers returned with the news. K'awiil had been captured, and the battle raged under the command of K'awiil's second. On the sixth day, I was with Ix Chel when the messengers appeared, running up the hill to the city. We had continued our teaching even during these days of war. She told me her mind needed other work than worry. But she was tight with worry when we rushed into the audience room to hear the messenger's words.

His face was dark with anger and grief. His breath came in gasps. He had run through the night to reach us.

"Tell us," my Father Ahaw commanded. His face was still as a stone mask.

"K'ul Ahaw," the messenger began. "Never have I spoken such terrible words. Never again can I say them. Ba Ch'aak K'awiil, your son, is tortured, mutilated."

My Father Ahaw looked to the ceiling and moaned. His face creased in pain, and his right arm crossed his chest to grasp his breaking heart. "Tell me how it was," he whispered, his mighty voice become small.

"K'ul Ahaw, he was captured in the middle of battle. We thought to win the day and bring him back. But Ux Ch'akan bound him and carried him up to their highest temple platform where all could see. Their *ahaw caan* snake-priest cut strips from his flesh and offered them in their temple while he bravely stood without a scream. They burnt his wounds with hot copper to stop the blood so he would not die too soon."

My Father groaned again. He swayed on his feet, and I helped him collapse to the stone bench behind him.

My guts clenched when I learned of this torture. In that moment, I might have become a warrior myself, filled with bloodlust for revenge. But the part of me that remembered K'awiil as he gave me my own scars was satisfied in some terrible way. This I can never write or confess.

The messenger still breathed loudly, catching his wind. "Then Ahaw Ux Ch'akan himself came out to taunt Ba Ch'aak K'awiil. He told his men of K'awiil's deeds at Ux B'alam, of how he had slain the little boy, his sister's son. 'You have cut my family and taken life from one of the best of them,' he told K'awiil. 'You have denied our future as I will deny yours.' He ordered his priest to take Ba Ch'aak K'awiil's man-parts and feed them to his dog."

A roar of outrage filled the great hall. Father K'ul Ahaw rose on unsteady feet and above the noise cried out to the one who sits on his left, "Send two hundred more men. Go. And tell them to leave nothing standing." He sank down with lips that had turned dark blue with passion.

Lady Chel clutched my arm, her nails digging ridges deep in my skin. What this news meant to her, I could only imagine. A fine, whole man had left her. A scarred, angry, impotent shell would return.

She howled, a long coyote wail. Lightning cracked just beyond the window, lighting her face with a terrible glare. She turned from me to fall into the arms of Ix Imul. Thunder growled. Ix Imul led her away toward her chamber.

The goddess looked back to me once, her eyes filled with tears of fury. Outside the rain pelted down.

We thought we had already heard the worst.

I woke in a strange place that reeked of sweat and puke.

My head spun as I sat up and looked at myself to survey the damage. What happened here? I gingerly patted myself down. Nothing hurt, but I was covered in dried blood. I suspected it was someone else's. My legs were coated in the sour remains of someone's supper. I suspected it was mine. "Oh gods, what a mess," I said loudly.

A girl darted into the room at the sound of my voice. She must have been listening at the doorway for signs of life. She carried a bowl and cloths with her. The girl bowed low and said in a sweet, young voice, "If you please, Lady Chel. I will help you with your bath."

"Thanks," I said. How had she known I was here? Had I ordered her last night? Everything was a blur.

"Ba Ch'aak K'awiil asked for me to take care of you," she said, answering the question that must have shown in my face. She wet a towel in the bowl.

"Ba Ch'aak K'awiil?" I echoed. "K'awiil? When did...why did...oh. Oh, xit."

Memory trigger, cascade of vivid unpleasant images, flood of embarrassment. "How can I face him?" I muttered more to myself than her.

She raised her earnest brown eyes as she began washing my legs. "He is already gone. With his men." She added at my blank look, "To march north for battle."

Good gods. What had I done? I'd thrown up on my future husband and sent a frustrated, angry warrior off to battle.

No farewell. No good luck token. No come-back-safely-my-love. Xit.

I thought I could handle this. I honestly did. It all made sense right until the moment he touched me, which I had been so bold as to invite, and then I freaked out on him.

It was too much all at once, that's all. Just nerves. Jitters.

There was no courtship in this society to get comfortable with each other. You were just supposed to get married and work it out from there. Those were the rules of this world, I guess. I didn't write them, I didn't like them, but I had to find a way to live with them. Romantic dinners and moonlit walks would have to come later. If at all.

I'd make it up to K'awiil somehow when he got back. I'd be a...a goddess in bed. Pull out some twenty-first century tricks. I hoped my future husband and king could overlook a little vomit the first time he made a pass at me. I hoped to the gods he had a sense of humor.

When I was cleaned and dressed, I thanked the servant girl sincerely. "You can just throw those away," I said, pointing to the bloodied dress and sheets.

"No, no, Lady Chel. They will come clean with scrubbing."

"You...you want help with that?" I asked.

She looked appalled. "You think I cannot—"

"No, no. Never mind," I said. "Your job, not mine." More rules.

When I made my way to my chamber, I found Imul in there, watching the babies sleep. She sat weaving a width of cloth with dyed cotton cord on a small lap loom. A yellow and red geometric pattern was taking shape.

"That's pretty," I said in a hushed voice.

"It is a marriage gift for you," Imul said. "It will be a cover for your feather sack *pi'lo* that you told me about."

"Marriage present!" I said faintly. "Oh, thank you, Imul. Gods, I hope there is a marriage. I hope K'awiil still wants me after last night."

Imul's eyes flashed with humor. "Yes, last night. You slept elsewhere." She laughed at my silence. "It is fine, Chel. The first is not the best. Believe me. He will still want you."

"That's not...I mean. Nothing happened. Except..."

"What?" she prompted, all ears and eyes.

"Except I threw up on him."

She fell into peals of laughter. "Oh, what a story. What a wonderful story. The great K'awiil!" She wiped her eyes with the back of her hand. "I can just imagine."

"I would rather not," I said sadly.

"I will tell you how to make him forget," she offered and launched into another of her Mayan Kama Sutra lectures. The difference was that this time it was light and she acted out the information she was trying to share. I realized then that in this department, there was nothing new invented since ancient days.

Even in this benighted age without cell phones or news at eleven, runners brought two or three daily updates on our soldiers' progress. On the third day, they told us the first city had fallen with hardly a struggle and sworn loyalty to our royal family. K'awiil was so confident of taking the next town as swiftly, he pressed on, even so close to the wedding. Awful thoughts forced their way into my head. Maybe he had no intention of coming back after all. Maybe he'd keep on marching and conquering until he ran out of reasons not to come home. He'd probably take some pretty little spoil-of-war to bed with him to erase the memory of my cowardice. I had no illusions that he hadn't experienced many willing women, as handsome and masculine and powerful as he was. I was terrified that I wouldn't measure up.

Future queens should be made of sterner stuff than I was. Xit. Joan of Arc led an entire army to victory when she was about my age. And she was only a peasant, not a goddess. It did end badly, as I recall, but she was sainted in the long run.

I'd be lucky to get my name and profile engraved on a big rock.

On the fifth day, runners appeared in the distance at first light, announced by the clamor of barking guard dogs, followed by the yells of our sentries. They must have run all night, either to bring news of another wonderful victory or else....I grabbed Imul's hand and dragged her with me to the audience room.

"What does it mean?" I pressed her. "Good or bad?"

She didn't answer, which made the nervous acid in my stomach churn.

We arrived at the audience room in time to hear the terrible news. K'awiil was taken captive while the battle raged. The distraught king immediately called his counselors to discuss how many reinforcements to send to ensure the soldiers took the city and freed K'awiil. The best had been sent first, and, of course, a second battalion required preparation.

I paced anxiously across the plaza, waiting for a decision, waiting for action. Night fell. Our supper was silent and tense. I sat beside K'awiil's mother and held her hand. Neither of us could eat a bite. Imul suggested that I sleep in Lady K'uk's room that night. Both of us pretended to sleep as we watched the bright patterns on the insides of our eyelids and listened to each other breathe.

It was a relief when morning came.

Men Ch'o and I feigned interest in our usual lessons, but the moment a blasting conch announced that a runner had been spotted, we dropped our brushes and ran to hear.

As the messenger unfolded his story, so cruel and horrible, my knees gave way. I leaned heavily on Imul, who wept openly. K'awiil the handsome, flayed alive, burnt, disfigured. K'awiil the mighty, cut down in his prime, suffering the most grievous and irretrievable insult—castrated like an animal. Now he would never father a lineage of kings.

I ran to my room and threw myself down on the jaguar pelts. Their softness was an insult to the pain I felt, the pain I deserved. I cursed myself for rejecting him. If I had been strong, been Mayan, been the goddess I claimed to be, even now, I might have been carrying the first of his line. I wondered if Imul would still forgive me for my maidenly modesty. I couldn't.

Nothing is ever so bad that it can't get worse—another one of Mom's sayings when she was in the glass half-empty mode. While we still reeled from shock of our prince's capture and torture, while we still provisioned the two hundred who were being sent to recover him, more news came.

The messenger looked like he would rather cut out his own tongue than tell the king what he had to say. "Divine King, forgive me," he said. "Ba Ch'aak K'awiil is dead. His great heart kept him alive in spite of all the demons of Ux Ch'akan did to him. Through the night he roared defiance and called them disobedient dogs and stupid, slow tapirs and monkeys without a brain. He told them Yaxmuul would strip their ancestors from their graves and feed their bones to his dogs."

The king turned gray as he listened.

"Finally, Ux Ch'akan complained that the shouting disturbed his sleep. In the middle of the night, without honor or ceremony, he had Ba Ch'aak K'awiil beheaded."

The king clutched his chest with both hands and ordered, "Tell them to retrieve my son's body." His voice fell to a growling whisper. "Or do not return." He had to be helped from the room, leaning on the arms of two men.

In the morning, we learned he too was dead.

Men Ch'o was now the K'ul Ahaw, the divine king of Yaxmuul.

The first act of a new king is to order the burial ceremonies for the former king.

It is a heavy responsibility—far heavier than the serpent scepter I must now take up—and one that must be done with all speed. Lady K'uk' had seen to it that servant women dressed his skin with fragrant oil and cinnabar. She herself had dressed him in his finest robe and decorated his arms and legs with the jewels he would take with him into the afterlife. She knew which were his favorites. She placed the jade bead and four grains of maize on his tongue. Hers were the last lips to kiss his on this earth.

Lady Imul saw to the preparation of the funerary pots. She was too dismayed to be near my Father's body. She filled the special pots—one with fresh water, one with ground maize, one with cacao, and one with strong fermented pulque to please the gods.

Mine was the duty of slaying his faithful companion Sac-tz'ul. The animal already refused all food, knowing his duty to follow his master into Xibalba. To send him quickly was a mercy. He died without whimper or complaint.

Stone cutters opened the way into the chamber where Mother's bones lay, where her spirit waited for my Father's to take the last journey together. Although she had earned her warrior's place in the world above with women who fall in the battle of birth, I knew she still waited. She came to me often in my dreams, a restless spirit. Finally she would be at peace.

Before sealing closed the stone chamber, I ordered that we wait two more days, hoping to inter K'awiil with our Father.

I began to write the difficult words for a monument that would tell the story of how war divided them and how death wove them together.

Messengers reported news from the battle—it had turned in our favor, but too late to save K'awiil. When they learned of his ignoble death, our soldiers turned ferocious as jaguars. The king Ux Ch'akan fell at the front with many of his men. Our captain and his best took charge of the city while they sent me word. Our soldiers marched home victorious with captives, the four sons of Ux Ch'akan.

Their sacrifice would be a fitting tribute to my Father and brother.

There was ill news as well. K'awiil's body could not be found for burial. No one would ever place the maize and jade in his mouth. I was, in that moment, glad my Father Ahaw had not lived to know this.

The day of the funeral, Ix Chel walked with Ix Imul, the two of them a tragic sight to many eyes. They took their place in the high seats of the ball court.

The four captives waited on the field. Four ball players, muscled and quick, also waited. I gave the signal for the game to begin, and the eight rushed together with loud cries and hard knocks. The people cheered loudly for the men of our city. They called, "K'awiil. Remember K'awiil," which inspired the players to great efforts.

The captives fought hard, being the sons of kings. Our players fought better, avenging their lost ba ch'aak. When I declared victory for my men, the captive ones knelt at my feet in submission. It would be a good death. I ordered strong aqa to quench their thirst and numb them for the end. It is what I would have wanted in their place.

All the city gathered in the plaza and made a path for our procession. Priests waited atop the tallest temple, where we climbed to make the sacrifice. They chanted Ix Chel's name and K'awiil's. They knew what his murder had stolen from them.

Ix Chel climbed without tiring. Her eyes had a strange look to them, like undisturbed water that hides a caiman beneath. Her shoulders were straight. All signs of her grief were erased, but still her face was dreadful to see, carved in solemn purpose, frozen as a stone maiden. It was as though a single glance from her could kill a man without touching him. People shrank back, feeling the divine power shine from her.

At the temple platform, I met her eyes without speaking. Her thoughts came into my head. This was her sacrifice, her vengeance to perform. As goddess, she would speak directly to the gods. The four captives also saw her powerful look. They began to tremble, in spite of the liquor.

I wore myself out with pacing, stomping my feet with every step. Traipsing up and down the green mountain. Climbing up and down El Castillo. Anger drove every step.

Abandoned, again. Marooned, again. Just when I thought I had it all figured out, just when I had a plan to survive in this pitiless age of battle and blood.

I blamed myself for sending K'awiil off in frustration and disgust. I blamed the king for allowing K'awiil to start this war. I blamed K'awiil for seeking more guts and glory when he was supposed to come home for our marriage. I blamed the king Ux Ch'akan for his merciless treatment. No man escaped my blame.

I blamed the sons of Ux Ch'akan just for being his sons. I saw where the soldiers imprisoned them. I walked past them every day and stared. I wished they would plead for mercy just so I could spit on them and tell them "You had no mercy, dogs." And ask them, "Where is the body of my husband? The mutilated body of my warrior husband?"

Maniacal pacing wasn't enough to help me sleep at night, though. Exhausted as I was, I lay awake in the dark, my furious crying loud enough to disturb poor Imul. It seemed my anger would never end. It poured out of me like the rain that poured down at night, turning the unpaved ground to mud.

Finally, I understood, Men Ch'o could wait no longer to hold the funeral ceremonies of the old king. Sweet oil only went so far in covering the inevitable decay, and it was time to move him to his tomb, deep inside the temple of El Castillo. To consecrate the temple to hold his remains, a special sacrifice would be performed.

Oh yes, very special, I promised his angry spirit.

We held a solemn procession to the ball court. Imul and I led, as the two widows. The crowds in the plaza split open, leaving us a path, and the common women wept loudly around us and tore at their hair. I was frozen, hard as the ice I would never again see here in the tropics. Imul was softer, more sweetly despairing, but she had her two babies to comfort her. I had nothing to nurse but my rage.

The ball court stands were packed with the city elite. The common people stood back where they could hear, but not see the game. I had imagined this scene the day Hernán had taken us to Xunantunich, almost ten weeks ago, or eleven hundred years from now. Maybe I had heard the echoes down the years—the cries of the spectators, calling for blood, for vengeance, for the memory of K'awiil. I cheered with them in my silent, stony heart, but my lips were tight and pale.

At the inevitable end of the game, our men were victorious and bruised, the four princes of Ux Ch'akan battered but proud. They had known their fate for days. We treated them with far more honor than they had treated K'awiil, and my blood boiled for the unfairness.

Men Ch'o and the priests gave the captives a cup, which they drank deeply. I saw by the look in their eyes and their unsteady steps that it was some kind of intoxicant—another sign of our mercy. I glared at them with the full force of my hatred, and it pieced even through their drunken haze. They quailed, these strong warriors, at the force of the goddess's wrath. As well they should.

At the sacrificial platform, I ordered the priests to arrange them at the four compass points, a perfect square, which symbolized the maize fields to my people. The priests understood the symbolism—this sacrifice would bring fertility to the fields. The executioner stood in the center, all the men within his arm's reach. Symbolically, he stood at the center of earth and heaven, touching both, like the great Ceiba tree, the tree of life, which reaches its roots into the third world, Xibalba.

I stood at the edge of the platform, gathering strength from the people below me in the plaza. The wind whistled on this high platform on this high temple on this high green mountain. The people shouted to me, to the memory of K'awiil. Their voices rose as one, honoring, imploring, praising, worshiping. I lifted my arms to them and let their adulation cover me, fill my senses, drive away my desperate anger and replace it with pure power. They roared my name and K'awiil's in a deafening chant. My heart pounded in response.

Why had I ever thought this a nightmare? My spirit swelled, growing to twice my puny mortal size, filled with intoxicating strength.

"Strike!" I called out in a voice that rang to the next mountain.

When I turned back, the four warriors lay dead at my feet. Their sightless eyes gazed skyward as their heads rolled to a stop. Blood spattered the celebratory garments of the priests. Blood spilled over the temple platform, pooling around our feet. Men Ch'o watched me with pride and fascination written on his face.

There was just a hint of fear in his eyes.

I woke screaming from the nightmare, disoriented, confused, surrounded by night. My arms tangled in animal furs. The pitch black room smelled of burnt sweet oil. The crickets chirruping loudly from outside the windows mocked the roar of five thousand voices raised in cheers of approval that still echoed in my ears.

I jumped up to close the window, to drown out their sound, and my hand closed on rough fabric. I pulled it aside and stared out into an unfamiliar sky. Then the realization stole over me. The truth smacked me. My skin crawled with the sting of a million fire ants. My arm hairs bristled. My entire body went hollow, and my knees wavered, threatening to buckle completely.

It wasn't a nightmare. Or rather, the nightmare had become reality. My reality. My mouth shouting, "Strike."

"Chel, what is it?" a soft voice asked in the dark. Imul.

I turned from the window. A black knife flashed in my memory.

"Bad dreams?" she asked. "After such a day as this?"

"Terrible," I replied. Four heads rolling at my feet. "But not dreams. What I did...to those young men...." My voice stopped as my stomach heaved acid into my throat.

"Glorious," Imul said with admiration. "Ba Ch'aak K'awiil's spirit must rejoice in the tribute you paid him."

Hot blood poured out on stone. I squeezed my eyes tight and the image remained, burned into memory. "But more needless death..."

"Death repays death. Honor erases dishonor," she said with certainty.

"But I did it," I moaned. Four pairs of sightless eyes accused me. "And I was proud to."

"As so you should be," she insisted. "A proud goddess. How fortunate we are to have you make your home with us."

"I'm not..." I began and trailed off. Her dark eyes shined with trust and faith in me, lit with starlight as she came to me at the window.

"What is it?" she asked again, her voice soft with tender concern.

The gentleness in her voice completely undid me. A sob forced itself up from my deepest core. I struggled to breathe like a small child who has fallen, paralyzed with shock, waiting for the pain to explode.

"I...I...I'm..." was all I could force out. *I'm not a savage, bloodthirsty goddess*, I screamed inside.

She embraced me carefully, not sure how to handle a distraught goddess but wanting to help. She cupped my head to rest on her shoulder and stroked my hair with a mother's loving hands.

"I'm so lost," I whispered. "Everything, everyone is lost." I shuddered from head to toes. "I don't even know who I am any more."

Imul's voice took on the sound of a smile. She took my face in her hands and held me with worshipful eyes. "Oh Lady, Lady Chel. You are she whom we call to, pray to, Ix Chel. And you answer our prayers." Her eyes filled with ecstatic tears.

Oh gods, what had I done? I pushed her away. "No," I said harshly. "No! It's not true. Michelle. I'm Michelle. Oh gods. I'm Michelle." *And I've murdered four innocent boys*, my conscience wailed. What had they done but defend their city from K'awiil's preemptive attack? Anger and remorse burned a hole in my chest.

I twisted my fingers through my matted, tangled hair and pulled it out in handfuls. The pain anchored me to the world. Pain. I deserved pain, for what I had done. So much blood on my hands. I stared at the clean, white palms that concealed the truth about me.

As Imul stood frozen, I threw my washbowl against the stone wall and grabbed up a razor sharp shard. In four quick motions, I slashed the broken ceramic edge across my palms, two slices each, four new red life lines drawn in blood for the four boys whose life lines I had severed. I stared at the damage, not feeling a thing.

What had these people done to me? Damn them!

Days ago I thought I was surviving, fitting in, adapting, making a new life for myself. Now I saw it for what it truly was—a life based on power and desire and bloodlust and lies. They had turned me into their vengeful goddess.

But the kicker was—I had gone there willingly. And what did that say about me?

PART III - THE CODEX OF IX CHEL

The second act of a new king is to begin to rule.

I sent messengers to our other neighbors, telling them of our easy victories but revoking the formal challenge they had received from K'awiil. "We will not send force against you, but you will wish to join us as allies when you see our prosperity and power grow." That was my message.

I called in my counselors and took my new place at the head of the council mat to learn how things stood in our kingdom. My Father Ahaw had been a fine ruler, and even in times of drought, he had set aside a small surplus of maize and beans to carry us through worse. Thank the gods. I wondered if K'awiil would have proved so prudent a king.

It was fitting now that I should offer to wed the goddess. Ix Chel, the moon, is the consort of the Sun, the highest king, by name Ahaw. With the death of my Father and his proper heir K'awiil, I now embodied that divine role. I confess, I felt no different, and no new powers revealed themselves to me. So when I witnessed her strength and her anger, I shrank from asking.

In life, I did not shine brightly as K'awiil.

In his death, I think, he shined even brighter.

By day, Lady Chel walked and walked, speaking god-words to herself, hearing no one else. The cold fury she had poured on the captive princes now gave way to molten grief that burned all who came near. She was magnificent in the passion of her grieving. For a goddess to show such a mourning for a mere mortal honored K'awiil more than even he deserved. She allowed no one to speak words of comfort to her.

I left her to her walks and tears.

But an auspicious marriage date approached and, as I interpreted the calendar, a more favorable time would never be repeated in our lifetime. In less than one uinal, a twenty of days, was the turning of the bak'tun. Twelve generations of men had passed since the last such turning.

Even better, the ninth bak'tun would end on Seven Ahaw Eighteen Zip. The perfect long count date of 10.0.0.0.0 was matched with the name day of the sun Ahaw and the month of the moon goddess as healer, Zip.

The omens were overwhelming. I had no choice. The date must be chosen. There was no time to allow her to wear out her grief.

I asked K'awiil's mother, whom Lady Chel had taken as her own mother, to speak for me. Thus I began my reign with the heart of a coward, not afraid of a hundred warriors, but afraid of a scornful look from those sky-eyes.

All the time Ix Chel wept, the rains fell on the bare fields. The *chultunoh* and *tz'onots*, both the dug and the natural cisterns, filled to overflowing. We would have fresh water to spare for many, many months. Even as she suffered, she helped her people. She would be a fine queen...if she agreed.

I grieved and ranted and paced like a mad woman, frightening Imul and everyone else away from me. Imul found another place to sleep with the babies. The servants left food outside my doorway, which I scarcely touched. Men Ch'o never once came to see how I was. Maybe he was warned away or too busy establishing himself as the new king.

After two weeks by my count, Lady K'uk' was brave enough to come to me in my chamber. Her robes were in disarray, her hair was uncombed, and her macaw feathers were sadly crushed. I realized with some shame I wasn't the only one suffering. Her husband and only son had died within hours of each other. A fresh wave of grief washed over me. I should have gone to her and held her hand in the night, the way Imul tried to hold mine before I pushed her away.

I reached out and hugged this woman, and for a while, we clung to each other silently. Tears flowed over my cheeks and onto her hair. "Oh, gods," I whispered as we pulled apart. "I'm so sorry."

She took my damp face between her hands. "You are too thin," she said. "You must eat."

"I can't. I have no appetite." My stomach was tied in knots. Was I actually thin? No one had ever called me thin in my life. Results of the widowhood diet, living on sobs and sighs. I couldn't even call myself a widow, really. The wedding hadn't taken place. Neither had the wedding night. What do you call someone whose fiancé has died?

Lady K'uk' pulled a small ball of spiced honey candy from a pouch. She knew I could hardly resist them.

"Very well," I said. "I'll eat this one."

She put the pouch on the bench beside me and began to comb my hair, very gently through two weeks of tangles. I closed my eyes and pretended she was my own mother. Just a small indulgence, and just for a few moments.

"Oh, Mother K'uk'. What should we do?"

I had no plan beyond mere existence. I'd lived in the palace since my arrival. They waited on me hand and foot. They didn't demand anything of me. It was like I was a good luck charm goddess or something. But what was I supposed to do now? Find a nice single farmer to marry and settle down and raise a family? Become the first female scribe at the temple? I was utterly useless. And utterly alone.

Lady K'uk' carefully worked a knot as she answered in a low voice. "Men Ch'o, he asked me to speak to you."

"Oh gods. Poor Men Ch'o. How is he holding up?"

I'll bet he was even more in shock than I was, propelled to kingship with no warning, in the middle of a war. And he was sort of sensitive about his older brother. He probably couldn't help thinking that everyone was comparing him and wondering how it would have been if the battle had gone differently.

Lady K'uk' smiled sadly. "He is doing well. He has brought us back to peace with our neighbors. I know how the men lust for battles and captives, but for us women, it is far better if they stay home."

If K'awiil had stayed home, we would be married by now. I wondered how different my life would be.

"I haven't seen him since...since that day," I admitted. "Do you think he has time to see me? I should go to him. But he must be extremely busy kinging."

"I believe he is quite anxious to speak with you," she said with an odd gleam in her eye. "I am certain he has time."

"Yes, well, we had to stop all our lessons. Maybe he wants to get started again."

"Lessons?"

I blushed. I'm sure this was unheard of in this era. "I am teaching him the god-words, and he is teaching me writing and the calendar." I had to understand the calendar to know exactly how far back in time I'd been thrown. I was finally getting close to understanding enough to calculate it with Men Ch'o's help.

Curiously, Lady K'uk' nodded her approval. "That is good. It is good for the king to know the god-words. That is power without sharp spears."

"Should I...?" I began.

She put down the comb and stroked my hair. "Yes. Go to him now. He will see you. Wait." She reached up and pinched my face pink along my high cheekbones. "Yes, a bit better. Go."

My heart lightened a little as I walked the familiar path to the audience room. I stood in the doorway while Men Ch'o spoke with two merchants disputing a price and realized with a pang how I had missed him over the past two weeks, how stupid I had been to take solitary walks when we could have given each other sympathy and moral support.

He mediated earnestly between the two men until their difference was resolved. They clapped each other on the back and departed together. Three more petitioners entered the room, and I watched from the shadows as he listened in turn to their complaints. Each of them had a partial claim to a new litter of prized hunting dogs, but only five had been born, one female. Now they couldn't agree how to share five pups three ways, a problem with fractions.

With the wisdom of a Mayan Solomon, Men Ch'o suggested, "Let one man take the bitch puppy and two men take two males each. You choose."

I liked his math and his logic—a girl was worth two boys. Pretty enlightened for his age, I thought with the first smile to touch my lips in weeks.

He glanced in my direction, just catching the tail end of that smile. "Ix Chel," he said. His face broke into an answering grin.

He turned to his door guard. "Are there more waiting?" he asked.

"No. Those were the last, K'ul Ahaw."

"Good. You may go." He watched until the guard had left, then gestured me forward.

"Ix Chel," he said again. "Come."

I wasn't sure where to stand, on the floor, on the dais, or what. He came to me halfway and led me to sit beside him on the jaguar fur-covered bench.

He fidgeted uncertainly, a huge change from his handling of the petitioners. "Is it well?" he asked.

"Is what well?" I asked.

"Did Ix K'uk' speak to you?" He twisted his hands together.

"Yes, just now," I replied. "She said you wanted to see me."

"Oh," he said. "Did she tell you why?" The hand wringing grew more frantic.

"No. Was it about our lessons?" I placed a hand on his. I couldn't help myself.

"No. Not about the lessons." He stared at my fingers, avoiding my eyes. He took a deep breath. "It was...it was about the turning of the bak'tun."

"Oh?" I wasn't at all sure where this was going. He seemed a bit worked up to be discussing the calendar.

"In ten days will be the turning of the bak'tun, twenty twenty years. It will be the most important ceremony of our lifetimes."

Turning of the bak'tun. That rang a bell. "Write it," I demanded. "Show me."

"Show you?" He looked confused at my intensity. "Very well. Here." He pointed to a date inscription painted on the wall. "Remember the order of the date. Bak'tun first, then k'atun, tun, uinal, k'inal. Remember?"

I nodded. The Long Count date. I'd been concentrating on learning the day names. But if I knew the Long Count date, I could figure out when I was. I could get oriented at last.

He said, "It is almost ten bak'tuns and zero, zero, zero, zero. A great celebration."

"Cool," I said. "Like the new millennium." And now the purpose of my intense curiosity. I pointed to the wall. "And what about thirteen bak'tuns and zero, zero, zero, zero. How long until then?"

"Yes, the end of the age. That is three of twenty twenty eighteen twenty days."

"How many years? I asked.

"Which years? Haab or Tzolkin?" he asked.

"I don't know. I need something to write with."

"I have nothing here," he said.

"Damn."

"Is this a terrible problem?"

"Yes," I said.

"Wait here," he ordered.

I sat impatiently while he ran from the room.

A hundred years later he arrived with an ink pot, pen, and tablet. "Please," he said.

I worked out the multiplication part easily. Three times eighteen times twenty cubed. Keep track of all the zeroes. That's 432,000 days—days between a few days from now and when the world ended...will end. Close enough.

Men' Ch'o watched over my shoulder in fascination as I scribbled numbers, strange symbols I hadn't taught him yet.

"Please?" he asked. "Show me?"

I jotted down the translation table for the digits zero through nine. "That's all," I said. I'd have to explain about base ten to him later. "Now 432,000 divided by 365. Or should it be 365.25?"

How much would leap years throw it off? There were 24 leap days every century. A lot. So I'd have to use 365.25. Yuck. Long division without a calculator.

I bit my lip hard as I worked the numbers, careful not to make a mistake or smear the ink. Carry the four, subtract the six, borrow from the tens place. And the final answer made my head spin.

The world falls apart in 1182 and three quarters years from this coming festival. Subtract from December 21, 2012, and your answer is....

I had arrived near the end of 829 A.D. By now it was 830. Xit. Holy Xit.

Men Ch'o was studying my face. "What is it? Ix Chel? What is wrong? Is it a bad calendrical omen?"

I shook my head. "No, nothing like that. Men Ch'o, I just calculated how far from home I am."

His expression crumpled. "I had hoped you would remain with me," he whispered. "With us," he corrected. "Are you returning to your far home?"

"No, Men Ch'o. I can't. It's too far to find again. I'm...I'm lost."

I was surprised that saying the words aloud didn't change me, didn't make me break down. It was just a simple fact.

Men Ch'o tentatively put an arm around my shoulders. "It is fine. We will take care of you here, goddess. I will take care of you."

I leaned against him comfortably. His warm bulk was reassuring. At least I had a friend, a true friend.

His cleared his throat, but his voice still cracked a little as he asked me, "Are you...are you carrying his child?"

"What? His...what?"

"K'awiil's child," he whispered.

"Oh gods, no. No, no, no," I said. "Definitely no. He...I...we...didn't. No. No way."

"Ah." His face relaxed into a smile. "It is well, I think."

"Oh, yes," I said, thankful for escape from near disaster—unwed pregnant teenaged widow was never part of my plan. "It is *very* well. So what about this celebration?" I reminded him. "I'm sorry I got distracted. You wanted to tell me about the celebration."

His comfortable body suddenly turned tense, and he unwrapped his arm. My shoulder felt cold and exposed. He swallowed hard and blinked.

"What?" I prompted. "You were all set to tell me."

He focused on his hands, clasped together in his lap now. "You see, the date of the celebration is also an interesting coincidence of days. It is the day Seven Ahaw—which represents me, the king. And it is joined with Eighteen Zip, which is the month of the moon goddess, which as you know, already, of course, is you. They join, you see. On an important day."

He wouldn't meet my eyes. I didn't get it. What was he going on about?

"Men Ch'o, I'm sorry I don't understand."

Finally he looked up, his eyes wide and fearful. "They meet, they join, they become one together—the king and the moon on this important day."

I frowned in concentration. What on earth...? He raised his eyebrows hopefully.

"They join," I repeated. "They join? Wait, you mean you want to....think we should...?"

With a huge effort, Men Ch'o switched to English, his special god-words to speak his most important question. "A'wa uw cho'in mi?"

"Are you join me?" I asked.

He nodded. His face was bright red.

I laughed. I couldn't help myself. "You mean *will you marry me?*"

He laughed nervously. "Wiil uwa mawa mi?"

"You don't have to," I said. "I'm not truly your brother's widow. And I'm not, thank the gods, pregnant. You're not responsible for me."

"I want to," he said.

He wanted to?

Oh. It was true. Looking into his hopeful face I could tell, he really wanted to. Was I totally blind? How come I hadn't seen this coming?

Because he'd always stood so quietly in K'awiil's shadow.

"Let me think about it," I said.

This I have written of the sun and the moon, how they came closer together yet remained bakaanes apart.

On the great temple frieze, the face masks of the sun and moon looked toward the sunset side, the future that will be, together. I hoped it was a true prophecy.

With stammering words, I offered Lady Chel half the kingdom, half the throne, all of my heart.

"Let me think about it," she said.

"It is in ten days," I reminded her.

I waited while the day came closer. I did not ask again, but at meal times I searched Lady Chel's face for any sign that she had decided. For this time, my food tasted like sand, and even though Lady K'uk' and her slaves tried their best to serve me, I did not eat well.

Affairs of state and settling the peace with our neighbors after K'awiil's bold words and bolder attacks took much time. It was time that I would have preferred to spend in lessons. Only during lesson time could Ix Chel and I put our heads together over a tablet with no awkwardness between us. Now there was nothing but awkwardness. I do not know if she felt it as I did.

Finally she came to me in the audience chamber at the very end of the last day. "I have decided I will marry you," she said with no joy in her face, all seriousness.

How could I answer except with matching seriousness? "Then it is good," I said. "You will stay with us, and we will be blessed." I meant to say, "I will be blessed," but her solemn little face changed my words.

"There is one thing I would like," she said.

"Of course," I replied without thought. "Anything you desire, you may have."

"Thank you. I would like my own chamber."

"Of course," I repeated. "That would be customary."

"I mean, I would like to stay in my own chamber alone, with...with no disturbance."

I feared I understood the meaning of her words. We usually did understand each other well, even without words. I asked, with hope that I was wrong, "You wish me to stay in my chamber alone, with no disturbance as well? You wish to be married but...apart?"

She felt my pain, I believe. She took my hands in a way I supposed she meant to comfort, but her touch burned as the blistering sap of the chechem tree.

She said, "For a while. I am...this body...is so young. I'm not ready to bear children. But I will. I know you need heirs to rule after you...at some time...in the future."

Heirs. What did I care for heirs? Just to hear her quiet breath beside me in the night would be half of all I could want. But I agreed to her wishes. It was more than a man with my face and form could have hoped for, to marry a goddess. And I had little choice if I wanted to be married on the next day.

"Thank you for being so understanding," she said. She kissed my hand and left. I pressed it to my face as she walked away.

At supper, it was as if none of this had passed between us.

Men Ch'o accepted my terms, thank the gods. I wasn't ready to be married. I had scared myself spitless over the realities of being married to a man like K'awiil. Men Ch'o was certainly a gentler soul, but he was still a man of his times—and still, no doubt, a man. I was surprised, actually, that he agreed to a "marriage of convenience." Perhaps it suited his purposes for now. He could use me as a symbol of power and control, just as his father and K'awiil did, without sleeping with me. Maybe he didn't even like me that way. Maybe he had a mistress already. I wondered how I could find out.

I needed time, time to collect myself. I still hadn't recovered from sacrificing those four boys. Yes, their death had been inevitable according to this world's rules, but I couldn't forget that I gave the final execution order. I couldn't forget that I had been happy to do it, filled with the rush that the power of life and death gives a person. In that moment of frenzy, I was possessed by thoughts that shouldn't have been mine—they were primitive, cold, and bloodthirsty. I wasn't that kind of girl. But I was becoming that kind of woman. So I had a lot of thinking to do, and no shrink in sight to help me.

I didn't tell Imul about the proposal until after I had decided and informed Men Ch'o. She was thrilled, and declared herself the Mayan equivalent of matron of honor. Since preparations had started long ago for my marriage, my wedding clothes were ready. The festival of the new bak'tun had been planned by whoever plans these things. All I had to do was put on a pretty dress and show up in the morning.

Maybe I had failed to realize the importance of the festival.

In the morning, insulated in the palace dining room as I ate my maize porridge and papaya, I had no idea that crowds had been gathering since first light. When we stepped out of the palace complex to begin our walk to the temple, the crowd stretched as far as the eye could see. Even from the temple platform, the teeming sea of black-haired citizens covered the landscape for at least a half-mile. There had to be more than ten thousand gathered.

The first ceremony of the day was a dedication of the new bak'tun. I thought back to the new millennium when Mom and Dad let us stay up till midnight for the first time. It's my earliest memory. We were only two and a half, but Mom and Dad made such a big deal of it that my brain was engraved with an impression of confetti and party hats and honking paper horns. When we were old, they promised us, we'd be able to tell people that we saw the new millennium come in. But Maya never made it to old, and even if, against all odds, I did, I'd have no one to share the memory with.

Men Ch'o noticed the faraway look in my eyes. He patted the small of my back, and I forced away melancholy thoughts. All around me, our people were celebrating the potential of a new dawn. I was their goddess. I needed to be here for them.

There was a long break for feasting and games of skill. Dancers in the plaza re-enacted great scenes from history and legends. Then five handsome boys climbed partway up the temple steps and blew loud blasts on the conch to call people back to the next ceremony, the formal crowning of Men Ch'o.

He and I went through the back temple passages, so that to the people we would just appear on the platform high above them. The head priest, Ah K'uhun, removed the ridiculous top-heavy headdress from Men Ch'o's head and tied a white band around his brow, a reflection of the white band of the Milky Way. Men Ch'o held out his hands, palms open. Two of the junior priests brought forward a carved scepter and knelt at his feet, raising it up to him. Each end was the head of a snake with flame shooting from his head, and in between, the body twined around the trunk of a great tree. Men Ch'o grasped the scepter and raised it high.

The crowd roared their approval with an overwhelming explosion of sound and raised their waving arms.

In celebration of his accession to the throne, Men Ch'o retired his childhood name of Eagle Eyes and announced the name under which he would rule and be remembered—K'ul Ahaw Tikilik Ri Ik', the divine king of the full moon.

He whispered to me, "I hope it is acceptable to you. I chose it after you answered me yesterday. The impatient stone cutters have asked me night and day for the inscription. Today they are happy. It is a pun as well—a play on the word *tikiritajik*, which means *the beginning* as well as *celebrate*. It is perfect in every way."

I whispered back, "What should I call you now? To me you will always be Men Ch'o."

"So be it," he said. "You will call me Men Ch'o."

"And please," I added. "Just call me Chel from now on. In private, I don't need a title. Not with you."

When the priests completed their chants, there was another break for more feasting and music. I was afraid we would run through all the emergency stored grain at this rate, but Men Ch'o assured me that all the farms had made contributions toward the royal storehouse over the last quarter-year, just for such an occasion.

Finally, at mid-afternoon, the conch-boys summoned everyone again for the marriage ceremony. I had already worked through the idea that this would not be the wedding that little girls dream of. My Dad wouldn't walk me down the aisle. My Mom wouldn't be weeping with happiness in her pew. My sister wouldn't be standing beside me holding my huge bouquet of roses and lilies while I took my first communion as a married woman. I wouldn't kneel on a white runner with my long white silk dress and gauzy veil floating out behind me. I wouldn't leave my hometown church to the strains of Purcell played on the trumpet stops of the new organ, hop into a glossy limousine, and speed away to a reception where a mile-high wedding cake topped with a plastic bride and groom awaited.

And yet, even missing all these ingredients, it was a good wedding. I wore a heavy, colorful embroidered robe trimmed with jaguar fur. My arms hardly showed through the copper and abalone and jade bracelets Imul helped me put on. My hair was dressed with long, green quetzal feathers and white orchids. My cheeks sparkled with the powdered flakes of mica Imul had dusted onto them. The sandal maker had brought me new, soft, deer leather sandals for my not-so-dainty feet.

Flutes, drums, and tambourines played haunting and harmonious melodies. Imul and Lady K'uk' stood with me as my women-folk and led me to Men Ch'o, who stood alone with the high priest. We said the words of the ceremony that bound us together while the Ah K'uhun symbolically bound our hands together with a knotted rope.

Then we visited the four altars the priests had set with flowers. The altar on the North was strewn with red hibiscus. On that altar, I placed a pot of dried red beans. The altar on the East was decorated with yellow sunflowers. Imul placed a pot of ground yellow maize. The altar on the South was vibrantly purple with sprays of orchids. Lady K'uk' offered a bowl of dark purple papaya seeds. Finally, the altar to the West, the direction of the setting sun, was white with morning glory blossoms. Men Ch'o placed a white painted pot of clear water in the middle of the flowers.

The high priest completed the ceremony by tracing the same steps we had taken with a bowl of burning copan incense. He blew the fragrant smoke across each altar to direct the spirit of our gifts to the gods above. A cheer rang out from the watching crowd.

"Is that it?" I asked Men Ch'o. "Are we married now?"

"Yes," he said with a gentle smile. "We are married now."

"You may kiss the bride," I said in English. He tilted his head to the side in puzzlement as he tried to work out the words. I put my arms around his neck, looked him in his serious straight eyes, and said, "Thank you."

He leaned toward me and kissed me on the forehead. Not what I was expecting, but given the limits I had placed on him, probably a good idea.

After another round of feasting and music and games, the sky was turning pink toward sunset, and I was completely exhausted. Men Ch'o noticed me wilting on my feet. "Come, we can go in now. The celebration will last through the night. I do not think you will."

I kissed Imul and Lady K'uk' and thanked them for their support during the day. They winked at each other as Men Ch'o and I made our early departure. Who could blame them?

"I chose this chamber for you," he said. "I hope it is right."

He pushed aside the door curtain to reveal a room warm with flickering lamp light. The walls were painted a golden color, and the floor was completely covered with tawny fur, soft on the feet. A mattress leaned against the right-hand wall, and folded beside it sat a fine white cloth and a dark red blanket. A pile of tablets, a pot of ink, and a bowl of brushes rested on a three-legged table in front of the stone bench along the left-hand wall. My Coke can and granola bar were placed in a wall niche, like a tiny shrine. The dry bag hung from a wooden peg driven into a bore hole in the wall. My clothes were neatly folded in another wall niche. A curtain of cloth covered a window on the back wall. I moved it and gazed out at the glorious sunset that now streaked the western sky.

"It's beautiful, Men Ch'o," I said with gratitude.

And that reminded me. I had a wedding gift for him back in Imul's room. He admitted that he had one, too, and we agreed to meet back in the room as soon as we retrieved them. I came back first, with a pillow under each armpit and a vase I had stayed up too late painting. When Men Ch'o returned, he also was carrying a vase. We looked at each other's gifts and burst out laughing.

"Ladies first," I said. "I thought I was being original."

I handed him my pot, which was pale red, painted with black writing. I read the words first as they were written in English on one side. The glyphs I had carefully painted on the other side. In English, it worked out as a haiku, but it was more like free verse in ancient Mayan.

On the green mountain
Moon and Sun meet together
Turning night to day.

"I have never heard that verse before." Men Ch'o sounded both pleased and curious.

"Yes, well, I composed it for you," I said.

"Your own words?"

"Yes. My own words."

"It is a very fine gift," he said with awe in his voice. "This is more practical."

I offered him the down pillow I had painstakingly sewn by hand, using part of a sheet for the case. It took weeks for the duck-boy to bring me enough soft down to stuff it. "It should help you sleep more comfortably."

"That would be welcome," he said with enthusiasm. "I have not slept well at all these past days. Here is my gift. They are not my own words, but a traditional song-poem for a marriage. I wrote out the glyphs, of course."

He must have used a brush with only ten hairs, the writing was so tiny and fine. It must have taken days. He must have begun as soon as he asked me. And I had made him wait so desperately long for an answer.

I traced the perfect lettering, dozens of glyphs I had yet to learn. "Can you please read it?" I asked.

He blushed, but nodded. He held the pot without looking at it and sang from memory in a fine tenor voice:

Wear beautiful clothes for the day of your wedding;
Comb out all the knots from your raven dark hair;
Put on your most beautiful gown and your leather;
Hang great copper rings from your delicate ears;

Tie on a gold belt and wear garlands around your throat,
No one more glorious than you will be seen.
Now wrap your soft arms in these bright shining jade coils.
Your loveliness reigns on this hillside of green.

Beloved and beautiful lady you sparkle
Above all the rest like a comet or star.
Because they desire you up to the moon's height
Or standing on earth in a field full of flowers.

Pure white are the clothes of the pure-hearted maiden,
Pure happiness flows at the sound of your laugh.
Share joy from your heart in this moment of festival.
People will follow your steps on the path.

I found it hard to breathe or swallow when he finished and turned his black shining eyes toward me. "Oh Men Ch'o," I said. "That's a wonderful song-poem. What is it called?"

If possible, his blush deepened. "It is named 'To kiss your lips beside the fence rails.'"

"Oh." I turned my head slightly, hiding my own warm cheeks. "Thank you," I said, feeling the words were entirely inadequate to express the mixed feelings raging through me.

"Good night, dear Chel. Sleep well." He turned to go.

I stopped him with an outstretched hand. "Good night, dear king."

I leaned closer to kiss him quickly on the left cheek. He turned his face in the same direction, and with a shock, our lips brushed. Without thinking, I relaxed forward, wrapping my arms around his shoulders and falling into the warmth and strength of his embrace. His arms came up around my waist and pressed me even closer. My heart pounded. My feet tingled with fear and excitement. My whole being wanted to disappear inside this kiss, which deepened and went on and on. I drew a slow, shuddery breath through my nose. My eyes fluttered open a crack and flew wide with surprise as they met Men Ch'o's. His eyes held a question which I was suddenly too scared to answer. But he read my hesitation. He unlocked his arms from around me and stepped away. Before I could unlock my brain, he was gone, his wedding gifts left behind.

This I have written of the Codex Ix Chel, the prophecies and warnings of the goddess Ix Chel in human form.

Lady Chel, my Chel, was bored and restless. I had no time for our lessons as we began our rule. She helped Ix Imul with the babies, having none of her own, nor wanting them. Yet. She asked whether she could continue her writing lessons with Ah K'uhun, but I worried that the high priest was old and would not like to teach a woman the power of writing, even if she were queen. I asked why this was so important to her.

"I want to keep a durable record, a xurnal," she said. "I asked the pottery workshop for blank tall pots. Each uinal, I will write of what has happened, and the pots will tell my story, if they are ever found."

"Found? What do you mean, found? Who would find them when they are not lost?"

She became sad and hesitated before speaking again. "I don't want...No, I misspoke. I didn't mean *found*. I meant *read*—if they are ever read by my descendents. They would tell my story. But I don't have enough words yet."

"I understand," I said. "We do need more time together. I would still like to learn your god-words. I was learning much before all this,"—I gestured to the open door—"usurped my time."

"When?" she asked.

"The evening. Before sleeping," I suggested. I was not thinking of the breath-stealing, mind-stealing, soul-stealing kiss of our marriage night. Not at all.

No one waited to see me right then. I said, "Let us walk to the stone cutters to see progress on the bak'tun stela. They had much still to carve the last time I went, but I would like to dedicate it soon. Maybe they will work faster for you."

She laughed at that idea, and it was like the sun breaking through rain clouds when she smiled with her eyes.

We left the palace, crossed the plaza with curious gazes following us. The craft shops were busy in the mornings. All this my Chel devoured with her gaze as though she had never seen such industry. Her interest made it fresh to my eyes.

Potters were preparing the new pots for the day to dry by sunlight and fire during the night. The weavers were dipping long strands of their cotton yarns in pots of deep-colored plant dyes. Point-makers chipped obsidian blades into lethal weapons and fastened them to knives, spears, clubs, and lances. Rope-makers pounded and peeled agave fibers and twisted them into strong cords. Tablet-makers pounded softened bark into thin pages while others painted them white with lime and hung them to dry in the afternoon heat. The people raised their heads from their work and greeted us as we passed by. I knew many of the names of the old ones from watching them as a boy. Now their children were masters of their craft.

The ring of hammer on stone greeted us as we came to the stonecutters. They had finished the date panels long ago. Today, I saw, they had finished the portion concerning my seating after the deaths of my Father Ahaw and K'awiil. K'awiil they credited with taking four captive princes before his death, a poetic flourish that no one would contradict.

The stela was marked with charcoal for the rest of the carvings, announcing the marriage of the ruler of Yaxmuul to Lady Chel's human incarnation. They would be finished soon.

Chel ran her hands over the part that was complete and admired their fine work. The stone cutters swelled with pride to be noticed so. Yes, for her they would be finished soon.

"This is the date," she said to me. "I can read it. And here is your child name." She touched the eagle-face glyph beside a tipped up pair of eyes. "And here is the city, Yaxmuul. I recognize that now."

She had a fine mind to learn and remember things so well.

Suddenly, she put her hands over her eyes and held her head as if it pained her. Then she grabbed my arm with terrible, piercing strength. "Men Ch'o, when will they carve the next important date stela?"

"I can not tell that now," I said. "If there is a war or a royal birth or death or a new building to dedicate..."

"What if it is none of those, just the next important date?"

I thought hard to understand what she meant. "Then it would be the turning of the next k'atun, at ten, one, zero, zero, zero."

She ran her hands over the glyphs, muttering numbers as she had on the day I had asked to be her husband. "Eight forty-nine," she said. "Xit. Eight forty-nine. Hernán said that was the last one." She spoke only to herself. The stone cutters and I could not follow her thoughts.

"The last one they found," she said. "What happened? What will happen here?" she asked the sky.

I put my arm around her to call her back to our presence.

She looked at me with huge, despairing eyes. "Men Ch'o, terrible things are going to happen. And it will be soon."

"A vision?" I asked.

"I wish it were only a vision. I have walked in the future on the last day of the age, and this is what I know. In one k'atun, we will erect the last stone stela in Yaxmuul. Before that date, Yax Mutul will fall and be abandoned by its people. And some time after that Yaxmuul will also be abandoned."

"Yax Mutul? Abandoned?" I could not believe my ears. "Yax Mutul is huge, powerful. Have you never seen it?"

"Yes, Men Ch'o. I have seen Yax Mutul. We call it Tikal. I have seen it abandoned and in ruins. The cenotes are empty and dry. The fields are dead. The people starved or fled to villages. A hundred, maybe two hundred thousand of them. The forest will return to cover the city for almost three bak'tuns before men find the ruins again and try to understand the silent voices of the monuments. The men of the future will ask, 'What happened here?' as I did."

"And Yaxmuul?" I asked with pain.

"The men who find Yaxmuul will call the city Xunantunich, Stone Maiden. Even the true name of this place will be drowned in the well of time."

I bit my lip until I tasted blood. "This is a terrible future. The gods must hate us."

"I wonder if they do," she said.

"You must ask them," I said. "You are our goddess. You must ask them what we must do to change their hearts. I will gladly sacrifice my own life if that is—"

She interrupted. "Men Ch'o, I'm not...I'm just..."

She stopped. The stone cutters watched her with round, frightened eyes. "I'll figure this out. There must be something we can do. I'll figure this out." She looked around at the busy artisans, her eyes full of questions. I knew she was thinking, "What will happen here?"

After that, Chel kept to her room except for meals. She had a stack of fig bark tablets sent in every day, and all day, she sat writing, writing god-words I could not read.

One evening, after supper, we went to her room as we usually did to spend only a short time with lessons. She was distracted and folded a page back and forth until it was shaped like an arrow. She tossed it from her hand, and it floated on air until it had crossed the room and smacked into the wall. It fell to the ground with a bent beak.

"A bird," I said. "You have created a paper bird. Show me how."

She sighed with a twisted smile. "This, Men Ch'o, is a paper *plen*. In my future, huge plens will carry men across great distances, entire lands, above the clouds."

I laughed aloud at her jest. "Only if the gods rise up and throw them, I think. Would they not fall to their deaths?"

"Well, yes. Sometimes," she said.

"How cruel the gods can be," I said, then flinched. I wondered if she would strike me for my careless words.

But she folded another plen and looked at it with such sorrow, I asked, "Can I help you somehow, Lady Chel?"

"You will," she said. "You will, soon."

Finally, after fifteen days of writing, she had a stack of pages as high as her knees. "Now I can use your help, Men Ch'o. We need to translate these into Mayan and put them together."

"Together? Like your brown-skin xurnal?" I asked.

"Yes," she said.

I imagined it. "A codex. You have written a codex." The codex of Ix Chel.

"I have written a prophecy," she said. "And now we have less than a twenty of years to make sure it never comes to pass."

Who, what, when, where—all those questions had been answered. The one left haunting me was "why?" Why me? Why was I stranded in 830 A.D. in ancient Belize?

When I touched the stone stela, felt the date under my fingers, I knew. I understood. Whether the Mayan gods were true or not, whether any of the interpretations of God in the twenty-first century were true or not, some force had opened a way and sent me back in time. And that *had* to change everything.

Was I actually chosen to be the instrument of change? Me? Surely the gods must be crazy. There were five of us together at the end. Maybe it was supposed to be my father or mother or sister or Enrique. An actual historian would make way more sense. But speculating was pointless. The reality is, it *was* me, chosen on purpose or dumped here at random. And just the fact that I was here, knowing what I knew about the future, *would* change things.

But maybe there was even more I could do. I just had so little time.

Our civilization had developed along a certain path that led to the world I knew, a world that was wonderful in many ways—modern medicine, productive agriculture, individual rights, global communications and trade—but it was awful in many ways as well—especially comparing the countries that benefited from all those wonders and the ones that remained stuck in poverty, ignorance, and conflict.

What if the world had taken another path? Things would be different. Would they be better? I had to believe so, or there was no point in trying.

I *had* caught part of the vision, listening to K'awiil's Napoleonic plans. I just caught the wrong part, the conquer and rule part, not the unify and strengthen part. Not the part about saving it all from waste and ruin. And that's why I was here. That would be my calling, my job, my purpose.

Men Ch'o recognized my urgency and was desperate to help me. He made sure I was well supplied with brush and bark, food and drink, so I could dedicate myself to my work. In the evenings we spent a little time together drinking herbal tea and working on language and writing. His mind was so quick, and his pronunciation of the English words was getting better all the time, giving me hope. There was no rerun of the one passionate kiss we had shared that had nearly swept me away. Just as well. That was a complication I couldn't handle now, anyway.

When I had written the history of the future, I also wrote what I hoped would be a remedy, a positive change. After fifteen days of living and breathing it, I believed I had a strategy for trying again. I said a prayer to every God I could think of, and we began the heavy work of translating into Mayan.

Men Ch'o and I had to spend more and more time together. I read my text and explained to him everything I knew about theories of the Mayan collapse—the endless warfare between city states, the long periods of drought, the overpopulation that resulted in over-planting that destroyed the soil. I told him about the great Aztec empire that would emerge in five hundred years. I had him bring me a rubber ball, and I painted on it with white paint a map of the world. His eyes filled with fear when he saw the great landmass of

Eurasia on the opposite side of the globe, completely unreachable by canoe. And then, I explained about the European conquest of the Americas and saw a terrible look of defeat on his face.

"There is nothing we can do against gods who can cross waters as wide as the sky."

"They aren't gods, Men Ch'o," I reminded him. "They are only men in fancy clothes who learned how to do certain things before your people did. But right now, they are in a time called the Dark Ages. They are fighting battles between cities as you are, fighting hunger and cold and disease. They are only men. And there are things we can do now to prepare for them. Our children's children's children in the twelfth bak'tun will not be taken for fools when the pale-skinned men arrive. They will have read my words, and they will know what to do."

Then Men Ch'o looked at me with trust and pride. I only hoped I was right, that we could make a difference.

While Men Ch'o worked all day, I made more copies of the text he had translated the night before. I was still slow, making two copies in an entire day of what he could translate and write in two hours. Still, we made progress.

One day, with an aching back, I went for a walk in the plaza. I was dazzled by the light. I'd been spending too much time inside working by a west-facing window. I strolled over to the crafting workshops to see what was being made, what was going on. At the weavers stall, I saw a pile of something like pillowcases up against a wall. There was one demonstration pillow on display. I laughed to myself. That was one little change I had made only for my own comfort, and somehow it was spreading on its own.

Behind a stall where two women sat grinding spices for sale, their little boys were tossing a paper plane back and forth. A coatimundi on a tether reached up to bat at it as it flew past, and the boys giggled every time. They smiled and waved at me. "Plen!" they yelled, and fell down in more giggles.

Over at the stone cutters, the bak'tun stela was nearly complete. How on earth were the stonecutters going to move that huge slab of stone to the permanent site? I had no idea. Wait, yes I did.

I ran back to the potters and begged a lump of soft clay from them. Yes, I had an idea. An idea that was going to blow them away.

By the time Men Ch'o came by that evening, I had almost nothing written, but the clay had hardened, and I had something special to show him.

"Look at this," I called to him as soon as I heard the door curtain rustling.

The smell of turkey stew wafted into the room ahead of him. He held a bowl and a drinking cup. "You never came to supper. I thought you might be unwell," he said.

"No, I forgot. I was so busy working."

He looked at the tiny pile of new pages and raised his eyebrows. "I see."

"Not on those. On this." I placed a small clay model of a handcart on the table and rolled it back and forth. It was crude, and no doubt someone could improve on my axle design, but it was enough for a smart person to copy and scale up in wood.

"What is it?" he asked.

"It's a cart, for carrying heavy things, like supplies and grain and even stones. Isn't it great?"

He studied it dubiously and chose his words carefully. "A k'art. It does not look as if would carry more than two handfuls of sea salt. But it is great. Very great."

"No, no. Men Ch'o, this is a model. A small copy. The real one would be made from wood and much larger. One or two men would push or pull on these handles. See, it rolls. It is much easier than carrying or dragging. It would be even better if we had horses, but that's long in the future."

"Jorses and ouweels," he said.

"What?"

"You said that long ago. That we needed jorses and ouweels."

"You remember? I don't even remember saying that. Wow. These,"—I spun one dramatically—"are wheels."

"Those are the sacred shape, the shape of the universe, the shape of an altar. You have pierced it and turned it on edge. We cannot do this."

"What do you mean, you can't do this? I did."

"Yes, you are a goddess. You can turn the world over so that it spins. If I did that, I know the gods would destroy me for profaning their creation. The perfect round is sacred. We cannot corrupt it just to make carrying things easier."

I sighed. "Of course you can. Try it." I pushed the little toy cart toward him.

He looked back and forth between me and the cart. "You mean to test me? Is this a test of obedience or of courage?"

"This is not a test," I replied, somewhat testily.

I had expected him to leap with joy at my re-invention of the wheel. If it was this hard, he was going to hate the pulley I planned on showing him next. "Touch it," I ordered. "Make it move."

He was literally shaking as he stretched out a finger to touch the profane object. It hovered an inch away.

Sometimes a goddess just had to pull rank. This was too important to let superstition stand in the way of progress. "Do it now," I said in my most goddess voice.

He touched the cart and closed his eyes, no doubt preparing for annihilation.

"Push it," I commanded.

He opened his eyes a squint and pushed the cart. It flew off the table and onto the fur floor covering.

I picked it up and inspected. Still in one piece. "Gently," I suggested.

Men Ch'o squatted down so that the table was at eye level and gingerly pushed the cart back and forth. He watched the wheels going around with fascination, like a three-year-old with his first Hot Wheels racecar. "It almost floats," he said. "Only one place touches the ground."

"Now try this," I said, placing my full drinking cup in the cart. "Gently."

He pushed the cart and his eyes lit with surprise. "It is the same, no harder."

"Voila. The power of the wheel," I said.

"So. I will ask the woodshop to begin working on a k'art for me to push," he said.

"How about a cart for everyone? Every farmer and every merchant who carries goods around. And a caravan of carts for your traders to take on the road?"

"No, no. I am sure the gods spared me because the Ahaw is half-divine. For common men to use this would be disaster."

"Only if they put internal combustion engines in all of them," I muttered in English. "I promise you, Men Ch'o, the gods won't be angry."

I added the final icing on the cupcake of temptation—competition. "You know, the Spanish men use carts with wheels."

"And jorses?" he asked.

"Yup." I nodded.

"Then we will make jorses, too. What is jorses?"

I had to smile at the boyish enthusiasm on his face. He would have loved horses. "They are tall, strong animals with four legs who do our bidding if we care for them."

"Like dogs?" he asked.

"Much bigger. Bigger than tapirs." I think. But that gave me an idea. How many generations would it take to breed our fifty-pound guard dogs into cart-pulling Great Danes? It might be worth a try.

"Like llamas?" he asked.

"Oh gods. You know about llamas?"

"They are a creature of legend that the canoe traders of the coast tell about. Taller than a man, covered with thick hair, and they have evil eyes and spit venom."

"Yikes." What a wonderful image—venomous llamas. "Actually, they just spit spit. And they are very soft. We have to get some llamas. But definitely not in canoes. I'll think about that one."

"Maybe in k'arts with ouweels," Men Ch'o suggested.

"Good idea," I said. "I'll think about it." I also had to think about how to coat the rims of our wheels with rubber so they wouldn't disintegrate on unpaved roads. The stone sacbe only ran so far across the territory. Now I needed a highway project across Mesoamerica connecting all the cities. Poor Men Ch'o had no idea what he'd gotten himself into.

"Your supper is cold, I think," he said.

But my mind was on fire.

With Chel, I watched the stone cutters lift the great stela using *pulis* onto the k'art that the woodcrafters had made. Four men did the work of ten or more.

"Isn't this a great time to be alive?" she asked. Her face was as bright with happiness as the sun itself.

I remembered the words of the vase which I had given to her on our wedding night. I spoke them aloud: "Pure happiness flows at the sound of your laugh. Share joy from your heart in this moment of festival. People will follow your steps on the path."

Chel was pointing me along a new path. This ouweel and puli and k'art. My mind began to spin around as an ouweel in the night, considering new things and new ways.

It was the day of dedication of the bak'tun stela. Six men pushed the k'art to the great plaza where the stone would be stood up. The foundation hole was prepared on the west side of the plaza. A great round altar stone was in place for the dedication. Since we had been at peace, we had no captives to sacrifice, and I had little desire to begin a new war just to dedicate the stela with proper order. I discussed this problem with Chel. She provided the answer.

How wise she was to guide us to a new way yet again.

The Ah K'uhun, our chief priest, watched the k'art arrive through half-closed eyes. I could feel his anger that the stone rode on four worlds turned over. The younger priests watched him with unease. They were unsure whether to follow my calm or his displeasure. In turn, the crowd watched them, trying to figure their own reaction to this creaking, wooden *mah'xin*, as Chel called it. Ah K'uhun's wrath was magnified by the lack of proper sacrifice. But I did not plan this day for his peace of mind.

This was my day, the day on which I would depart from the past and create a future in which my people had a place.

The six strong men hoisted the stela into place at the edge of the foundation hole and tipped the forward edge so that it slid into place with a loud thump. The huge pox drums took up an echoing beat, and rattles shook like snakes about to strike. Ah K'uhun burned copan and chanted the proper words as Lady Chel and I poured water and maize-flour on the round altar stone.

Then, to the surprise of everyone, I cupped my hands for her foot and lifted her up to the top of the stela. I glanced up to make sure she landed safely. She balanced above me.

"Ready," she whispered for my ears only.

I filled my chest with good air so that all could hear my important words. "I dedicate the new bak'tun to the maiden of the stone, Xunantunich. By the grace of the goddess Ix Chel, our state of Yaxmuul will become the head of a vast body of states stretching West across the lands of the Mexica, North to the turk'oiz workers, and South to the llama lands. Together we will create the largest holpop the world has ever seen. Yaxmuul will sit at the head of the mat, and all the other kingdoms will take their places there, too, to exchange trade goods and wealth and ideas and scholars. The new bak'tun will not witness the end of our people, but the beginning of their most glorious future."

With one motion, Lady Chel and I both drew the stingray spines from our waist pouches. She cried out across the heads of the crowd, "Let the blood sacrifice from now and always be freely given, and never taken. That is the will of the gods."

I could not turn my head to look, but I knew she was doing as I did, stabbing the spine through her tongue with a wide spatter of blood. This is what we as rulers could do for our people—bleed for them. This was the sealing of our royal bargain.

The young priests brought paper strips to catch my blood and place it in the bowl of burning copan to send the offering skyward. Finally, I turned to look up at Chel, splendid against the clouds. Her chin ran red with blood that flowed down the face of the stela. Her eyes were steady and calm.

My heart nearly burst with joy and pride. She was my queen. No man has ever been as blessed.

Men Ch'o and I met for a quiet supper of warm broth while the crowds outside feasted on roasted deer. This would be a day they would never forget. Neither would I. My tongue ached and throbbed, swollen and raw inside my mouth. I wished uselessly for an antibiotic.

"How are you?" Men Ch'o asked with tender concern as he watched my eyes fill with tears.

"I'm fine. Weally. It jush hutsh sho mush. How long till it shtopsh?"

"I don't know," he said. "I've never done that before. Not through my tongue."

I ran a hand across his broad smooth-skinned chest. "Not your chesht like K'awiil did."

"No," he said. "Only through my man parts."

"Only...through...good godsh." My stomach clenched. I didn't even want to imagine how awful that must have been. "I won't complain any more," I promised.

He laughed. "It is good that one forgets the pain when it is gone."

"Yeah," I agreed. "Otherwishe women would never have more than one shild."

"Stop talking," he said with a crooked smile.

He passed me a cup of cocoa, the way I liked it, without peppers, with lots of honey. If only we had a source of milk, I thought with longing. Mayan cocoa was sort of black coffee that tasted like chocolate. Could you milk a tapir? Definitely worth a try. I could start a whole new dairy industry.

I sipped my broth painfully to the last drop. Men Ch'o watched me through tired looking eyes, the same silly smile on his face. "There'sh sho mush to do," I said, sighing.

"We have time."

"Gods, I hope you're right."

He reached across the table and stroked my hair. "Chel, it has already changed. The canoe is untied from the water's edge. Now we just have to paddle it to safety."

"What about crocodiles?" I asked, picking up his metaphor. "Are there any hidden crocodiles?"

"I suppose we will find out when a log turns and tries to bite us!" Men Ch'o let out a huge laugh. "And then we will beat it on the snout with our paddles."

"Sounds like a plan," I agreed.

So many, many things were on my list. Men Ch'o and I still hadn't finished a complete pass through my codex. We hadn't gotten to the part yet about teaching everyone the god-talk. And so far, Men Ch'o and I had only tackled English. I still had to teach him Spanish, at least up to high school first semester Spanish III. That's as good as it got. But I figured, if the conquistadores ran up against a greeting committee that spoke a semblance of their own language, they wouldn't dismiss them as ignorant savages. And maybe, if some of my wilder ideas worked, we'd actually have the upper hand when the explorers showed up in, what, six hundred years? Maybe my people would develop to the point that the Europeans looked like ignorant savages.

It was possible.

"Men Ch'o, when do you think we should hold our meeting of the many states, the round mat?"

"Not until the summer solstice," he said, "at the earliest. We need time to weave the special *pop* and even more time to build the gifts, a k'art for each of the kings."

"How many?"

"I think to begin, the nearest thirty kingdoms. I worry that Yax Mutul will hear of this too soon and crush it in fear. And if not Yax Mutul, its angry twin Oxwitza."

"Tikal, I mean Yax Mutul, is already falling," I said.

I remembered what Hernán had told us when we visited. There had been a lot of competition between the biggest city-states in this region—Tikal, Caracol, and Calakmul.

Men Ch'o sighed. "I do not want them to pull us down, too. And we *must* help Yax Mutul remain strong. It is a most magnificent city."

"I know. I've seen it."

"You have seen only its ghost, dear Chel. We will travel there some day, a state visit. You know how I love our green mountain, but we are as a pineapple compared to the Ceiba tree, when first you see Yax Mutul."

In the morning a distraction arrived. I woke to the sound of conch horns and ran to see Imul. Was war marching to us?

Imul reassured me. That call was for honored guests, not warriors. She quickly cleaned the babies and dressed them in fresh cotton shifts. We had no time to prepare. The travelers had been spotted about two miles away.

"Who is it?" I asked. "How many are there?"

Imul dragged me to a window overlooking the approach. "I can't count the number from here, but as they come from the West along that road, and I see several palanquins with bearers, I suspect it is Ix Yo Imix, the oldest daughter of my husband, with her slaves and attendants. She comes from the direction of Saal."

"Men Ch'o's sister? I didn't know he had a sister. Why wasn't she invited for our wedding? And for the king, her father's funeral?" This was amazing. I had acquired an extended family I didn't even know about.

"Oh, she was," Imul reassured me. "But she was still carrying a child and could not travel. Men Ch'o would have sent you to her birthbed, I have no doubt, if we had not been having burials and weddings here. So, the sign that she is coming means the baby has been safely born and now she has come to meet you, her half-brother's wife."

"Half-brother?"

"She is full sister to K'awiil. She will also wish to mourn his death with their mother, Lady K'uk'."

"Is she queen in Saal?" My mind tripped off on a fantasy of a Victorian-type dynasty, siblings ruling the adjoining city-states.

"No," Imul answered. "Her husband is the left-hand advisor of the king, and the king has no heir. I do not think she would refuse the throne if it came to her and her husband."

"Ambitious, is she?" I asked.

"Consider her brother," Imul said.

Good point.

Imul and I dressed ourselves in our second best, careful not to outshine someone who had been traveling the dusty road, but still to honor her visit. Breakfast was set out and waiting in the dining room. Men Ch'o came from the direction of his chamber, and we greeted each other with a smile. He put his hands on my shoulders, and I felt the sudden impulse to kiss him good morning, but he spoke before I could move.

"You may forget anything you planned to do today," he warned me. "Lady Yo Imix will expect you to entertain her."

"What does she like to do?" I asked.

"Gossip. And listen to music. And see the shops."

"Maybe I'll take her for a walk, show her our new projects."

"First, I think some food and drink."

We didn't have long to wait before Lady Yo Imix swept in the door with her husband B'olon Muluk. He was splendidly dressed for someone who had been on the road for a couple of days. Huge golden ear spools hung from his earlobes. His belt and breechclout were dyed a deep blue color. His cape was a startling bright yellow made of thousands of tiny yellow feathers. His shiny hair was gathered in a neat, tight topknot. Exotic red plumes sprayed out in all directions. He was a study in bold, primary colors.

Lady Yo Imix was also dressed beautifully, in a deep wine-colored skirt and a white fur cape that barely covered her breasts. I had noticed that women of high social rank covered themselves more modestly than the townspeople, but I wasn't sure whether that was truly from modesty or to show off their wealth. Looking at Ix Yo Imix's showy cape and ample cleavage, I had no doubt that in her case, the message was "look at me, look at me." Kind of like Maya.

And thinking of Maya made me think of shoes. I glanced down at the embroidered deerskin slippers on her feet. It was obvious that they had never touched the road—she had been carried the whole distance by her slaves. A large-breasted woman stood behind her, chest fully exposed, holding the new baby, and I wondered if Lady Yo Imix was nursing the baby herself. As much as I wanted to like her, she didn't look like the nurturing type. She looked just like K'awiil.

I held out my hands in greeting. "Be most welcome here."

She touched my fingertips and lifted her chin. "And so this giantess is your new queen?" she asked Men Ch'o. "I understand she uses the name of Ix Chel."

I answered for myself. "Ix Yo Imix, please call me Chel. I was to marry K'awiil before his death in battle. You and I would have been sisters. Now I have married Men Ch'o."

"Ah well, my dear. It is a tragedy." She rubbed her hand over my stomach and raised her eyebrows in a question.

"No," I answered.

She sighed. "No? Ah, a pity, indeed. He should have sired twenty sons. He was a fine man, my brother."

I slipped my arm through Men Ch'o's. "So is this brother. The gods have smiled on me."

Men Ch'o caught his breath and stood taller beside me. "Chel is the goddess," he said. "She is the incarnated Ix Chel, Lady of Rainbows."

Ix Yo Imix gave my face the once over with her piercing black eyes. "Goddess? You're sure?" she said in what was supposed to be a friendly voice, but I heard a threat underneath it.

"Yes. The goddess," Men Ch'o said. "I found her in the mouth of Xibalba."

"Really." Lady Yo Imix arched her sculpted eyebrows. The tattooed dots above them rose as well, emphasizing the effect. "How interesting. He found her in the mouth of Xibalba," she repeated to her husband, B'olon Muluk, who had been standing, quietly observing the whole time through half-closed eyes.

"Oh yes. She's already performed several miracles for us," Men Ch'o said, a little too enthusiastically for my taste.

It had the effect I feared.

"Perhaps she'll perform another little miracle for us while we are visiting," she said.

"May I see your baby?" I asked, hoping to get onto another subject.

"Of course. Only a girl." She gestured behind her.

The servant girl gave her to me to hold. I'd grown used to the size of the twin princes already. This one was so tiny by comparison. She was a beautiful baby, but she still wore the head flattening board tied to her forehead to make it slope back, and a jade bead dangled on the bridge of her nose. I wanted to rip off the board and squish her skull back to a normal shape. While everyone had their own standards of beauty, I wasn't into ritual deformations. My own kids would be round heads, whether or not anyone objected.

As Yo Imix cast an assessing sweep around the room, Lady K'uk', her mother, arrived from the kitchen with a steaming bowl of maize porridge and mango. Somewhat deaf, she'd slept through the conches, and no one had woken her to tell her about the company. She nearly dropped the bowl in surprise at seeing her daughter and granddaughter.

"Praise all the gods," she cried. "I never hoped to see you so soon again."

"The little one came early this time, Mother," Ix Yo Imix said. "And so I came late. Father has traveled on ahead, has he?"

I was shocked at the lightness of her tone.

Mother K'uk' shook her head sadly. "Ah, what happened to K'awiil broke his heart."

"But not yours?" Ix Yo Imix asked.

Her mother met her accusing eye unflinching. "Mothers are stronger than men. Else we'd never survive these little ones. I mourn in my own time and way. Ix Chel and Men Ch'o have been a great comfort to me. Ix Imul has also, along with her two boys."

"But where are they?" Yo Imix asked.

"Napping," Imul responded. "I chose to let them be."

"Eat before the *ul* grows cold," Lady K'uk' reminded us. "Your room will be prepared while you eat." She hurried off to make the arrangements I should have already seen to.

Lady Yo Imix looked me over well. "Is that one of my *old* dresses?" she asked.

I blushed. I wore a fine white shift with beautifully embroidered images of fish and shells along the hem.

"Yes, thank you, I suppose it must be. My clothing was...lost in Xibalba. Men Ch'o provided these new garments. Do you mind?"

"No, not at all. But perhaps you will allow me to call on the dressmaker with you and have her make up a wardrobe more becoming. What do you say?"

I swallowed a sarcastic retort. Not politic. "Yes, thank you. That would be lovely."

She nodded regally, bestowing a special favor on me. Then she gestured for one of her slaves to bring forward a pitcher and bowl as large as a chamber pot. The pair were exquisitely painted with battle scenes. "A trifle. A gift for your table," she said. "Saal ceramics well deserve their fame for beauty, do you agree?"

"Lovely," I repeated. "I thank you."

There was something about this woman that just didn't sit right with me. I was sure I'd figure it out, given the amount of time we were going to spend together.

"How long can you stay?" I asked in my sweetest voice.

"I hope we'll see you through the summer solstice at least. If you are carrying soon, you'll be laid low with breakfast sickness and need another woman's help around here."

I glanced over at Imul, who was rolling her eyes skyward. I had to agree.

As Chel said, there was too much to do. If night had been day, we would still have had trouble working as fast as I wished. The morning my half-sister Ix Yo Imix arrived was a surprise to us all. It was kind of her to travel so soon after giving birth, and she was quite interested in becoming friends with Ix Chel. But the interruption of a visit by guests who demanded attention made it much harder for Lady Chel to do what she had planned. She bore it with remarkable patience.

The woodcrafting shop was training apprentices, fifteen in all, to help with the k'arts-making. Chel watched the ballmakers work with saps to create rubber balls and strips. She was figuring a way to make tah'yars, which she said were coverings for ouweels. Ix Yo Imix crossed her arms in boredom, and Chel hurried on to supervise other workers. She knew of many things that would help us if only we could learn to make them the right way.

Lady Chel's other project was called wah'yars. Wah'yars were different from tah'yars. She said that clicking sounds could run along these wah'yars and allow us to send messages without messengers. She said the clicking sounds ran faster than even our fastest runners. I could not imagine how long threads of copper covered with rubber sap could be a road, a sacbe, for clicking sounds. She promised it was so.

Now, in private, she said, we must only speak in god-words so that I would learn faster. She called the god-tongue Enk'lix. She said I must soon become master of this Enk'lix because there was another god-tongue to learn as well—Ispah'nol. I tried hard to please her in this, but the words and ideas and the order of words were so different from what I knew. It was harder even than speaking with the Yukatek.

"Why must I do this?" I asked. Why the gods needed two tongues was more than I could understand.

She replied, "I am learning how to be a teacher. When I understand how best to teach you the god-words, I can start a sk'ul."

"A sk'ul?"

She wrote the god-letters S...C...H...O...O...L. "A place for learning," she explained. "Imagine this. If I can teach twenty people in two years, then we can build ten new schools for them work in pairs. The twenty can teach two hundred in the next two years. The two hundred can teach two thousand in the next two years."

My mouth fell open. "And the two thousand can teach a good-sized city." The numbers grew and grew like the number of stones in the levels of a pyramid. "Like a pyramid," I said.

"You get it," she cried with great delight. "And I won't just teach the teachers. We need to start a school for small children."

"Small children?" I asked. "But they know nothing except how to play, or simple things like grinding maize. Husking the ears. How can they learn your words? It is difficult, you know, even for a king."

She laughed. "Believe it or not, it is easier for children to learn a new way of speaking than adults. Their minds are more open to new patterns."

"Ah. I understand," I said. "One of the woodcrafters made two tiny k'arts, like the first one you made to show me. His wife averts her eyes and spits on the floor when she sees the ouweels. But his boys run them down hills filled with different things to see whose k'art rolls faster."

"And so *nazkar* was born," Chel said. It was a most mysterious comment.

We worked hard by day, harder by night when we were left in peace.

I shared some of these plans with my brother-by-marriage, B'olon Muluk. I would need Saal's support when we called the many cities council together. I suggested that his king would sit at my left, in the next most senior position.

"Perhaps," he said, "it would be best if it appeared that you sat at his left and Yax Mutul at his right."

"I think not," I said firmly. "My place is *ha holpop*, the head of the mat. I am the one the goddess chose to carry out her plan. She has told me of the future."

My brother-by-marriage showed me a sour face. "A future in which you rule over us all? How convenient for her. She and my wife would make quite a pair."

I confess, the image of Chel as ambitious as my half-sister Yo Imix startled me, and for one moment I questioned her motives, but only for a moment. I knew that her desire was to avoid the ruin of our entire people, not to place herself at the top of the mountain.

Why would she work through men when she had only to command us all with her power to give and take the rain? To cause babies to be born alive or dead? It was a stupid thought, that she would use me as a sharp tool. I sent B'olon Muluk's comments from my mind.

Late in the night, I woke to a disturbance in the sleeping chambers. I rose from my sleeping mat and followed the sound of loud argument to the room where the infant girl and her nursemaid slept. Through the door curtain, I recognized Chel's voice raised in anger over the sound of the infant's howling.

I peeked into the room. Chel had the infant across her lap, and she rubbed the tiny stomach in circles.

"Yes, you did," she said to the nursemaid. "I saw you eating the hot peppers. You can't do that when you are nursing."

The baby twisted and waved angry little fists as she screamed.

"Lady Chel," I said, letting them know of my presence. "Can I do anything?"

"Oh, Men Ch'o," she said and switched to god-words. "This stupid woman ate food that gave the baby wind."

She heaved the baby onto her shoulder and rubbed the back as she had been rubbing the front. Suddenly, the baby erupted with noise. Loud wind flew from her mouth and a wet, bubbling sound flew from her bottom end. Then the baby put her head down on Chel's shoulder and was instantly asleep. Such goddess magic! She who had never borne a child knew how to draw the wind out of a howling infant.

"There," she said. "All better." She turned to the nursemaid and sternly scolded her. "You must never eat pepper seeds again until the baby is off the breast. Understand?"

The woman nodded and took the baby from Lady Chel.

"Haven't you ever done this before?" Lady Chel asked.

The nursemaid dropped her eyes and shook her head, no. She whispered, "No, Lady Goddess. I lost my first born just as the Lady Yo Imix took to her childbed. She gave me this little one to nurse instead, but I have no mother and no sisters. No one told me about pepper seeds. Please forgive me."

"Oh gods," Ix Chel said. Her eyes filled with tears. "No, no. You must forgive me for speaking so to you. Oh, you poor thing. I'm so, so sorry."

She wrapped her arms around the woman, who finally let her own tears fall. They cried gently together while I stood useless at the door.

Oh, the power of those goddess tears. I knew the nursemaid would soon be blessed with another child after Chel embraced her so.

I slipped away quietly. I was not needed.

Lady Yo Imix followed me around relentlessly, poking her nose into all my projects. Her eyes were curious, but disdainful at the same time. The k'arts, she said, were not so helpful, when it took four men to pull what would take ten men to carry. I couldn't explain to her that I was still trying to figure out the whole idea of draft animals. Giant dogs? Imported llamas? Domesticated tapirs? I'd probably spend the next decade trying all three approaches to see which would work out best.

Imagine a ten-year biology experiment.

Yo Imix averted her nose and vigorously waved her small wicker fan whenever we approached the rubber curing vats. That was my chemistry project, getting the ball makers to create a rubber that was sticky enough to coat the edges of the wooden wheels and strong enough to run over stone roads. I had no idea how steel-belted Michelins had been made, and there was a lot more riding on my tires—an entirely new transportation system for trade and communication.

And, speaking of communication, I had a physics problem. Long ago, in the future, I'd made that battery out of copper pennies, paper, and salty vinegar in the science lab. All of the ingredients were available here. I just had to figure out how to get enough voltage to do anything.

I wish I'd paid more attention to those TV shows on how things are made. Once I had the entire knowledge of Western civilization at the touch of a remote control, and I watched sitcom reruns instead. How lame.

But all those experiments would have to wait until the company left. I was beginning to wonder if they ever would.

The other person who watched me but from a greater distance was the chief priest, Ah K'uhun. Many days as I headed out of the palace and over to the workshop area to check on progress, I felt a warning prickle on the back of my neck. And sure enough, whenever I subtly turned my head, he was standing there, watching. He and Lady Yo Imix would exchange a brief, slow nod. Apparently they went way back— he had been her religious tutor when she was a girl.

At supper time, they often sat with their heads bent together, Yo Imix, her husband B'olon Muluk, and the chief priest. They spoke softly so that the sound of flute playing covered their words to each other. They darted glances at me and at Men Ch'o. They made me nervous.

An echo of Dad's voice came back to me. "Chel, always remember. Where there's smoke, there's fire." Something did seem kind of smoky about those three, and it wasn't just the smell of ash drifting in from the burning fields.

After I entertained Yo Imix nonstop for more than two weeks, she lost interest in following me. Instead, she went to the kitchens to stay with her mother. Since supposedly her original purpose in visiting, at least part of it, was to grieve with her mother, I thought it strange how little time they spent together. At least she was making up for it now. I saw a brighter look on Lady K'uk's face, especially when she held her little granddaughter. Now that her stomach pains were gone, the baby was plumping up, with chubby dimples at her knees and elbows.

Imul's twins had learned to roll over and could balance in a sitting position if they were well-cushioned with props of folded cloth. Soon it would be time for their hetzmek ceremony, celebrating their four months of life and formally baptizing them into the community. Sometimes I had to stand and stare at them. Their changes were a measuring stick of how long I had been here. Living this new life.

To think, I had wanted a more authentic experience. Ha. There was a haiku in that:

> *You seek something lost.*
> *It will always be found in*
> *The last place you look.*

One night, Men Ch'o and I had a special reason to celebrate. The giant mat was woven. Beautifully. The fifteenth cart had rolled off the assembly line. We were more than halfway there. At supper, he announced to B'olon Muluk that he expected to be prepared by summer solstice to hold his many states meeting. It was time to send out the messengers with gifts and invitations.

"I hope," Men Ch'o said, "that you will personally convey my invitation to your king. You understand my aims, I think, and could express them better than even my messengers."

B'olon narrowed his eyes in that peculiar way of his and replied, "Yes, I understand. I would be happy to take my leave and convey your invitation to my lord. Your sister may remain here under your care so that I travel faster."

"Very well," Men Ch'o said, although I'm sure that's not what he had in mind when he asked them to leave. "Then let us drink to your speedy return." The two men drained their glasses. Lady Yo Imix refilled her husband's cup with the last of the fruit wine in the Saal pitcher, which now sat on the high table.

"Oh pity," she said. "That's the last of it. I will run to the kitchen for some more."

"Send a slave," Men Ch'o said.

"No, no. I will only take a moment," she protested.

As she left the room, someone passed another half-full pitcher down the table, and both men drained another glass. Men Ch'o was in a fine mood, happy with the progress, excited at the idea of meeting with all his peers and offering them the chance to join in something greater, a confederacy based on cooperation instead of competition, a structure designed to last a thousand years.

He pulled me in to dance with him and ordered the flute players to pipe a tune more upbeat. The *tunkul* drummers quickened their tempo, and soon we weren't the only ones dancing. I found a cup slipped into my hand, and Men Ch'o was offered another. We tapped them together. As I was about to drink, my nose reminded me that this was the same soured fruit drink that had caused me horrendous problems before. My stomach flipped over at the memory, and I put the cup down on the edge of a table. Men Ch'o laughed when he saw me getting rid of it. He tossed his down his throat and then drank mine.

"Oh gods," I said. "I hope you don't regret that in the morning."

"You'll grow used to it, Chel, when you have a stomach of rubber as I do."

"I doubt it," I said.

I regretted my words when they turned out prophetic. In the morning, Men Ch'o never showed up for breakfast. I made him a cup of unsweetened hot chocolate, the closest thing to coffee I could think of, and wandered back to his room. I'd never been there. He always came to mine to work.

As I came close, the sound of retching grew louder, and the smell of vomit wafted through the door. Ugh. This was even worse than I imagined. Was I up to it? I never actually said "for better or for worse."

I peered in the door to see Men Ch'o crouched over a large round cauldron. He heard me enter and turned his head.

Oh gods, what a sight. His eyes were red and his face clammy with sweat. I stepped forward, feeling stupid to be holding a cup of chocolate.

"Let me get some towels," I said, and backed out as he turned to heave into the cauldron.

I ran to my room and soaked some cleaning cloths in the water the servants had brought for my sponge bath. I dashed back to his room to find him lying on his sleep mat, breathing shallowly. I pressed a cool cloth to his head.

"This has never happened," he croaked.

"Rubber stomach let you down?" I joked, trying to let him know I wasn't too shocked.

"Feels like knives," he said. "Blades slicing my insides. I cannot stop." And true to his words, he pushed me out of the way to get to the cauldron again.

"When did this start? Why didn't you call anyone?"

"All night," he said weakly. "I did not want to disturb anyone because of my foolish...Aaahh." He bent double with another spasm and clutched his stomach. "I think I am cursed," he said.

I peered into the cauldron. Xit. There was more stuff in there than I could imagine coming out of a human body. Way more than he'd had in his stomach last night. Where was it all coming from?

"I'm going to get you some water," I said. "You've got to be really dehydrated by now."

He waved a weak thanks at me. Before I even took a step, he groaned and spit onto the floor next to him. Bright red.

"Oh gods," I said nervously. "Did you bite your tongue? Please tell me you just bit your tongue."

Vomiting blood wasn't likely from too much to drink.

He shook his head. "Not my tongue. Told you, knives inside. Cutting me in half."

He fell back onto his mat. His hand fluttered toward me. "Help me, please, Lady Chel, healing goddess." He closed his eyes, rolled onto his side, knees pulled into his chest, his breathing slow and labored.

I put a hand to his head and found it burning and slick with sweat. What made you bleed inside? Was Ebola only in Africa? I had no idea what this could be. What could come on like this out of the blue?

"I promise I'll be back," I whispered. "Hold on."

I knew only one person with enough experience to help, and I ran to find Lady K'uk'. She wasn't in the kitchen, so I ran back to her room, my sides splitting with cramps. She wasn't there either. Surely someone knew where she was. I had to find her. I couldn't call 911 for the gods' sake.

I crashed into a serving girl on my way back to Imul's room. "Have you seen Ix K'uk'? Any idea where she might be?" I asked frantically.

"She went into the herb garden," the girl said. "Or maybe into the woods to collect foods for later."

Xit. How would I ever find her?

"Come," I ordered, pulling the girl toward Imul's room. "You will stay and watch the babies."

She nodded with wide, frightened eyes.

We burst into Imul's chamber, and she knew with one look at my face that something was desperately wrong. "What has happened?" she asked.

"Oh, Imul help me!" I wailed. "Men Ch'o is sick and I must find Lady K'uk'. This girl says she is out harvesting herbs, and I don't know where to look."

Imul frowned at me uncertainly. "Why do you need Lady K'uk'? You could just put your hands on him and heal him."

Ha. How I wished that were true. "It doesn't work that way, Imul. I need healing plants, and Lady K'uk' will tell me where to find them." And, I hope, she'd know what we were looking for.

"So, we'll find her," she said, pulling on her sandals. She led me out to an area behind one of the nobles' apartments that I'd never seen. My hope soared when I saw Lady K'uk' bent over a patch of plants, a gathering basket at her feet.

"Mother K'uk', Mother K'uk'," I called.

She stood, hands on the backs of her hips.

"Men Ch'o is terribly ill," I said.

She smiled and made a gesture to wave away my worries. "Last night—" she began.

"No, not the wine," I said. "He can't stop vomiting and now there's blood in what he is bringing up." I tried to sound factual, like I was giving a medical history, but my voice betrayed me.

Her brows drew together. Of course, I could imagine her thoughts—why wasn't the goddess just godding away the illness.

"I need you to help me prepare the right medicines for him before I...before I empower them. Do you know where to find them?" I asked.

"In the kitchen, of course," she said. "Come. Blood, you say?" She moved fast for a woman her age. She muttered as we strode along. "Coconut milk for calming, ginger for healing. Yes, both should be there."

She deftly pounded open a coconut with an obsidian tipped mallet and poured the milk into a cup. She placed this over the glowing coals in the kitchen brazier to warm. In a granite pestle, she crushed ginger root and squeezed the juice from the pulp into the coconut milk.

"Add some honey," I suggested. I had to make some contribution.

"Interesting," she commented. She handed me the honey pot and a carved wooden spoon. I acted like I knew what I was doing.

"The words," she hinted. "As you stir nine times."

"Of course," I said.

As I gently swirled the heating mixture, I said over and over again in English, "Please let this work, please let this work..." After nine incantations, I laid down the spoon and picked up the warm cup with a cloth. All three of us hurried with the steaming liquid.

The stench from the room hit us as we got close. Lady K'uk' gasped, her nose wrinkling. Imul drew up a corner of her dress to cover her face.

Men Ch'o was curled, gripping his stomach with both hands, eyes clenched tightly.

"Men Ch'o," I said. "We've got medicine for you. Can you sit up?"

Weakly, he tried to prop himself, but his arms collapsed under his weight and wouldn't respond. I handed the cup to Lady K'uk' and sat down at his head, lifting him up to rest his back against me. He opened his eyes and stared wildly.

"They're in here!" he cried. "Who let them in here? Make them fly away!"

"Fly away? Men Ch'o, who's in here? What do you see?"

"The butterflies! The blue butterflies! Send them away goddess. Please send them away before they kill me."

I turned anxiously to the other women, who only shrugged.

I pressed the cup to his lips. "Drink this. Drink this and try to hold it in, keep it down."

While I murmured encouragement in his ear, Imul gathered up all the filthy bedding, anywhere the vomit had splashed. Lady K'uk' crouched over the vomit cauldron and sniffed.

She stepped back with a cry. "Poison!" she spat out. "He's been poisoned."

"How? When?" I demanded helplessly.

"Last night, it had to be," she said. "It comes on very fast. Quick, send for Lady Yo Imix, my daughter. She is a student of poisons and remedies. The Ah K'uhun himself taught her. Send quickly."

Imul ran off while I continued cradling my poisoned husband. We'd all had the same food last night. We had all poured from the same jug, hadn't we?

Imul returned pale and out of breath after an age. "She's already gone," she said between gasps. "Early with her husband. They went at first light."

Strange. That wasn't the plan I remembered from last night. B'olon Muluk had told us she was supposed to remain here so as not to slow their travel. This didn't sound right at all.

"Send for Ah K'uhun, then," I said. "If he taught Yo Imix, he can help."

It seemed like forever that we waited. Lady K'uk' said nothing. When Men Ch'o finally sipped the last of the fragrant potion, his eyes rolled back, and he slumped heavily against me. Sick with dread, I felt for a pulse.

Lady K'uk' put a hand on his heart and shook her head.

I nearly fainted. "Dead?" I whispered in shock.

"No. Very slow. Very bad," she said.

Then I felt it at his wrist. There it was, his pulse, weak and sluggish, but there it was.

"Not dead." I exhaled. "Not dead."

"Not yet," she replied. "But it is bad."

My mind tumbled. The cups, the pitchers, the dinner plates, when? Then I remembered someone handing the two of us cups as we danced. Men Ch'o drank both. Xit. One of them was meant for me. He must have taken a double dose, his and mine, double what someone thought was enough to get rid of each of us.

Fear clutched at my throat now. No way was this was an accident. It was an assassination attempt. Maybe a successful one. Tears of terror welled up in my eyes. I squeezed Men Ch'o as I held him. "Don't die," I whispered. "Please. Don't die. I need you, Men Ch'o. I love you. You can't leave me. Please."

He never heard a word.

What a crazy, terrible, stupid time to realize how much I'd come to love him. I knew he was my best friend, my teacher, my student, my king, and my husband. Somehow in all our time together, I never saw that he had become my everything.

I rested my cheek on his head and willed him to live with all my strength.

Finally Imul returned with Ah K'uhun. The chief priest tsked with his tongue as he took in the scene. "How is he?" he asked in a neutral voice.

"Terrible," I said, reeling off symptoms: "Feverish, weak, palpitations, hallucinations, bloody vomit."

"Ah, I see. Not spoiled food, then. Nor too much wine."

"Obviously not," I hissed. "Someone poisoned him. Do you know what it might be?"

"And how should I know that?" he asked. The weird tone in his voice infuriated me.

"Because you're an expert in poison remedies, I was told." Of course, half my mind argued, that would make him an expert in poisons as well.

"Yes, yes. So I am," he conceded.

"What is it?" I demanded. "What do you think?"

He pursed his thick lips. "Perhaps a toadstool. Perhaps nightshade. Perhaps essence of blue morpho..."

"How do we counteract it?" I said through clenched teeth. "This is the king's life we're talking about. Can you help us out here?"

He shook his head. "My dear Goddess, I'm afraid my mortal powers can't add anything to what you have already done. Thank the powers you are looking well. Imagine if you had both been struck."

My skin crawled at the threatening undertone in his words. I had no doubt now who had cooked up this wicked plot.

"Yeah, just imagine," I said with acid in my stomach. "It's a good thing we goddesses aren't vulnerable to poison."

"Yes, how fortunate. And how interesting, dear Goddess," he drawled. He leaned on the word goddess with great insolence. "I'm afraid it's up to you to save him."

"Get out of here, then. Leave us." My eyes narrowed. "If I find proof that you had anything to do with this, I'll see you dragged into hell."

Imul gasped.

When I was sure he had gone beyond our passage, I said, "Mother K'uk', do not let that man anywhere near your kitchen. I will eat only food that comes straight from your hands to my mouth."

She nodded, wearing a stunned expression.

I took her hands between mine. "Please prepare more cups of coconut and ginger and bring them straight to me. I will stay here until Men Ch'o recovers. He is strong."

Pray the gods he was strong enough to survive a double dose of deadly poison.

All I can remember of those dark days, I will write.

All was fire around me and knives within me. Monstrous blue butterflies as large as bats flew around my chamber and tortured me with their wings. Black iguanas crept across my bed, tearing out my innards with their sharp claws. I lay in my chamber, wracked with agony.

Through the red mist covering my vision, I saw women approach. They commanded me, cleaned me, but I could understand none of their words, and I could not move my own body to help. It was all I could do to force the air into my body and out. With what little breath I had, I called to Ix Chel, goddess of healing, to save me.

Yet she did not.

I pleaded to her, shamefully revealing all my weakness, and she refused me comfort. A touch of her hands could have stopped this in a moment. In my confusion I begged her, ordered her as her king and husband, even cursed her for leaving me in this state. The agonies went on and on as my life poured out of me. All I could reason was that this must be a test—a test of my strength and my worth to rule, to be her husband, to be her partner in the hard work ahead.

It seemed to me that in my despair I left the chamber, and for unknown days I walked through Xibalba. I cried for a guide in the blackness, for help, but none came. Ix Chel had abandoned me and I wandered alone. The air grew colder and colder as my feet trod a downward path.

Invisible hands from all sides touched and pushed me; forced my lips apart and poured hot liquids down my throat. I choked and gagged, but they continued to torture me. They pressed on my chest, squeezing the air from me until it was impossible to inhale.

Then finally through the darkness, I saw a crack of light and pushed toward it. The darkness fell away, and I stood on a gleaming field of white stone, cold to the feet. The sky above was also a cold gray, with no touch of sun. I lay down on the stone plain and the pain seeped from my body into the ground. I could finally rest here.

My limbs turned numb with cold, peaceful. One day, maybe, I would find my way back to Ix Chel, but for now...for now, to lie here with no feeling at all was what I desired. Perhaps she would be displeased that I had failed her test, but as my flesh sank into the white stone, I could not raise the energy to care.

My heart paused between beats, longer and longer. And stopped.

Then the cold gray sky split with a crash. Lightning shot from above and stabbed at my chest. My mouth was forced open and a fierce wind the size of a hundred breaths blew in and out. Scalding rain burst from the heavens, burning the feeling back into my flesh and forcing me into wakefulness.

"Leave me," I pleaded. "Let be."

The heavens rocked with thunder, rumbling, "No. You must live. Men Ch'o." They called me by name. "You must live."

"If it is your will," I replied.

I tore my arms and legs in agony from the stone they had become. I drew breath and forced my heart to beat again.

On another plane, my eyes opened in a barely lit room I hardly recognized. I saw the face of Ix Chel above me, raining boiling tears onto my cheeks.

"I'm sorry I failed your test," I whispered and turned my head away in shame.

By far, those were the longest two days of my life. I hardly moved from Men Ch'o's side, watching him get worse and worse. Once the vomiting stopped, I hoped for a turnaround, but he sank deep inside himself. His pulse grew slower and weaker, his breathing more labored, his skin colder. We tried to warm him from the inside with hot ginger-coconut and then, stupid, I know, started adding ground herbs and seeds at random, hoping something would work, would counteract the unknown poison that was quickly killing him. I was working completely blind, and patient Imul and the earnest Lady K'uk' hardly better.

I didn't have the heart to tell Lady K'uk' I suspected her daughter Yo Imix of conspiring to assassinate her own half-brother; I didn't have the brains to ask whether her daughter Yo Imix had any favorite poisons.

As Men Ch'o's body grew stiffer and cold, Imul and I rubbed his arms and legs, trying to keep the blood moving and muscles flexible. His eyelids didn't even twitch. If not for the slight rise and fall of his chest, he might easily have been mistaken for dead.

At one point, on the morning of the third day, I did have to leave to find his left-hand advisor and ask him what Men Ch'o would normally be doing, what arrangements needed to be made to keep the city running as usual. So soon after the deaths of the old king and K'awiil, I didn't want public panic to set in.

"How bad is he?" the man asked me, a serious and nervous look on his face.

"He will recover," I insisted, refusing to face the alternative. "But it may be days before he is ready to take on a busy schedule of meetings and audiences."

"Then you may act in his stead."

"Can't you?" I asked in a panic. "My place is by his side."

"And my place is at the left, not the head of the mat," my advisor insisted. At least he wasn't ambitious to take over. "And if, if the worst should happen, I believe the council would prefer you as ruling regent for the twin princes rather than their mother Ix Imul."

Regent? Pray the gods it wouldn't come to that. I'd already lost and mourned one family, one life. I'd lost and mourned a fiancé, a near stranger. But Men Ch'o had become the beat of my heart, the hope of my soul. I couldn't imagine going on without him. And so I wouldn't.

I agreed to come back when Men Ch'o was clearly on the way to recovery. "You have to keep things going until then," I ordered. "I'm relying on you and your discretion."

He stood straighter and lifted his chin. "Yes, goddess. I won't disappoint you."

By the time I got back to the dark sick-chamber, Imul had fallen asleep in a pile of furs in the corner. Poor thing. I'd been awake for forty-eight hours at least, and she'd spent much of it awake with me. Lady K'uk' sat quietly holding Men Ch'o's hand. The room felt deeply hushed, waiting.

I sank to the floor next to her. I stroked my husband's chill, limp arm. "I'll take a turn," I said to her. "You get some rest."

She turned a tear-streaked face to me. "No," she said. "I'll watch with you. It won't be long now." Her voice cracked.

"What won't?" I asked stupidly.

She gestured with her chin toward Men Ch'o.

I raised an oil lamp to light his face. It was peaceful and still and faraway. His dark lips were purplish-blue. I passed a hand in front of his nose and mouth and hardly felt a flutter of air. His cheeks were icy cold. I checked for the pulse in his neck, and as I pressed the beats paused. I waited for the next beat. And waited.

"Men Ch'o," I screamed, startling Imul awake. "Men Ch'o, you are not going to die on me. Not today."

I smashed my fist onto the left side of his chest. I pushed Lady K'uk' out of the way, tilted his head back, and began blowing air deep into his lungs. I leaned on his chest with all my might, and started quick, firm compressions. I lost count of how many breaths, how many compressions as I turned myself into a life-support machine. The other two women watched in awe and helplessness. My head swam with dizziness, my arms ached with exhaustion but I couldn't stop, because that would be the end.

"Live, damn you, live," I sobbed between breaths. I pounded the words with my hands. And then his eyes blinked open and a tiny sound, almost below hearing came from his lips. "Oh, Men Ch'o," I cried. I put my head on his chest and left it there, filled with the joy of hearing a strong, steady thrum inside. He was back.

I allowed myself the luxury of sleep at last, my ear pressed to his skin, comforted by the sounds of life.

Lady K'uk' tapped me on the shoulder, recalling me to consciousness.

"What is it?" I whispered. I sat up and gathered my wits. Men Ch'o was resting peacefully. His lips had returned to a normal red-brown, and his skin was slightly flushed with warmth.

"They need you in the audience room. Two men call for K'ul Ahaw Tikilik Ri-Ik' to settle a dispute."

"About?" I asked.

"A dog, it seems," she answered.

"Good gods. Couldn't that wait a few days?" There was nothing I wanted less than to leave Men Ch'o before we could talk, before I could tell him what had happened to him, before I could confess what he meant to me and how I almost never had a chance to tell him.

Lady K'uk' shook her head. "The council have put them off as long as possible and offered to arbitrate the dispute themselves, but the men want only the king. They have come to blows in the audience room."

I rose stiffly. "Then the queen will have to do."

My voice was firm, but my stomach was not. I had to cover for Men Ch'o. I couldn't let anyone outside our inner circle know how close this plot had come to succeeding. They needed to think that Men Ch'o and I were invulnerable or someone else might try the next power play.

Political murder, military conquest, blood sacrifice. This society had a long way to go.

In the audience room, I found a frustrated left-hand advisor, two disheveled guards, two young men wearing angry expressions, and a handsome black dog standing between the two men. Her long nose twitched as I entered the room. Her eyes were bright and her large upright ears alert. Her tightly muscled body bulged slightly.

I moved to the stone bench and made myself comfortable on the pelts, while the men waited with taut lips. I wasn't who they had asked for.

"What is your complaint?" I asked.

"Where is the king?" the man on the left asked.

"At the moment," I said, "he is dealing with important affairs of state, not squabbles between brothers."

The man on the right gasped. "How did you know we were brothers?" They couldn't have looked more different, in face, that is. However, they stood in exactly the same way, each holding his right elbow with his left hand, chins held at the exact same angle, and eyes squinted to the same degree. And they both had a huge bruise around their right eyes—both southpaws.

"Twins," I said, hazarding a safe guess.

The men turned to each other in the same moment with the exact same astonished expression, which completely confirmed my suspicion.

"Why are you arguing? Why has it reached this level?" I fixed them with a disapproving look, borrowed from my mother's repertoire.

"We lay claim to the same bitch," the man on the right announced.

What?!

"You're sleeping with the same woman?" I asked.

It was their turn to look confused. They pointed to each other.

"You're not...?"

"No, of course not, idiot brother."

"I'll kill you if you..." He raised his hands to the other's neck.

"WAIT," I commanded. "Someone explain more fully. You first," I said, choosing the right-hand brother randomly.

"We have shared this dog Xolo all of her life. She sleeps between us. She eats from both of our hands. She hunts with both of us. Now only one of us can have her."

"Why?" I asked with a touch of impatience.

The other brother answered. "We are each marrying, leaving our family home, and building a new, small *xamil nah*."

"Far apart?" I asked.

"No," he answered hesitantly. "Next door to each other. On the same mound. I claim the dog to live with me and my wife. He claims the dog to live with them."

"This is the stupidest argument I've ever heard," I said.

The men looked at their feet.

I thought of some of the stupid arguments Maya and I had left unresolved, both of us too stubborn in our own ways to budge. I thought of the words I'd had with her over the last week we were together. It was agony to remember. And in my heart, I had called her cheap and easy, a hopeless slob, a whiny wimp. The last time I saw her alive, I was thinking how stupid and selfish she was to capsize our canoe. The pain of all those negative feelings burned me. There was no way to make up for them now, not with Maya. But maybe I could help these two before they blew it.

I called the dog to my side with a whistle and a slap on my leg. "Sit," I commanded.

The dog dropped to the floor with her long snout on her paws. I rested a hand on her head and felt the heat pouring off her. No wonder people loved to sleep with them.

"Here's the deal," I said. "The dog will have the choice. I can ask her to decide now, by letting her go to one of you, and she will belong to that brother only. Or you can allow her to decide anew each day by leaving a hole in the walls between your houses so she can pass back and forth. Consider well. Is half a tortilla better than none?" Dad's proverbs came in handy, culturally translated of course.

The young men glared at each other.

"Rats will come in," the first one said.

"Babies will crawl out," the second brother added.

"Maybe one shared wall with a hole," the first one suggested.

"Maybe one large house," the second supplied.

His brother smiled and nodded. "Done."

"Go consult your wives," I ordered. "They are part of this decision, too."

"Thank you, wise queen goddess," the men said together. "Come, Xolo." The dog obediently trotted out, perfectly spaced between them, favoring neither one. Smart dog.

"I hope they're all this easy," I said to the guards.

Of course, they weren't. There were more serious disputes over land and over water shares and over unpaid debts. While Men Ch'o kept to his chamber, recovering and throwing off the longer lasting effects of the poison, I did the best I could in the audience room.

I collected an odd assortment of gifts from the petitioners—a pot of honey, a little round flute that resembled a turtle, a flask of vanilla scent, a carved duck. By the time I dragged myself away, he was sleeping soundly. And I'd had no chance to talk to him yet.

I collapsed for a few hours' rest in my chamber, copied out a few manuscript pages of glyphs, and went back to duty in the public eye. For days, this became my routine.

In the whirl of exhaustion, my sweet sixteenth birthday came and went, unrecognized, unshared. I starred the date in my journal. But there was no cake, no party. I had time only to raise a cup of cocoa to Maya's memory—no time for the luxury of tears.

Men Ch'o had made overtures of friendship to the cities that K'awiil had angered, and some of them sent back word that they accepted his gifts, accepted him at his word. I sincerely hoped no crises with the others came up while he was healing.

There was still no response from Naranjo, that is, Saal, where B'olon Muluk and Yo Imix had taken their tales of Men Ch'o's plans for unity—poisonous tales, no doubt.

And our would-be assassins remained free.

I am yet too weak to draw with a brush, so these words are written only in my heart. It is best that way, I know.

Each time I woke, I hoped to see my Lady Chel, to thank her for saving me at the last when I failed her test of faith and strength. Great was her disappointment. Great was her indifference. She was never there.

My legs were still too weak to take me from the room, although with Ix Imul's help, I could begin eating to rebuild my strength. I could not ask Imul to send for Chel for fear of hearing her refusal.

Lady K'uk' was as a mother with a newborn, caring me back to health. I owed her much. A great sadness weighed on her, perhaps the memory that she could not have saved her true son.

Day and night blended, not countable, not separated by regular meals and waking times. At last my trembling legs would hold. I had no time to waste relaxing in the room of steam. I bathed the remaining stink of illness from me with a bowl and a cloth, dressed in my finest robe, and departed my sickroom, touching the wall for support.

My first destination was Lady Chel's room. Whatever my fate, I had to face her again. Could she forgive my mortal weakness? Could she ever forget my humiliation? The small anger that still gnawed at my insides—that she watched the curse take me to the brink of agonizing death—I had to put aside. She must have had reasons. I could not believe her heart was so cruel.

I parted the curtain to her chamber to lay eyes on the strangest sight. Lady Chel sat writing, or rather, her hand still held a brush, but her forehead pressed down on the words she had been writing, and a glyph stained her cheek as she slept on a pile of new painted pages. A stack of completed papers had fallen to the floor. I gathered and re-ordered them. Then I lifted her from her writing bench to her sleeping pad and covered her with a rabbit skin blanket. She stirred and mumbled, but did not wake.

I watched her sleeping like a mortal woman. For a moment I imagined how it might be for me if she were only what she appeared to be.

For a moment, I wished it.

Air moved between her dark red lips. The glyph for *chami*, we die, faced backward, decorating her cheek where the ink had transferred. If only she could press that cheek to another paper and put the glyph onto it, how much quicker the copying process might be. The idea of a line of women with backward cheek glyphs jumped into my head. I imagined walking behind them and pressing them onto a piece of paper-bark over and over again.

It struck me strongly. That might do, I thought. Not with women, though. Maybe with a clay glyph, or better, a copper glyph that would hold shape forever. A fever of idea seized me then. Maybe I could earn my dear Chel's good regard if this worked. I stole a kiss lighter than a butterfly's wing from her lips and went out to see the coppersmith.

Sunlight dazzled my eyes, and I squinted blindly for a moment. A firm hand on my chest stopped me on the platform of the palace.

"K'ul Ahaw," said a familiar voice. It was Ah K'uhun, in all his priestly splendor. Blue paint covered his forearms and decorated his chest. He had just come from offering sacrifices, then. "Do I see you are almost recovered?"

"Ah K'uhun. Yes," I said with some relief. "I thank you and your priests for your prayers on my behalf. You see how they are answered."

"So I do," he replied. "So I do."

I started to edge past him, but he stopped me with a hand. "Is it wise, do you think, to be out under the darkening sun?"

How could it be the time of the darkening sun? When I fell ill, that had been far ahead, an event we had not yet begun preparing for. "How many days have I been ill?" I did not like to reveal my uncertainty or let it be known how far out of my mind I had traveled, but I needed to know how things stood, and Ah K'uhun was a most trusted advisor. He had steadied my hands when I drew my very first glyphs as a child.

The priest raised an eyebrow in concern. "Can you not remember? Well, the moon has traveled half a journey since."

Fourteen days and nights! What a disarray the court must have fallen into. I glanced through my fingers at the sky. "The sun still shines. Have I time to complete my errand before the darkness begins?"

"What is the errand that brings you out alone?" he asked. "I could take the burden from you."

"A surprise," I said. "A gift for my Lady Chel when she wakes. I go only to the jeweler. You need not worry."

Ah K'uhun replied. "Be quick. When you are finished then, will you come to me at the temple? We will burn incense and share a cup of pineapple juice. I will tell you all that happened while you were...indisposed."

"Thank you, I will," I said. I left my old friend and hurried to the jeweler. I sketched out the two signs I wished him to engrave and left him to it, to form and mount them.

On my way back to the temple complex to meet again with the Ah K'uhun, I saw Ix Imul in the plaza under the great Ceiba tree that shaded the very center. She embraced me with joy.

"Men Ch'o," she exclaimed. "I couldn't find you. How glad I am to see you about."

'Yes, finally," I agreed. "There is much to put in order. Fourteen days, I understand."

"Chel will be so happy," she said.

My face told her I was not so sure.

"You do not know how hard she has been working," Imul went on. "She takes her turn tending you in the night, runs the court by day, and scribbles in her room in the evening. I do not think she ever sleeps, unless it is in the early morning."

"Running the court?"

"She said no one was to know how ill you were, and she took your place in the audience chamber."

"The council as well?" I asked.

"No. She would not convene the holpop without you. I hear they are restless, wondering what is to become of your plans for the many-cities meeting. We have heard nothing from Saal."

I considered this. "Fourteen days since my brother-by-marriage B'olon Muluk carried back my invitation and nothing heard?"

Imul shook her head.

Now I would have to send my own runners to Saal. Lady Chel's fast running clicks on wah'yars would have been most helpful.

"And how is my sister Yo Imix? Must I thank her as well for nursing me in my illness? I do not remember."

Imul turned an odd, pale color. "No, I think not. She left unannounced and, I must say, unmissed, with her husband. She was of no help." Imul would not meet my eyes as she spoke.

"Lady Chel is sleeping now. When she wakes," I said, "please tell her I am recovered and will come to her as soon as I can."

The leaves of the great Ceiba above me trembled in the wind, and I watched their shadows move across the ground. Through the tiny holes that the worms had eaten, I saw the image of the sun, now lopsided as the darkness of the eclipse began to creep across his face.

"Imul, it is beginning. Now, please go inside and stay with my lady. I must join the Ah K'uhun in prayers and chants until the sun is renewed."

Imul's eyes flew round and open to mine. "You go to the temple? Then take great care," she said before she darted off into the palace.

An insistent hand tugged me awake. I dragged myself from deep sleep, from the middle of the first pleasant dream I'd had in months.

In the broken dream, an old woman, grandmotherly in age and face, held my hand and walked me up to the top of El Castillo, although in the dream, the warm breeze lofted us up to the top with no effort. She gestured to the surrounding lands, rich green with healthy maize and beans and squash crops. She pointed to the white roads, the sacbe, leading away from Yaxmuul to the cities north and south, east and west. Branchless trees lined the sacbe, an endless black snake of cable running from trunk to trunk. Carts drawn by teams of tall, strong animals came and went along the roads, but too far in the distance to make out the features of the animals. At the foot of the temple mound, a new building, a school, I supposed, rang with the shouts of children reciting the alphabet at the top of their lungs. The wind carried their voices up to our ears.

"It is well done," the old grandmother said, and she lifted my scarred palm to her lips to kiss it. My hand was as bony and wrinkled as her own, but I felt that it was profoundly right.

The hand shook my shoulder. "Chel, Lady Chel," Imul demanded. "You must wake. I don't know what to do."

"About what?" I asked with a yawn, imagining it had something to do with the boys.

"It's Men Ch'o," she began.

I leapt to alertness. "What? Not a relapse? He's not worse, is he?" My heart paused between beats, waiting for her answer.

"No, no. He is well enough to walk out today," she said. "But he has gone to see Ah K'uhun because of the dark sun."

"What? When? How do you know this?" I asked in a rush.

"I met him in the plaza, and he told me he was on his way. I'm sorry. I did not know what to do....how to tell him what you suspect."

"Oh gods," I roared. "You told him nothing?"

She shrank back, clearly afraid of my fury. "I told him to be careful," she choked out.

I shook my head in frustration and fear. I glanced around for my sandals, and not seeing them, took off at top speed in my bare feet.

Her voice faded behind me. "But my lady...you can't...the darkness..."

The plaza was strangely vacant. The sky outside had turned a sickly pale yellow, and a chill wind blew across my arms, raising the hairs. The greater chill lay in my heart, though, as I ran across the empty expanse to the temple. Please let me be in time, I prayed.

I burst into the temple complex and demanded that a young priest take me to Ah K'uhun and Men Ch'o. My worst fears were realized when I found them sitting at a table on triangular stools, a cup before each of them.

Was I too late? Weak as he was, another dose of poison would surely kill him. This time, Ah K'uhun knew exactly how strong to prepare it.

"Don't touch that, Men Ch'o," I yelled in warning. I dashed the cup from the table, and it shattered on the floor, but not a drop of liquid was left. I turned furiously on Ah K'uhun, who sat unblinking. "I would tear you apart with my own hands," I growled, "But I need the antidote. Give it to me. Now."

Ah K'uhun tilted his lips in the most twisted, sinister smile I have ever seen. "Dear goddess, such drama. And what a shame the audience is so small. Antidote? There is no antidote."

Men Ch'o's eyes flicked back and forth between me and the priest who had betrayed his trust and friendship. He sighed deeply and shook his head. The look on his face was sad, deeply sad—not alarmed, not panicked. After what he had just been through, I couldn't understand it.

"Men Ch'o," I said, kneeling at his side. "This man has poisoned you, just as he did before. With...with the help of your sister Lady Yo Imix."

Men Ch'o's face squeezed as though the emotional pain were already physical.

I felt it, too. My eyes filled with tears. "Oh gods. Oh, Men Ch'o. What can we do?"

He placed a hand under my chin, tilting my damp face to him. His own expression relaxed, and a strange calm flowed from him. Acceptance of his fate? Or was it something else?

"It is well, sweet Chel. Dry your tears. The first rule of kingship my Father Ahaw ever shared with me—never drink alone, even with your most trusted, without switching the cups."

Ah K'uhun's hands flew to his own stomach.

Men Ch'o regarded him sadly. "You see how trust and caution are balanced. My old friend, I am sorry. In the end, you have betrayed yourself."

My mind boggled. Men Ch'o was apologizing to someone who had just tried to assassinate him? Again?

Ah K'uhun threw himself on the floor, his head at Men Ch'o's feet. "I beg, I implore you. There is no antidote. I spoke truth. The goddess saved your life, but I know it is useless to ask her for mine." He raised his eyes to me hopefully.

I shook my head. "I...can't."

Men Ch'o studied my face in silence. The blood pounded in my ears, making my head ache, turning my vision dark. Even if it had been in my power, how could I save someone who had knowingly put his pupil, his friend, his king through such torture and planned to do it again. He'd used up my mercy.

But perhaps not Men Ch'o's. "Get up," he commanded.

A spasm of pain crossed the old priest's face as he stood. Men Ch'o watched and closed his eyes a moment, maybe reliving his own agonies.

"Please, my king," the old man asked. He reached into his robe and withdrew a small obsidian dagger. I was about to slap it from his grasp, but Men Ch'o stopped me with a glance. Ah K'uhun held the dagger in outstretched hand to his king. "Spare me that death," he begged.

"That's more than you would have done for him," I hissed in fury.

Men Ch'o looked to me with a question in his eyes.

"Your decision," I said. I held up my scarred palms for him to see. "I won't have any more blood on these hands, guilty or innocent." I whirled around and left the temple. Part of my deepest primal core wanted to stand over the writhing, tormented body of the priest and watch his death throes; part of my atavistic soul wanted to take the obsidian blade and plunge it into his heart myself with all my anger and desperate hate.

But I couldn't, wouldn't be that person. I ran through the stone rooms and out into the half-light. I breathed in the clean outside air, purging the primitive feelings of revenge and blood lust. I counted my breaths to block out all other thoughts, all imaginings of what was going on inside the temple. Gradually, the pounding in my head stopped, and my heart emptied itself of dark emotions.

I leaned against the warm, green trunk of the chaka tree and ran my hands over the peeling bark. At the hint of a soft tread behind me, I turned to see Men Ch'o.

He walked all the way up to me, inside the circle of my reserve, and pressed his forehead against mine. His arms reached across my shoulders to the strong tree at my back. He closed his eyes and whispered, "It is done. It was not well done, not gloriously, not honorably done, but just...done. I could not let him suffer as I did."

I heard the pain in his voice, the pain of having no right answer, just one a little less wrong. His loss tore at me as if it were my own. My arms came up around his waist, and I tilted my face until our lips met, there in the shade of the tree. His tears flowed freely now, and their salt flavored the kiss with bittersweet regret.

"My Chel," he murmured against my cheek. "Forgive my weakness. I only wish I were a better man for your sake."

"Men Ch'o," I said. "You are the bravest, strongest, wisest man I know."

His eyes smiled at me, glistening. "You have not met many men, I think."

"True," I said. "But I've met enough to know that much. And I love you. Really, I do."

"Then I count myself the most fortunate mortal alive."

This was the point where I knew I was supposed to flow into his arms, kiss passionately, and live happily ever after. I could feel it. This was where our convenient marriage was supposed to end and our real one begin. Except there was one terrible lie, one awful misunderstanding still between us. And

I had to end the lie, even if it meant the end of everything else.

Men Ch'o loved Ix Chel, that was obvious to me now. But would he love plain old Chel? Michelle? Sixteen-year-old castaway from the future?

"I have to...," I began. "I need to...." Then I lost my courage.

"Yes?" he asked patiently.

I shrugged and turned toward the palace. "I need to get back to my work," I said. Damn. Xit.

When I glanced back, he stood watching me with puzzled eyes. He tilted his head, opened his hands, and begged me silently to speak what was on my mind. But I couldn't. I had too much to lose. Again.

The day after Ah K'uhun's terrible, merciful death at my hands, I took my seat again in the place of power. I promoted a young priest to take the senior position in the temple. He had always been kind to me and to others, and often I had enjoyed thoughtful discussions with him.

I dispatched messengers to Saal with a public message to the king inviting him to sit at my left at the giant round mat. I sent also a private message telling him of my sister's treachery toward me. Did I seek her life? No. I could not, for that would be the final blow to a lady I held dear, Lady K'uk'. At last I understood the true cause of her heavy heart. It was not sorrow that I lived while K'awiil her own son died alone. She carried a burden of guilt, suspecting that her daughter was the architect of my near death. I would not add another quetzal feather to the weight carried by a woman who had already lost both husband and son.

But I am not foolish. I recommended to my elder cousin at Saal that he banish Yo Imix and B'olon Muluk to the faraway land of the Mexica. They had shown ambition for my throne. It was possible they would show the same for his.

At midday, the coppersmith arrived. I saw him ahead of the others who waited, so great was my excitement to see what he had made. He handed me the ring mounted with the glyphs reversed, the glyphs for Ix Chel.

"The shaping here was very tricky," he boasted as I admired his work. "And I still wonder that you insisted I mount them wrong, the lady facing to the right. Is it a cipher, divine majesty?"

I reached for a brush and ink, and blackened his carefully polished work before his disbelieving eyes. He reached for a cloth to clean it again, but I said, "Watch this." I pressed the ring to a piece of paper, lifted, and pressed again.

His eyes widened in quick understanding. "How wonderful!" he said. "Will there be more?"

"Ah yes," I said. "Many, many more. Prepare your workshop and I will send instructions." I paid him generously for the ring, and he left most pleased.

At supper, my eyes betrayed my secret delight.

Chel smiled at me and asked, "What? What are you thinking about?"

I did not answer, but my heart jumped with the thought of how much larger her smile would grow when she knew the reason.

I found her in her chamber later, copying. I counted ten full stacks of her codex and twenty more yet to do. We had never made so many copies of one writing before. There had never been the need.

She dropped the brush into the inkpot when I entered and rubbed her tired hands together. "Oh, thank the gods. An excuse to rest. What are you hiding behind your back?"

I held out my empty hand palm up, and she gave me her right hand. First I kissed her fingertips, stained with ink, then I slid the ring onto her pointing finger.

She examined it carefully. Her eyebrows drew together into a single line. "Men Ch'o, thank you. It's very fine."

"Your name," I said. "Ix Chel."

"Ah, my name." She laughed a little and tilted her head. "But it's backward. Chel Ix. Did you see that?" she asked.

Without a word, I picked up the ink brush and painted the surface of the glyphs. Then I rolled her fist over to press into the middle of a blank white paper. She blinked several times as she looked between the paper and the ring.

She swore by a god I had never heard named. "Holy Gutenberg," she cried. "Men Ch'o, you're wonderful. You invented moveable type. Six hundred years before Gutenberg! I knew you were brilliant."

She threw her arms around my neck, knocking ink over the floor and my clothes, but I paid no attention. For the moment, I enjoyed the press of her warmth before she could grow strange to me again.

"Just wait till the Spanix see this," she said with a wild, mysterious gleam in her eye. "They've got nothing on us. Oh, I just thought of something else we need."

"Anything you wish," I said with haste and without caution.

"A science academy."

Although I had made good progress in the god-tongue, the words were unknown to me.

She laughed at my blank response. "Your wisest, most creative people and those from our neighbor cities. They will meet together and figure things out—things like how we turn these copper glyphs into a printing press, like how to make tah'yars and wah'yars. And we'll need people who understand breeding of animals and...and better crop rotation." The ideas flew from her mouth faster than I could catch them and bounced off my head. "We'll announce it at the holpop," she ordered.

I smiled in agreement. It seemed the wisest path.

That was just one of her plans for our landmark meeting, the first time ever that so many kings would be assembled together. She also insisted that we begin to plan a voyage by ocean to the llama lands, taking men from many cities to share the risk and the reward. A shared adventure would draw the cities together. When I worried that such a voyage by canoe would doom them all, she said, "Not canoes, Men Ch'o. Great sail boats."

"Sel botz?" It was my turn to look confused.

"Oh gods," she said. "We have a long way to go, don't we?" Then she painted a picture of a broad canoe with wings to make it fly across the water. What things she had seen in the times to come!

I set several scribes to help Chel copy her great codex. It was too much work for one person and the complete glyphs for a *print'n pres* could not be finished in time. The scribes were sworn to secrecy. It was too soon to tell everyone of the terrible world that would come unless we followed Chel's new path. This news had to be handled very carefully or thirty kings would pack their sacks and leave me standing alone, an idiot. Would they be convinced by Chel's prophecy as I had been? They did not know her as I did.

The kings and their retinues started to arrive four days before the summer's longest day. Preparations consumed every waking hour. Servants arranged rooms for thirty visiting kings, their left-hand advisors, and their servants. All the guest rooms in the nobles' palaces had been claimed as well, with so many to sleep. Chel and Lady K'uk' worked tirelessly planning to feed so great a number. It would be a great drain on our reserves. The kings brought such wonderful gifts to us—long necklaces of chaak-red shell, carvings made in green river stone, and cloaks sewn from coats of animals we had never seen—but nothing that we could eat.

Now my hands shook as I wondered whether we would even succeed in convincing them to accept the k'arts we had built and filled with gifts. I remembered how fearful I had been of the small clay model. I remembered how fear of the ouweel and the changes it brought had driven Ah K'uhun to treason and death. Yet, after only three or four uinals, as I walked about the city, I saw nearly every child had a tiny toy k'art among his other playthings. The woodsmith's sons had built a k'art large enough to pull their baby sister to avoid the chore of carrying her, and I wondered how long before every new mother wanted one just that size.

The future belonged to these children, who so easily accepted and improved on something new. It was my responsibility to make sure that all we did here ensured their future. I knew that with Chel at my side, we could do it. Yes. I could do it.

My arms, eyes, and neck ached by the morning of the opening ceremonies, but the copying was done. Men Ch'o and I had discussed whether to kick off the meeting with blood-letting, self-sacrifice, but I argued that we wouldn't be able to speak properly for the rest of the day. Besides I wanted to get away from the idea that every important event had to be drenched in blood. I suggested a breakfast feast, music, and dancers on the patio—actually, the platform above the plaza.

As the meal was winding down and the visiting kings began to ask what this was all about, I signaled the conch blower, who signaled the parade leader. All heads turned at the sound of drums as the carts appeared from behind the great Castillo where they had been concealed. Teams of four strong men pulled each of the thirty carts along the pathway and into the great plaza. Each cart was filled with gifts— woven blankets, casks of liquor, jars of precious cacao beans, and baskets of jade, obsidian, and other valuable stones. And feather pillows.

I watched the mixed expressions of delight and interest on some faces, disdain or fear on others.

Men Ch'o addressed his fellow kings. "These gifts will be yours at the end of our council as well as more valuable others which cannot be carried—peace, knowledge, and good will between cities. These wooden boxes are called k'arts, and they roll on ouweels, allowing four men to bring more than they could carry. These are also gifts for you. I will give you the woodsmithing plans so your cities can make as many as you have need for."

Excited murmurs passed between the kings and their advisors. I strained to hear the words but some of the regional accents were hard to understand. I had the impression that they were largely positive.

Men Ch'o's plan for the morning was to dazzle them with our new ideas in an open and giving way. His statesmanship came naturally, not nurtured by his father, but by his character. Now I understood the difference, saw that K'awiil would have lorded it over these kings, some from far more powerful cities, demanded recognition as the greatest among them, and controlled access to anything we developed in Yaxmuul. His approach to regional unity would have been through conquest and submission. "All for one" with the "one" being him.

My turn to speak would come later, in the evening, after the men had relaxed with food and drink. I would have to tell them of my world and somehow convince them that I wasn't insane. One thought was at the front of my mind and refused to let go. The supposedly civilized French had burned Joan of Arc as a witch and a heretic when she showed them a way out of their century of war. What would these guys do to us if they didn't believe me?

Men Ch'o found me in my chamber, pacing restlessly, wringing my sweating hands, and muttering rehearsed words to myself. My stomach churned with the remains of lunch. I don't know why I ever thought I could pull this off.

"It is going well, do you think?" he asked, watching my breakdown with confusion.

"Yes. No. I don't know," I said. "You're fine. You're brilliant. You were made for this. I just don't know if I can do it."

"Yes, of course you can. You must."

"But what should I say?" I whined. "I don't know how to convince them. They'll think I'm crazy when I tell them about the fall of the Mayan cities, and...and about Montezuma and Cortes and everything else. How can I tell the king of Tikal, Yax Mutul, that his topknot is coming unraveled and his city will be abandoned in another generation? It will humiliate him. He'll want to kill me."

I started to breathe faster. Panic was setting in.

Men Ch'o placed a strong hand on my shoulder. "Ix Chel, my goddess, you will find the words and you will convince them. You convinced me," he added simply.

"I'm not...I'm really not..."

"Ready?" he suggested. "No one ever feels ready for something like this. I wasn't ready to be king. Ha. Look at me now. King nonetheless."

I turned away from him. I couldn't say it to those trusting eyes. So I told the wall instead. "I'm not Ix Chel. My true name is Michelle Balam. I'm not a goddess. I'm not immortal. I'm not magical. I'm a normal sixteen-year-old girl who is lost and alone and scared and..."

"Look at me," Men Ch'o said. His voice held no emotion.

I stared at the wall still, watched the colors blur. Terrified to turn around and read his—what?—shock, anger, dismissal, disappointment.

"Chel," he commanded. "Face me, now."

I turned.

"Have you walked on the last day?"

"Yes," I whispered.

"Have you seen Yax Mutul and Yaxmuul in ruins?"

"Yes," I said again.

"Have you knowledge of things hundreds of tuns in the future days."

"Yes, Men Ch'o. I do." I choked on a sob.

He lifted my chin and forced me to meet his gaze. "Then you are the messenger who changes us. And if you are not Ix Chel herself, surely she stands beside you. She works with and through you. Do you not understand?"

"What do you mean?" My voice was small, soft.

"Why do you think it rains every time you shed tears?"

"It does?"

"It rains even now," Men Ch'o said. He pointed to the open window.

"Coincidence?" I said.

He raised an eyebrow. "And why do you think your hands and tears have healing power, the power to save lives?"

"That's called CPR," I insisted.

"And are you the daughter of the jaguar, B'alam?"

"But that's just my last name. And my Mom is...was... Swedish," I said weakly.

"Why do you think you speak our tongue as one born to it, but you came to our world knowing nothing?"

That one I couldn't explain. But for someone raised as a mixture of Catholic and Lutheran, the idea that a Mayan goddess was channeling power into me was a bit too much to absorb. I stood silent.

Men Ch'o cupped my face in his hands and kissed me hard and fast. "Chel. Believe me. I know who you are, I know what you can do, and I know this is where and when you are meant to be. This is your reason. Right now. Tonight. Come."

His eyes poured strength into me. All his faith filled up the hole in my own. I would be who he wanted me to be for him, for all of them.

"But I'm not a goddess," I said once more for the record.

"Perhaps not," he said, his expression softening. "But with my eagle's eyes, I surely see her standing behind you."

Then he kissed me slowly and deeply, and I felt a powerful answer within myself.

I sensed a hand at the small of my back pushing me forward, tighter into Men Ch'o's embrace, and as I returned his kiss with rising passion, an invisible voice whispered in my ear, *tonight begins the future*.

EPILOGUE
10.1.0.0.0
November 24, 849 A.D.

I pulled aside the woven curtain, and sunlight streamed through the open window, casting a beam of light across my sleeping husband's face. It was late morning, but many were lying in. Last night we'd stayed awake late celebrating the final moments of the first k'atun, like a glorified New Year's Eve that came once every twenty years. Today at noon we would dedicate the new stela marking this ripple in the stream of time. The first turn of the k'atun in the eleventh bak'tun.

The stone carvers had been at a loss—what to write after the date? Only the names of the rulers? There were no wars, captives, or human sacrifices to commemorate. No important births, deaths, royal marriages, or anniversaries in this year. Our son Balam Ch'o had not quite reached his first k'atun, still nineteen according to my journals and also by the Mayan calendar.

Men Ch'o stirred as the sun touched his eyes. "You rose early, Chel."

True. I had been awake for two hours, working on a new collection of poems. It still felt to me like vanity publishing when Men Ch'o insisted on printing and sending copies out to all of his friends. Better that I should be working on another text book for one of our many schools.

Put that on the stela, I had instructed the carvers. How many teachers we had trained, how many schools we had built, how many children spoke Mayan and English and my rudimentary Spanish. How many were now literate in glyphs and alphabet. Those were the accomplishments of the past twenty years.

Fourteen good harvests, six bad, but the soil was improving under careful stewardship. Twenty meetings of the many-cities holpop, which had grown to fifty members. Tikal, Caracol, Calakmul had exchanged their competitive drive on the battlefield for competition in inventiveness and productivity. The breakthrough we needed so badly in telegraphy had come from a team at Tikal, and the first cables were now being built by engineers from Caracol. The code had been worked out by a linguist in Naranjo. Our own builders had installed the millwheel on the Mopan that ground our maize and freed so many women to become teachers.

"And you're rising late, lazy bones," I chided Men Ch'o.

The years had been kind to him. His face was still round and youthful, not a gray hair in sight. Our daughters at six and ten were the jewels in his crown, and our son was his greatest pride and hope for the future. Back when our Balam Ch'o, jaguar's eyes, reached his manhood ceremony at thirteen, we confided in him—my origins, the old future, the plan for a new path—and we were rewarded doubly by the look of determination in his man-boy eyes. He saw the future through my eyes and the present through his father's. In fact, he found it more miraculous to think that I had come from a real place and time than from the unknowable realms of the gods.

"Are we late?" Men Ch'o asked, still refusing to open his eyes or leave the warmth of bed.

"Not yet," I said. "We've missed our breakfast, though. You'll have to go hungry." I poked him in the stomach, which was still as firm as in his youth.

"I thought I was the king," he said. "First-meal is whenever I say it is."

"And is it now?" I asked.

"Not yet!" His arms reached up and grabbed mine, and he pulled me down to the sleeping mat on top of him. His eyes widened with a familiar look that I found irresistible. I buried my face in his neck.

The sound of four little feet pattered through the doorway. "Xit," he mumbled in my ear.

"Mama, mama," our little hummingbird Tz'unun called. "Look what Balam Ch'o found. He said show you."

I tickled Men Ch'o under the covers and winked. "Raincheck," I said in English.

He looked at me blankly.

"Later," I explained in a whisper.

"Okay, let's see, my sweet," I said, extracting myself from the bed furs. The two girls were holding out a bright orange bag, their eyes wide.

My head whirled so fast I nearly snapped my neck. No, it wasn't *my* dry bag. That still hung on the wall next to the Coke shrine. The granola bar had disappeared in the night long ago—probably a coatimundi had sniffed it out.

Men Ch'o was sitting up, wide awake and alert now as well. I held out my hands, trying to control their shaking.

"Here, Mama. What is it?" Chaya, with the command of an older sister, took the bag from Tz'unun and reached in. She pulled out something I hadn't seen in a lifetime.

My eyes devoured the sleek black case, the shiny Nikon logo. Maya's camera.

"Careful, oh careful, my sweet," I gasped.

My heart drummed so hard I was certain Men Ch'o could hear. He put a warm, comforting hand between my shoulder blades. I'm here for you, it said.

I steadied my fingers and uttered a prayer to all the gods who had ever been or ever would be. The switch slid with an easy click from OFF to ON. A chirp sounded. It was still alive. The batteries still held a charge. It must have just come through.

My voice quavered as I asked, "Where...where did Balam get this?"

Chaya answered. "He said at the cave river, early this morning. When they went to leave the gods offerings for the dawn of the new k'atun."

I shook my head in hope, in disbelief. Quickly, so as not to waste the battery, I pressed the review button. The LED screen lit with an image long forgotten, a face long missed. Maya, close up, cheek to cheek with Enrique before we entered the cave.

My heart nearly exploded, so full of memories, regrets, hopes. Too many emotions for a fist-sized organ to hold at once.

"That's the lady," Tz'unun said.

"Which lady?" Men Ch'o asked.

"The lady Balam brought back from the cave. I talked to her in Enk'lix," she reported proudly.

Men Ch'o and I exchanged a telepathic look.

"Where?" I begged. "Where are they?"

"I think on the palace steps still."

Before she stopped speaking, I was on my bare feet and running, running out of the palace and into the sun. I stopped in my tracks at the sight in front of me. It reopened a closed room in my brain, flipped my world upside down, past and present overlapping.

Balam Ch'o stood on the palace steps, one arm around a teenaged girl in shorts and a tank top and totally impractical sandals, the other pointing to the plaza, the temple, the nobles' palaces. Tourguiding. Their attention finally swiveled to where I stood, frozen in place.

"Ho there, Mama," Balam hailed me. His brilliant grin was triumphant and something else. "A surprise visitor," he said in our tongue. "See what the early kingfisher has found in the stream." He led Maya forward, toward me.

Her look of polite curiosity turned to puzzled recognition, then outright shock. "Oh my god. Chel...?"

The spell on my feet was broken at the sound of her voice. I ran forward and hugged her with all the strength of twenty years of regretful longing.

She pulled back first. "What the hell happened?" she asked. "What is this place, some kind of historical village? And why do you look, excuse the expression, like old?"

"Thanks. Thanks a lot," I said, forgiving her instantly. "Three kids will do that to a girl."

"Three kids?" Her nose wrinkled in confusion.

"So will twenty years," I added.

"What the hell are you talking about?" she asked. "Wait. Wait. Can we go somewhere inside and sit? My feet are killing me. We've been hiking for like three hours and this handsome hunk here,"—she squeezed his arm for emphasis and batted her lashes at him—"wouldn't let me stop for anything."

"This handsome hunk is your nephew Balam Ch'o, my dear sister," I said.

He threw me a look over the top of Maya's head, a "back off mom" kind of look. I sighed. Already caught in her net. Well, that might serve a purpose. Already my head was spinning with plans for her. Fluent in Spanish, wildly artistic, and very good at making friends. Could we actually pull off the Industrial Revolution *and* the Renaissance at the same time?

She kept her tight hold on his arm and laughed lightly. "Nephew? As if," she said dismissively. "Where's Mom and Dad? I bet Mom hates all this realistic re-creation stuff and Dad's in seventh heaven."

My heart skipped a beat. So they hadn't come through with her. Well, we'd have to deal with that soon, but not now, not on the steps of the palace. I felt for her. I knew what was in store for her when she realized there was no more mascara or music videos or blow dryers. I'd been there, too, a lifetime ago.

"Come. Let's go inside," Balam urged gently. He tucked Maya protectively under one arm. Now he caught my gaze, and from the sad, knowing look in his eyes, I knew he had just realized the intense emotional journey ahead for this pretty, lighthearted girl. With an answering look, I gave him my blessing to be there for her.

Smoothing the roadbed,
The sacbe to the future,
Every stone is new.

BIBLIOGRAPHY

Ancient American Poets, complied and translated by John Curl, Bilingual Review Press, Arizona State University, 2005.

The Ancient Maya-New Perspectives, Heather McKillop, ABC-CLIO, 2004.

Chronicle of the Maya Kings and Queens: Deciphering the Dynasties of the Ancient Maya, Simon Martin and Nikolai Grube, Thames & Hudson, 2000.

The Code of Kings: The Language of Seven Sacred Maya Temples and Tombs, Linda Schele and Peter Mathews, Scribner, 1998.

Collapse, Jared Diamond, Penguin Books, 2005.

Daily Life in Maya Civilization, Robert J. Sharer, Greenwood Press, 1996.

The de la Cruz-Badiano Aztec Herbal of 1552, English Translation by William Gates, The Maya Society, 1939.

The Fall of the Ancient Maya, David Webster, Thames & Hudson, 2002.

Guns, Germs, and Steel, Jared Diamond, W. W. Norton & Company, 1999.

Handbook to Life in the Ancient World, Lynn V. Foster, Facts on File, Inc., 2002.

The Maya, 7th Edition, Michael D. Coe, Thames & Hudson, 2005.

Maya History and Religion, Eric S. Thompson, University of Oklahoma Press, 1990.

Rainforest Remedies; One Hundred Healing Herbs of Belize. Rosita Arvigo and Michael Balick, Lotus Press, 1998.

Secrets of the Maya, Ed. Archaeology Magazine, Hatherleigh Press, 2003.

WEBSITES

eclipse.gsfc.nasa.gov/SEpubs/5MCSE.html
FAMSI.org
maps.google.com
precolumbianwheels.com
space.com/snserver/snweb.php
users.hartwick.edu/hartleyc/mayacalendar/mayacalendar.html

ABOUT THE AUTHOR

Liz Coley at Xunantunich

Liz Coley is author of numerous published short stories in some unusual places: The Last Man Anthology, More Scary Kisses, Cosmos Magazine, Bride of the Golem, and Strange Worlds Anthology. She has always been a fan of speculative fiction, ever since the first Tripods marched across her imagination to rule the world.

She lives in Ohio with her husband, three kids, a white dog, an orange cat, and seven Macs between the five of them.

In 1969 San Diego celebrated its bicentennial with a festival that recreated a ceremony with Aztec sky dancers and the sacrifice of a beautiful girl. Seeing this woman's heart apparently ripped out while still beating made an indelible impression on young Liz. Forever after she was fascinated by ancient Mesoamerican cultures. This novel represents the culmination of study, travel, and a burning "what if...?"

Made in the USA
Middletown, DE
19 May 2015